The
Tale
Of
Two Rivers

By David W. Firmes

THE TALE OF TWO RIVERS

This is a work of fiction. Many locations are real and some of the historical events are real but many of events in those locations are from the imagination of the author. Some of the people referred to in the historical settings are real but any dialogue relating to those people is the fabrication of the author to create this work of fiction.

"WHEN YOU ELIMINATE THE IMPOSSIBLE, WHATEVER REMAINS, NO MATTER HOW IMPROBABLE, MUST BE THE TRUTH."

SHERLOCK HOLMES

INTRODUCTION

Spring 1962 - Jackson Village

Flowers finally broke through the hardened ground from the previous winter. Snow eventually lost its grip on the many mountain peaks, which caused gushing sounds as the waters streamed to their riverbeds. It was a long wait for the smells and colors of spring. The valley was ready for another season of tourists to roam the countryside. Hikers, mountain climbers and shoppers were starting to filter into the many inns and resorts throughout the valley.

Gallagher Brady's life finally had normalized after dealing with the knowledge of the tragic circumstances surrounding the death of his parents. It took more than a year to heal emotionally but Anna has remained a real strength and comfort to him as they move on with their plans to spend the rest of their lives together.

Gallagher returned to his passion of mountain climbing and his pursuit of rare and hard to find literary works to compliment his bookshop, the Turning Page and to fill the newly constructed Antiquarian Museum.

Peace, and a much needed calm had settled over the valley after the strange and bizarre death of Gordon Hayes. Gallagher and his close friend Jonathan Henry were able to solve the mystery surrounding his death but the circumstances around the case was something that would linger in their minds for many days. Also, the FBI finally broke up the infiltration of the Fifth Column group, which was exposed by the duo.

Gallagher finally popped the question of marriage to Anna and she accepted and were engaged in

October of 1961. An autumn wedding is planned for the following year.

It wasn't long after the new year of 1961 came into existence that a new threat to the peace of the valley and the world's came into existence. Before his inauguration, John F. Kennedy was briefed on a plan by the Central Intelligence Agency, which was developed during the Eisenhower administration to train Cuban exiles for an invasion of their homeland. The plan anticipated that the Cuban people and elements of the Cuban military would support the invasion. The ultimate goal was the overthrow of Castro and the establishment of a non-communist government friendly to the United States. A new war had begun where words were used instead of weapons but the threat of their use was ever present causing tensions throughout the entire world. With that happening on the world scene there were those working undetected in the peaceful mountains of the North Country creating an upheaval of long established traditions and memories. The very heart of the land was on the brink of ruin. It's with these thoughts in mind that our story begins. The events that you're about to read have been written down in the order they occurred.

***

PART ONE

The Message

1

Friday morning...March 2, 1962

John Russell woke up at the crack of dawn and made his way to the banks of the Saco River at Hart's Location and started to do what he loves most in the world; fish. The air was mild for an early March day and there was a fresh blanket of snow that looked like powdered sugar on top of the surrounding mountains. The sun was glistening down on the river revealing its crystal clear water, which nourished the valley for the local farmers. Being a long time resident of Hart's Location early morning fishing was a routine John's father introduced him to just like his father did for him when he was a boy. In late winter the river flows strong and swift due to the heavy snows that melt down into the small streams that run through the valley below when the midday sun heats up the mountaintops. The rushing water makes fishing a challenge for everyone but John because of his skill at plucking fish out of the cold water with his bare hands. It was a method used for centuries by his ancestors.

John was given the name Little Hands at birth echoing his Abenaki heritage. The Abenaki Indians are part of the larger tribe called the Wôbanakiak. Their people settled in the region migrating from the Great Lakes and strengthening throughout New Hampshire, Vermont and Massachusetts. The Penobscots, Micmacs and the Mohawks are all part of the larger tribe called, 'People of the Dawn Land'.

John's a gentle man by nature and was named Little Hands by his father. Some have said it was a joke on his part to give his son such a name. At birth everyone who saw John as a baby knew he was going to be a big man when he grew up. He weighed in at fourteen pounds at birth and the striking feature about him was his unusually large hands. A story is told that one time when he was thirteen years old he strangled a black bear with those large hands to save his friend.

On this particular day John was enjoying his time fishing when he noticed four men further down the river hammering signposts into the ground along the side of Saco's riverbank. One of the men proceeds to paint something on each sign in bright red paint. After he finishes the last sign he clumsily tips over the paint can and spills the remaining red paint onto the side of the riverbank. Instead of trying to clean it up he and the other three leave the area in a hurry.

After they were out of sight John decides to walk over to where they had placed the signs. The signs read; PRIVATE PROPERTY - NO FISHING. He looks down on the ground and notices the spilled red paint had oozed into the muddy riverbank.

John Russell, being a gentle man, always minded his own business but anger started to creep in on him so he impulsively pulled the signposts out of the ground in a rage. He then took all the signs and carried them away and threw them into the back of his pickup truck. During the whole time he was gathering up the signs he was unaware the four men had hidden themselves in the nearby woods and were watching his every move.

Despite being very upset over the signs being posted John continued his morning fishing and eventually drove off to work the fields of his families farm. He still planned to come back another day to fish despite the posted signs.

**

2

Monday morning...March 5, 1962

Mary Ann's Gift Shop...

"It's looking great," Valerie Blair says to her sister Mary Ann as she finishes hanging the final curtain in the front window of her gift shop.

With a look of satisfaction Mary Ann says, "I'm so happy the shop has this gorgeous view of the Presidential Range and its centerpiece, Mount Washington. It would be great to add on a little tea room so folks could sit and enjoy the view while they take a rest from their shopping."

"Sounds wonderful. Now you just need some customers to come in so you can pay for your dreams."

Mary Ann smiles and says, "Just being together in this idyllic little village has already fulfilled my dreams."

Valerie gives Mary Ann a big hug and says, "We can thank Gallagher and Jonathan for making it all happen. Who would have ever thought our lives would have changed as much as it has in the past year. I was living alone and was seeking someone like Jonathan and you were working all kinds of hours in a job you despised with people you didn't trust."

Just as Mary Ann was about to respond a tall distinguished looking man sporting a well-groomed white beard came into the shop carrying two large leather bound books. "Excuse me but is the shop's proprietor in today?"

Mary Ann looks the man over and says, "That would be me. My name is Mary Ann Blair. How can I help you Mr....?"

"My name is not important. I've come with a gift for your little shop. I heard you just had your grand opening and I was hoping you would find these books of some value. These are two rare editions of Sir Conan Doyle's 'The Hound of the Baskervilles' and they have been in my family for almost sixty years."

Mary Ann takes the books from him and places them on the counter and says, "I don't know what to say; they are in perfect condition. Are you sure you want to part with them?"

She opens one book and notices the author's signature. "It's even autographed. These books must be worth a fortune."

The man nods and says, "The novels were originally serialized in *Strand's Magazine* from August 1901 to April 1902 in London. My father was able to acquire these leather-bound hardcover editions as soon as they were published."

"I feel uncomfortable about just accepting your books. I'm just starting out and my working capital is very low at the moment so I couldn't offer you what they are really worth."

The man shakes his head adamantly and says, "I do not want your money. They are a gift like I said before. All I ask is that you take good care of them and hopefully they will land in the hands of someone who appreciates fine literature; maybe you know of someone who does in the valley."

Mary Ann thinks to herself why the man didn't bring them to Gallagher's bookshop, the Turning Page; it would be the perfect place to display the books. She shrugs off any attempt to question him about it, discerning he was a stranger to the area and didn't know about Gallagher being the foremost authority on rare and hard to find books.

Before leaving the man looks intently at the two volumes for the last time and says, "There are books of which the backs and covers are by far the best parts."

A puzzled look comes over Mary Ann's face by what he said but without saying another word the man turned towards the door and quickly leaves the shop. Valerie goes to the front window to see if she can see where he was going but he had quickly disappeared from her view around the corner. Valerie turned to Mary Ann and says, "Have you ever seen that man before?"

Mary Ann shakes her head and says, "He's never been in my shop before and I've never seen him anywhere in town. I think I would have recognized him with that gorgeous white beard of his and those mesmerizing blue eyes."

"Why don't I call Jonathan and see if he knows of anyone that fits the description?"

"Good idea. I'll just put these books in the back for now for safekeeping. I don't want to even consider selling them until I have them appraised. I'm sure Gallagher would know their value."

"They may be ideal for the new antiquarian museum Gallagher is building in the center of town."

"Valerie, I think that's a great idea. Maybe the man knows about the museum and thinks I might donate the books and that's why I didn't have to buy them."

Valerie nods and says, "It's very possible because I was in the Chamber of Commerce the other day and noticed a poster advertising the museum's grand opening this October and it said if anyone had any rare books in good condition and would like to contribute to the museum to call a particular number."

"Yes, I saw the same poster in Rawling's Grocery Store. I will let Gallagher know about these books right away."

***

3

Wednesday early morning...March 7, 1962

A cold front with heavy snow was coming down from Canada breaking the recent mild spell of weather. Skiers were hustling to get their last opportunity to tackle the black diamond trails before the season's end. A cozy fire is burning in the Village Tavern, which is busy with the local patrons enjoying breakfast and the day's gossip when John 'Little Hands' Russell walks through the front door looking like he has the weight of the world on his shoulders and wants to heave it on someone else.

Immediately Gus Swenson, one of the owners of the tavern comes over to his table and greets his dear friend, "Little Hands... good to see you so early this morning. Has the weather kept you away from your fishing today?"

Little Hands forms a big smile and says, "Gus you know better than to think a little wind and snow would keep me from my favorite pastime. There's something else on my mind, which has me fit to be tied."

"I can see you're bothered by something. It looks like you just lost your best friend."

Little Hands shakes his head in disgust and says, "I haven't fished for the past five days. Some inconsiderate fools have posted 'No Fishing and Private Property' signs all along the riverbank. In my anger I pulled them out of the ground. I don't know who they were because I was far down the river and didn't recognize them but I want to find out. I was just going to let it go but I found out new signs were posted."

Gus nods and points to Ben Willard who is sitting across from them talking with two men and says, "Ben's been involved in purchasing a parcel of land in Hart's Location to build a large shopping center and adjoining restaurant. The Land Management Board just approved the sale last week; it was in the local paper. For the past several weeks an increased amount of truck traffic has been seen traveling back and forth along Route 302. My guess is they have been delivering construction materials for the new shopping center way in advance. Ben must have been real confident the purchase would go through. I'm surprised you hadn't noticed the traffic up by your place."

"It's news to me. The signs were the first things I noticed. You know me; I don't get involved in the goings-on of the valley; I keep to myself if I can. I think what's been happening in the past few years have not been very beneficial to the area. This shopping center is another example."

Little Hands looks over at Ben Willard and begins to shake from his anger at the thought of his land being spoiled by greed and abruptly rises from his table and walks over to Ben. "Mr. Willard.... Can I speak with you for a moment in private?"

Ben looks up at Little Hands showing his irritation at the intrusion and says, "John...I'm sorry but can't you see I'm busy right now with some of my clients? Maybe later when I'm not so busy."

Little Hands walks closer to Ben and says, "I want to talk to you right now; it can't wait."

Ben looks around the room hoping no one was hearing them. "I said not now!"

Little Hands could see Ben was becoming nervous and says in a much louder voice, "I heard you bought land near where my family lives in Harts Location."

"That's right. Is there a problem?"

"My people have their homes and farms throughout the area along the river and some of our ancestors are even buried there. The land has been protected from commercial use by legal agreements made with the government and the Blackthorn family several years ago."

Ben rises from his chair and says, "Little Hands...I'm sorry to inform you but the statue of limitations on those agreements ended over a year ago. It's open land now to anyone who has the money to invest in it. I had the money and I invested and I don't care who lives or who has died there; it's ancient history. Today it all has to do with progress; understand?"

Little Hands can't hold back his anger and grabs Ben by the throat and easily lifts him up off the floor causing Ben to gasp for breath. The two men who were with Ben proceed to get up to help when Little Hands throws Ben across the table like he was a rag doll and then storms out of the Tavern.

***

4

Three days later...March 10, 1962

The Village Tavern was getting busy as usual on a Saturday during lunchtime. Gus and Lars Swenson are working in the kitchen when Gallagher sneaks in through the back door.

"Hi guys, what's cooking?"

They both smile and greet Gallagher in their usual Swedish manner, "god middag." Gus points to the newspaper in his hand and says, "Did you read in today's paper about the work that's been going on at Hart's Location? I guess the shopping center is becoming a reality."

Gallagher nods and says, "I did, but I thought the project would have fallen flat on its face when they realized the plot of land was historic to our native Indians, the Abenaki. My great grandfather purchased that land back in the early eighteen hundreds for the singular reason to preserve the Abenaki heritage in this valley. He eventually donated the land to the Abenaki Foundation for their oversight. The tribal council has been overseeing the property for the past twenty-five years."

"There was a statue of limitations that ended last year on the land," declares Lars Swenson as he joins in on the conversation. "One of the members on the planning board pushed the idea through so it will bring jobs and more tourism to the area; that's a laugh."

"I know...it seems unreasonable to place a shopping center on the last level piece of land in the entire area of Harts Location. The mountains are all around it and the people of the valley will not tolerate such a blot on the landscape. The reason why we have such an influx of tourists during the fall and winter seasons is because of the beauty of the land; not shopping centers. I would expect a petition to be passed around to stop the construction and reverse the decision."

"Gallagher...I hope your right. But times are changing and not for the better. John Russell was in here three days ago grumbling about not being able to fish anymore along the Saco River because of it now being private property."

"Who is the one that pushed the proposal through?"

"You're not going to like it but it's our old friend Ben Willard. Little Hands, in a rare moment of anger, threw Ben across a table after having words with him about it. He actually picked him up off the floor with one hand around his neck and threw him across a table like he was a sack of potatoes."

"Ben...? I thought he was involved in his own project on Thorn Hill. He was planning on building a first class Ski School and Resort. Why is he getting involved with a shopping center ten miles away in the opposite direction?"

"He was in here a few nights ago bragging about it saying it will help with his ski resort. He mentioned as an incentive he was going to offer ski and shopping packages for his guests. He also mentioned his father-in-law is the major stockholder and silent partner in the project and is adding one of his own famous steakhouses to the site."

"I see. Where have I been? I usually hear this kind of news from my patrons at the bookshop. I don't know how I missed hearing about it. This will definitely change the landscape around here and not for the best."

"Even Anna's brother Scott was in here that night and argued with Ben about how it would affect the small shopkeepers in the valley. He mentioned how his own family owned supermarket could suffer by bringing in some of the big chain stores who have the buying power to provide lower prices."

"Well we can complain about this all day but it won't get us anywhere. I will see if I can reason with Ben before it goes any further. But right now I need to fill my stomach before I do anything else today; I'm famished."

"What will you have today my good friend?" asks Gus.

"I could go for a plate of Swedish meatballs over noodles and a chicken and spinach salad to go."

Gus looks out the window and says, "The sky is clearing. You must be planning a climb today. It's cold and a little windy up on the ledges. You and Anna are definitely in need of a hearty lunch."

"Well I wish I was but climbing Cathedral Ledge will have to wait until I finalize the details of the museums construction. It's going well but there are always hurtles to jump over to get things done on time."

Gus nods and says, "It will be a great addition to the valley. I can see the local businesses benefiting from it. We have the skiing, we have the fall foliage, we have the hiking trails and now we will have some added culture to bring in the intellectuals."

"Something for everyone," Gallagher says with a big smile.

"That's right! Oh... by the way your friend Bill Waters came in about a half hour ago and is sitting over at the far end of the counter. He asked if you had been in yet. I will bring your order over there when its ready if that's okay."

"Thanks Gus."

Gallagher makes his way over to Bill as he is enjoying a bowl of his favorite New England clam chowder.

"Good to see you Bill. Clam chowder for breakfast?"

"Gallagher...my friend. Clam chowder for an old salt like myself is good anytime of the day."

"I forgot you were a commercial fisherman before you worked at the hospital. How's it going in Lincoln these days?"

"I couldn't be happier. It's really good to be out from under the grip of Anthony Kennedy and his brother and their web of corruption. Loon Mountain is even expanding their ski trails and adding on big new ski lodge with gift shops and two restaurants. Also, Toni's Restaurant has been sold and will become a first class dining establishment called Corelli's Trattoria."

"You mean Vince finally expanded outside the village?"

"He's always wanted his own restaurant. There's too much competition in the valley so Lincoln with its expanded ski trails was the ideal spot. Anyways...what I wanted to talk to you about is quite unsettling. I think there is something strange going on in the Swift River."

"What do you mean?"

"I've been trout fishing along the Kanc and I've been noticing dead fish floating along the water's edge for several days now. They don't stay very long because bears have been seen having a feast on the fish at night."

As they are talking Gus comes over with Gallagher's order. "I couldn't help overhearing your conversation about seeing bears by the Swift River. A gentleman came in for breakfast about an hour ago and mentioned finding a dead bear lying right outside his camper this morning. He said the bear didn't have a mark on it so he ruled out it having been shot by a hunter. He said he called the Ranger Service right away."

"Where is his camp site?"

"He's camping by the river off the Kanc at Jigger Johnson campground."

"Did you get his name?"

"I didn't think of it."

"I have to get back to Anna with her lunch. I will ask Jonathan to look into when he can."

Gallagher gives them both a big smile and says, "Something is very fishy about all this; no pun intended."

Gus and Bill both laugh as Gallagher leaves the Tavern. Gus looks at Bill and says, "I've seen that smile of Gallagher's many times before and I know his wheels are turning."

Bill nods in agreement and says, "I know what you mean. I'm sure he will find out what it's all about before the sun sets today."

***

Later that evening...

Gallagher hadn't seen much of Ben Willard since he was released from prison after being falsely accused of killing Gordon Hayes. He was exonerated when evidence provided by Gallagher cleared him of any involvement. His wife Jane had spoken several times to him thanking him for what he had done on Ben's behalf but Ben never showed any gratefulness towards Gallagher.

Gallagher called ahead to see if Ben would meet with him and he was reluctant at first but finally agreed and invited him to his home.

The Willard home is on Graustein Lane off of Thorn Hill road only a quarter of a mile from where the Brennan estate was before it was demolished. Ben and his wife purchased the property with intentions on building a state of the art ski resort. After going through several hurtles they were able to purchase the estate along with five hundred acres of land ideal for downhill skiing.

Gallagher approaches the house and immediately hears the Willard's dog barking away as it looks through the side window. Jane Willard meets him at the door. "It's so good to see you Gallagher, please come in. Ben is in the living room waiting for you. He has been quite uptight lately. I don't know what's going through his head. He won't talk about it with me."

Upon entering the room Gallagher quickly notices Ben lying on the couch with his head wrapped with a bandage. Gallagher speaks up and says, "Good to see you Ben. You haven't been tangling with Jonathan again; have you?"

Ben can't help but laugh and says; "I learned my lesson the last time I go poking around where I shouldn't. Please have a seat. I apologize for not getting back to you to thank you for all you did for us. I know it's been awhile. I just got involved in a big project and you know how time can get away from you."

Gallagher shakes his head and says, "Don't even think about it. I was happy I could help. You were definitely swept up in a tangled web of deceit. The truth had to come out sometime and thankfully it did."

"Well that being said and out of the way; what do you want to talk to me about?"

"It has to do with building a shopping center in Hart's Location."

"We have been surveying the land since the middle of last year and finally started breaking ground about three days ago after we got the okay to purchase the property."

"That's very interesting because what I've been hearing is not very good; there's been a lot of truck traffic coming and going through Hart's Location for the past several weeks."

Willard remains quiet for a moment and then sits up on the couch before responding to Gallagher's comment. "We were very confident of the outcome and took advantage of some timely deals on building materials and delivered near the site."

"Don't you think it was a little premature? You do realize you're building on sacred ground."

"You have been talking to John Russell I presume."

"No...not directly. It's the buzz all over town. You are not making many friends by your choice of Hart's Location. Many years ago my great grandfather had honorable intentions of protecting that land for the Abenaki's. It's true the statue of limitations is up on the property but I was hoping we could talk about it for the sake of the Abenaki's. They are good people and I don't want to see what happened to the great Sioux nation happen here. They lost their land because of greed disguised as Manifest Destiny."

Ben clears his throat and says, "I have no ill will against the Abenaki's or for that matter, Little Hands. I'm sure you heard about our altercation a few days ago. The problem is I'm being placed between a rock and a hard place. My father-in-law loaned me forty million dollars allowing us the working capital to build the ski resort on Thorn Hill; but it wasn't without a stipulation. The requirement was for Jane and I to purchase the property at Hart's Location so he could build a shopping center and one of his steakhouses. My father-in-law wanted to be a silent partner for an undisclosed reason. He's a difficult one to deal with so we didn't argue the point. He's used to getting his own way."

"I had heard he's your silent partner. You don't really know his reasoning for staying out of the picture publically?"

"I'm not at liberty to answer that question simple because he has been very closed mouthed about his personal affairs lately and wanted to be kept out of any negotiations for obtaining the property. It's really too late for me to do anything about it now anyways."

"Why did it have to be in Hart's Location? Why not on Thorn Hill? I would think it would be the ideal location for a steakhouse and shopping center. You have the land already and once the resort is completed it would draw people to the area."

"So does Jane and I but it goes deeper than that I'm afraid. I believe Jane's father has gotten himself involved in some shady venture and he will not divulge it to us on any circumstances. He says it's for our own protection not to know the details."

"You mean his hand is being forced?"

"Precisely. When Little Hands came into the Tavern that morning I was involved in serious discussions with two of the principle shareholders of Morgan Enterprises. I had no choice but to go along with the arrangement. My rudeness to Little Hands was an unfortunate knee-jerk reaction caused by the frustration I was feeling of my predicament. Personally I don't see the logic in building there. Hart's Location is a beautiful spot but not for a shopping center."

"I see. I knew there had to be something behind your actions. I suppose you're not on the best terms with your father-in-law right now because of your opposition to the sale of the land."

"Well let's just say it's strained at best. I am just going to stay involved with my resort and keep my distance with the shopping center as much as I can."

"What does Jane say about her father's involvement in this business venture?"

"She won't talk about it with him. You have to understand; he has spoiled her ever since she was a child. Her mother died when she was only five. He raised her alone. She won't go against him. I'm afraid my wife has influenced me to the point of becoming weak when it comes to fighting with her on business matters. She hides that side of her well but I live with her and I know her for what she can be like at times. She's her father's daughter."

Gallagher gets up to leave and says, "Ben, I'm glad we talked. I'm sorry about the predicament you've been forced into. I will smooth things over with Little Hands so you won't have to run the other way when you catch sight of him. He's really a big teddy bear when you get to know him. By the way; I never knew your father-in-laws name?"

"It's Randolph Morgan."

***

5

Early morning...March 11, 1962

Ben Willard was troubled after Gallagher's visit. He knew Gallagher was right. He could see why his actions in placing the signs at Hart's Location would cause consternation with the Abenaki people. It was weakness on his part to allow himself to give in to his father-in-laws demands. He was feeling angry and distraught over the position he'd been forced into. If he didn't go along with the shopping center project all the funds he was able to acquire would be taken away and his dream of a ski resort would go belly-up. He left the house without telling his wife and grabbed a coffee at the Tavern and headed for Hart's Location.

Ben approaches the construction site before the workers arrive so he walks over to the riverbank of the Saco River and makes sure the new 'Private Property and No Fishing' signs have been replaced where he had originally placed them. Everything looked good as he begins to walk over to secure the signs when John 'Little Hand' Russell approaches him from a distance and starts yelling at him at the top of his lungs. "Willard…. get off this land. My people will fight this all the way to the Supreme Court. You will regret the day you took this land away from us. Leave now before it's too late."

Even though Ben realizes Little Hands has good reason to be upset, his pride steps in and says, "Are you threatening me?"

"Take it anyway you like; just get off our land."

At that moment three hikers emerge from the woods and hears the altercation between the two. They remain out of sight behind some trees and wait for them to leave before they continue along the river.

Ben ignores the threat and yells back, "It's none of your business and you're the one who's standing on private property and I suggest you get off this land immediately."

Ben then continues examining all the signs along the riverbank making sure they were secure. Little Hands in frustration leaves the area in a huff and returns to his truck and sits inside and waits to cool off before he drives off realizing it's too late to stop the construction.

***

The next morning...

Gallagher slept unusually late and woke to the sound of the phone ringing. "Yes who is it?" Gallagher answers in a sleepy tone of voice.

"Gallagher...its Tom Perry. Sorry if I woke you but I thought you should know the latest news before you start your day. Your friend Little Hands was arrested two hours ago for suspicion of murder."

"The murder of who?"

"Ben Willard. He was found at Hart's Location by the riverbank strangled to death!"

"What? Why in the world would Little Hands be suspected of Ben's murder?"

"Three guys were hiking on the AM trail through Hart's Location and saw Little Hands and Ben on the site of the shopping center by the river arguing back and forth. They overheard Little Hands warning Ben, even threatening him, to get off the land and mentioned something about going to the Supreme Court if he had to. Ben yelled back and said it was none of his business and he needed to leave because he was standing on private property."

"Did the hikers see him kill Ben?"

"No. Two of them returned about an hour later and found Ben lying by the river in the mud."

Gallagher needs time to think about it. He knew in his heart Little Hands couldn't do such a thing and the evidence was only circumstantial at best.

"I hope you're not just taking their word for it. Are you going to investigate any further?"

"We took down their personal information and they said they could be reached at the Mount Washington Hotel in Bretton Woods."

"Pretty fancy place for a couple of hikers."

"They are both big wigs at a huge outfit in Boston and had just finished hiking Mount Eisenhower, the last 4000 footer for them to climb before they get their patch. Their wives were at the Hotel waiting to celebrate their accomplishments."

"You say it was just the two of them?"

"They are the ones who reported it. They did say another hiker had joined them right before they saw Ben and Little Hands arguing but he went off by himself and continued on the trail."

"Did they get his name?"

"No."

"He needs to be found whoever he is," Gallagher stresses.

"It looks bad for Little Hands. The ligature marks on the neck were definitely made from a strong pair of hands. No one I know of has hands like that except Little Hands."

***

After Gallagher gets off the phone with Lieutenant Perry his first order of business is to go to where they found Ben Willard's body. He travels to Hart's Location and parks right by where Ben had posted the signs and where his body was found. The area had been cordoned off by the police so he was unable to get too close to the riverbank but he was able to get close enough to notice footprints in the mud where the red paint had been dumped. He takes out his camera with its zoom lens and is able to recognize the brand of hiking boot by the sole imprint design in the mud. He snaps the picture and then drives away.

***

6

Early Saturday morning …March 17, 1962

Gallagher was in his study catching up on the latest news when Jonathan walks in and requests Gallagher's undivided attention.

"You have to listen to what I've put together for my speech to the senior class at Jackson High. I will cut to the chase and read the last few lines and tell me what you think."

Gallagher smiles and says, "I'm all ears."

Jonathan begins reading…"By the end of the Second World War the relations between the United States and the Soviet Union had become frosty due to the Soviet Union's political maneuvering to take control of Poland resulting in a communist Poland. Eventually in 1955 the Warsaw Pact was signed, which was in part, a Soviet military reaction to the integration of West Germany into NATO in 1955, per the Paris Pacts of 1954. The rivalry of the two super powers was in full swing by spring of 1961. On April 17th 1961 a counter revolutionary force attempted to overthrow the Cuban government. The invading force was defeated by Cuban armed forces under the command of Prime Minister Fidel Castro. The incident has come to be known as The Bay of Pigs."

"Well, what do you think?"

Gallagher thinks for a moment before he speaks, "I think it's clear and to the point. Are you sure the students at the high school will understand the implications of such an action taken by our military? Because to tell you the truth, I'm having a hard time swallowing it myself. It has to be one of the biggest blunders in the history of this country."

Jonathan thinks for a moment. "Maybe I should tone it down a little bit. I don't want to send the wrong signal to the students making them think I'm against the actions of our government. George Stevens wanted me to speak about the crisis and what led up to it as part of their world affairs lessons. I really don't know how to sugarcoat it anymore than I have. I'm just stating facts and leaving out my opinion which is probably equal to your thoughts on the subject."

"Well I don't believe you need to sugarcoat it but I think of my grandfather's desire to insulate the valley from the troubles of the outside world. That was what the Thorn Hill Covenant was all about if you remember. Until recently we've been able to provide an oasis from the negative side of the human condition. People want to get away from the harsh reality we call everyday life."

Jonathan smiles at his dear friend and says, "I think we found out it's almost impossible to screen off all the chaos this troubled world gets into. The evil thinking behind what man can do to man seems to be winning the fight like it has since Cain and Able walked the earth. Hiding from it or pretending it doesn't exist will not change it; if anything, it will have an appearance of toleration which in my opinion is equal to accepting it."

Gallagher acquiesces and says, "I can agree with you philosophically but I will always try to provide a shield to ward off the blows that come our way in this life. Man in general seems to be lost in the tangled maze of his existence."

"Woe…you're getting too heavy for me this morning. I just was looking for an opinion."

"Jonathan, I'm sorry if I'm sounding a little cynical but it looks like our little oasis is in danger of drying up."

Gallagher hands him a letter marked certified, "I received this letter yesterday afternoon by special delivery."

Jonathan opens the envelope and immediately stops before going on and says, "It says for your eyes only."

"My eyes are your eyes as long as we are a team."

Jonathan nods his head and with a smile and says, "I don't know whether I should cry or bust out laughing."

"Read it and weep! There's nothing to laugh about, I can assure you."

Jonathan decides to read it out loud.

To: Mr. Gallagher Brady,
Re: The Cause

Gallagher...I'm reluctant to inform you of a development that has recently come to my attention regarding the whereabouts of two individuals who were members of the Fifth Column group the Cause, who were not listed in the book of member names, which you found in Echo Lake during the Thorn Hill dilemma. A duplicate book was uncovered in Chicago recently, which originally had two additional names listed but evidence indicates the names were scratched off. We've had several specialists working on it trying to recover the names but have been unsuccessful so far. We believe whoever copied the list you found deliberately left out the two names for a reason.

My reason for passing this intelligence on to you is because we feel there still may be criminal activity in your area connected to the Cause. Whoever it was that placed that list in the lead box, which ended up in Echo Lake, had a long-range plan in mind. Those three individuals may be at work right now in your backyard, which would explain why the names were purposely omitted.

Please keep me informed on any strange or suspicious activity you may come across. Do not share your knowledge of this to anyone except Mr. Henry. I trust he will be the soul of discretion as he was in your last case together. I will keep you informed as to any new developments that surface on my end. When contacting me use the code name Echo because I strongly believe there is a mole in the Bureau.

On a more positive note, there is one bit if information you should know regarding the appointment of your new police Chief. A special committee had been set up since the beginning of the cold war to screen any new law enforcement positions in what we refer to as high impact zones. Chief James O'Reilly comes with impressive credentials and it's the Bureau's feeling that he's the right one to take John Peterson's place. In light of the possibility of more Fifth Column activity in your neck of the woods he will be of great assistance. He has been trained in martial arts and has received several awards including several wrestling championships in the military. I hope you will have the type of working relationship that you enjoyed with John. That's all for now. I look forward to hearing from you in the future.

Respectfully,
Paul Anderson
FBI Bureau Chief, Northeast Sector

Jonathan looks up at Gallagher after putting down the letter and says, "I don't like the sound of it at all. Why do we have to get involved? Just because we got involved in the Thorn Hill nightmare doesn't mean we are now the valley's resident investigators. You had a personal reason why you got involved in solving the Thorn Hill mystery but this is no business of ours. Let the experts handle this one."

"I think Paul feels we are the best to monitor the situation from here without dragging agents in which could cause suspicion; especially knowing there's possibly a mole at the Bureau. What we have to do is keep a low profile so as not to tip off anyone who might be lurking around in our village with evil intent. We can go about our business and if we hear or see something out of the ordinary we can pass it on to Anderson."

"Do you really think these two unknowns referred to in the letter are lurking around our backyard at this very moment? I would think they would've been scared off by what went down last year. All the members of the Cause have been rounded up and have been convicted of treason. If two of them had gone unnoticed you would think they would have left the country while they had the chance."

"From what we had to go through in the last case nothing would surprise me. There's obviously something on their agenda that's keeping them around and in seclusion. Remember how they work. They are patient and determined to achieve their objective. They seem to be driven by a force and are willing to die for it. You and I cannot understand it and that's good but what's also good is we're not ignorant of it."

Jonathan gets up from the breakfast table and says, "Well...I can't think anymore about all this right now. There's nothing much we can do until something surfaces. I have to run over to the library to print out some copies of my speech so I can present this brief synopsis of the world's current woes to the senior class. Also, I need to check out a report of some unusual traffic going in and out of Concord Airport recently."

"What type of traffic?"

"In the last several weeks there have been several cargo planes coming and going at an unusual rate in and out of the Concord Airport. There is no official manifest on each plane stating what they're shipping but according to Larry's last report someone told him it was medicine for humanitarian aid intended for overseas distribution."

"Concord?" Gallagher questions. "I would think Logan Airport would have been used to handle that amount of air traffic. It has a lot more runways."

"I know, it seems odd but Larry Nelson, one of my colleagues, who has been covering the case, has not reported in for the past two days so the

Observer asked me if I could pick up the story where he left off."

"Sounds a little suspicious!"

"Don't start. Everything that sounds a little different or strange doesn't mean our cold war buddies are behind it. Don't let Anderson's letter influence your thinking."

"I know, I know! I'm just playing with you. On a more local topic did you hear about the closing of the Kanc? An article was featured in your competitors paper, the Concord Sun, about roadwork being done for the remainder of the Spring and may extend into a good part of the Summer. There have been several small landslides reported. The shoulders of the road are being reinforced because of all the erosion that has occurred during the past year. Officials are saying it would definitely be ready by the time the leaf peepers come to the valley for the fall season."

"That ought to make the summer driving a challenge for us locals. We'll have to go the long way around to get to Lincoln."

"The article stated the stretch from Lincoln to Bear Notch Road will be passable. At least that's good news. We can cut right over to Route 302 from there."

Jonathan laughs, "That's good. Bear Notch Road comes to the rescue again."

***

Two hours later...

Jonathan arrives at the main terminal at Concord Airport and noticed several cargo planes refueling. He approached one of the security guards standing by the gate and was stopped abruptly by a man from behind dressed in plane clothes. "Can I help you with something? This area is temporarily off limits to civilians."

Jonathan flashes his ID and says, "I'm with the Jackson Observer and I'm here to report on the reason for the unusual high traffic flying in and out of here. Is there anything you can tell me?"

With an impatient look on his face the man says, "You're the second person from your paper to ask about it this week. I will tell you what I told the other gentleman; it's only medicine for clinics overseas; nothing more."

"So this is a military operation?"

"No comment."

"It's highly unusual for this airport to handle such large shipments of anything connected with the military. Pease Air Force Base in Portsmouth has been used for such operations in the past."

"No comment."

Jonathan starts to show his irritation about the man's lack of cooperation. "Can you at least tell me where the shipments are headed?"

"I'll have to get my supervisor."

"Okay, I'll wait."

Five minutes later two security guards armed with rifles approach Jonathan. "We have strict orders to keep the nature of these shipments out of the press because it's highly classified."

"If it's highly classified, like you say it is, why are you using an airport that's used by the general public for a highly classified operation? It's not making much sense and I believe our readers should know what their tax dollars are being used for."

Before Jonathan could get another word out of his mouth one of the guards grabs Jonathan securely by the arm and escorts him out of the immediate area. "I'm sorry you seem unable to grasp what we are saying. The product on board these planes is strictly classified and that should be sufficient for you and your readers. You must leave the premises now or we will have you arrested for trespassing."

Jonathan reluctantly leaves and eventually heads back to Jackson without proof to what was being shipped and why. The long ride back makes Jonathan's mind come to all sorts of conclusions on what was going on. He decides after much thought to let it drop and eventually drives to a small out of the way diner outside of Moultonborough to grab a bite to eat. He makes his way to the counter and notices everyone's eyes are glued to the television set. "What's happening?" He asks the waitress who is watching behind the counter.

A young woman sitting at the counter turns to Jonathan and says, "A fisherman discovered the body of a man in Penacook Lake right outside of Concord."

Jonathan sits down and places his order with the waitress while staring at the television like everyone else. Finally a news bulletin comes on and the commentator says, "An unidentified man was found dead in the shallow part of Penacook Lake. The policeman on the scene could only say he didn't have any identification on him but they had found a small notebook in his pants pocket. All indications point to an apparent robbery. No further details can be released at this time until a proper identification can be made of the victim."

Jonathan realizes he has time to kill so he has a few beers and a plate of corned beef and cabbage for lunch and catches up on the news in the local paper.

One half hour later he finishes his meal and continues his drive back to meet Gallagher and Anna. In all that time he did not make any connection in his mind about the news he had just heard on the television. As he is driving back to Jackson he catches sight of a large white box truck in his rearview mirror barreling toward him at a high rate of speed. Instinctively Jonathan quickly takes a right turn off of Rte. 16 and heads east on Main street through the center of Conway and then takes a left turn onto Eastman Road and drives north reconnecting onto Rte. 16 hoping to lose whoever was following him. After several minutes of waiting to see if the truck continues to follow him Jonathan puts the whole experience behind him chalking it up to his imagination.

***

7

Two days later...March 19, 1962

Tobey Jones leaves his house at seven o'clock as he usually does every morning to deliver newspapers. He has a lot on his mind and needs to talk to his newfound buddy, Gallagher Brady, before heading off to school. His last stop on his route everyday is the Turning Page Bookshop where he and many of his friends stop by on Saturday mornings and attend a reading group to listen to stories from Gallagher's extensive knowledge of literature. Gallagher has a way of making the stories he tells come alive and in the process encourages the youth in the valley to read more and watch television less. Teachers at the local schools have noticed a marked difference in the student's comprehension since the reading group was started.

"Miss Rawlings, is Gallagher in today?" asks Tobey as he walks through the entrance off the bookshop.

"Hi Tobey, good to see you this morning. I'm sorry but Gallagher's not here at the moment. He's on one of his book hunts. He's over at Mary Ann's and should be back soon. Is there anything I can help you with? I'm sure you're in a hurry to get to school."

"Well I'm not sure...probably not. I think it's something only Gallagher will be able to figure out."

Anna smiles and says, "I see! You can wait here if you have time before school starts; he won't be long."

Tobey looks at the clock on the wall and begins to fidget a little and says, I really have to go. Here's your morning paper. There's some pretty bad news right on the front page."

Anna smiles and ignores his remark about the bad news. "Thanks Tobey!"

Tobey looks at the note he has in his hand. "I just don't know if this means anything. It's really bothering me."

"What are you talking about; just tell me."

Tobey looks at the floor and says, "I stopped in to see if Chief O'Reilly was around but he hasn't come in yet this morning...anyways, I knew Gallagher would be the only one to figure this out."

Anna losing her patience and says, "Please Tobey, what is it? Maybe I can help. You definitely seem to be nervous about it."

Tobey looks at the note he has in his hand. "I wrote down this message I heard on our shortwave radio last night. I think it could mean something important. Some of it was garbled and there was a lot of static but I was able to make out a part of it and wrote it down."

Anna takes the message and begins reading it out loud..."*You have to stop this...found out...I'm sorry...for...happened...called...aricona...basker..... help...quickly...abandon...live...before............out of hand...come...it's too late.*"

Anna looks at Tobey. "What time did you hear this message?"

"It was after I finished my homework. Ma never lets me go on the radio until my homework is done. There's a big test today and I had to finish studying. It had to be a little after 8:30."

"Have you ever heard anything like this on the radio before?"

"No. Every night my father lets me roam the channels. Sometimes some of my classmates get on their radios and we talk for a while. Sometimes I find an interesting conversation going on and listen in but I've never come across anything like this before; the man sounded desperate and scared and there was a lot of static so it was hard to make out. Where I have the dotted lines is where I heard the static."

"Did you tell your father? He might know what it means."

"That's another thing. My father did not return home last Friday night after going to a seminar in Boston. He didn't call to say he was not coming home and he still hasn't come home. My mother is getting worried because that's not like my father not to call."

"Did he go with anyone?"

"Dr. Dredmeyer."

"I will give this to Gallagher as soon as he gets in?"

"Thanks Anna. I will come by after school."

Tobey Jones leaves the bookshop a little troubled because he has to wait all day for Gallagher's explanation of the strange message. He reluctantly gets on his bike and rides away not realizing he just became involved in reporting a horrific crime that had taken place the night before.

***

The night before around 8:45...

The large dog reacted violently after being injected with the experimental serum. It began foaming at the mouth. That's when everything went wrong. The dog immediately attacked the man who had just injected him with the serum and bit right through his leg puncturing his femoral artery causing him to bleed profusely. Then the dog leaped at the other man who was closest to him and started clawing and biting his legs. The man feebly attempted to fight off the dog but was easily overtaken by its size. The man struggled for a time and was able to break free and run behind a table where a telephone was and attempted to call for help. In his panic he forgot the phone was just an intercom connected to another building on the site. There was no phone line connected to the outside world. He and his research team were secluded and alone.

The dog lunged for him again then he remembered the shortwave radio across the room near the large walk-in cooler. He grabbed a nearby pushcart with several glass beakers on top and began throwing them at the dog. One of the beakers hit the dog square on the nose causing the dog to squeal and stumble. The glass shattered into the dog's eyes temporarily blinded it. While the dog was trying to recover from the blow the man kept the pushcart between him and the dog and made the distress call. The dog was fumbling and showing signs of fatigue but so was the man as he continued to bleed from his legs. The dog regained itself and leaped at him again and he flung the pushcart at the dog then quickly ran inside the walk-in cooler and slammed the door shut. The two other men in the room who had watched the whole thing were in complete shock and started to run out of the building in a panic when the dog turned towards them. They managed to get outside and shut the door to the building trapping the dog inside.

The man in the cooler wrapped his legs up with the sleeves of his lab coat. His thinking was the cold air in the cooler would slow down the bleeding. In a short time he started to become very sleepy. He thought to himself that no one would know he was in there if he passed out. The man knew the procedure; his superiors drilled it into him. His colleagues who witnessed the attack would have to deny any association with him if they were found and questioned. They would block the secluded road that led to the abandoned facility. They would chain and lock the gate. Any tire tracks they had made would be brushed away. Any trace of activity would be removed. His only hope was someone would have heard his plea for help over the radio.

***

Gallagher returns from Mary Ann's all smiles and says to Anna as he walks into the bookshop, "I have some great news. Mary Ann has donated two first edition copies of 'The Hound of the Baskervilles', signed by Sir. Arthur Conan Doyle himself to the museum. The books are authentic and are bound in high quality leather. They are probably worth over five thousand dollars each. Mary Ann will keep them in her safe until the museum opens."

"Did she say who brought them in and if they knew what they were worth?"

"She said he didn't give his name. He wanted to stay anonymous. He said he was not in need of any money and was more than happy to give them to her as a gift. Because of their high value she thought it would be best for the museum to have them. She felt she couldn't sell them for anywhere near their worth and said she owed a lot more to us than a couple of rare books."

Gallagher hesitates then says; "He did say something rather interesting before he left. He said, "There are books of which the backs and covers are by far the best parts."

"What an odd statement."

"Not really. It's a quote from Charles Dickens' book, Oliver Twist. He sounds like a collector like myself and knows his literature or maybe he's just an avid reader and appreciates fine literature."

"Did she say what he looked like?"

"She described him as tall and very distinguished and was wearing a well groomed white beard."

"There's no one that I can place at the top of my head. He's probably from out of town." She then hesitated for a moment..."Gallagher...I don't want to spoil your good mood but you need to read this message."

Gallagher studies the message and a bewildered look comes over his face. "Where did you get this?"

"Tobey brought it in about an hour ago. He said he heard it on his father's shortwave radio last night. Do you think it means anything?"

Gallagher rolls his eyes and says, "I don't know but here we go again. Just when I thought we could get back to our own simple lives another puzzling message comes our way to distract us. I should have never agreed to continue in helping the local police in any future investigations. I only became a licensed investigator for the sole purpose of finding out what happened to my parents. Now everyone thinks I'm available for solving every mystery that comes down the pike."

"Well you have to admit breaking up the Nazi conspirators and solving the Thorn Hill mystery and at the same time finding out who and what was behind your parents death was pretty amazing. Jonathan added to all that by writing all those articles chronicling your adventures together."

"I know, I know. I'm grateful I was able to accomplish all of that but it still doesn't change my thinking that I would prefer being a regular guy who owns a bookshop and who loves to climb mountains with the girl of his dreams. It that so bad?"

Anna shakes her head and says, "Aren't you just jumping to conclusions? It's probably nothing. Shortwave radios can pick up anything from just about anywhere. My cousins in Colorado use their radios to converse with friends of theirs in England. It might just be a silly prank."

Gallagher places it on his desk. "You're right. I am jumping to conclusions. This can wait for now. My first priority is to call Harry Fuller about the progress of the museum and tell him the good news about the books. I drove by there the other day and noticed the outside work is almost completed. He said the inside work would begin soon."

"That reminds me," Anna says while wrapping her arms around his waist. "Professor Meridian called and said you could stop by anytime today. The appointment he had this morning was a no-show. He sounded a little stressed about it. I hope he's okay and it's nothing serious."

"I will head over there right now. Is Kathy coming in today to help out?"

"Yes she should be here about 1:00. One more thing you should know before you go. Tobey said his father and Dr. Dredmeyer attended a seminar last Friday night in Boston but he never returned home. He never called to let Penny know he was not going to come home after it was over which is not like him."

"I heard about that seminar on the news. It was to be a closed door by invitation only affair. It had something to do with some new breakthroughs in nuclear research."

"Don't you find that a little strange?"

"If it was really out of the ordinary I'm sure Penny would've called the police about it. Tobey sometimes can have a vivid imagination."

***

Gallagher leaves the bookshop and starts walking towards the professor's home. As he is passing the police station, the newly appointed chief, James

44

O'Reilly, comes out and gently grabs him by the arm, "Gallagher do you have a minute?"

"Sure Chief. How are you this morning?"

"I'm doing fine. Still trying to get to know all the folks in town."

"Well you only have been here about six months now and I think you're doing better than I did during my first few months in the valley. So, what can I do for you?"

"I just got a call from Penny Jones and she's in a panic. I don't know her that well yet. Is she the emotional type?"

"Is it about her husband?"

"No, it's about Tobey. Have you seen Tobey this morning?"

"He was in the bookshop about an hour ago. Why, what's up?"

"According to Penny he was supposed to drop off a message to me after his paper route and then go off to school. I told her I never saw him this morning."

"He did deliver a message to Anna. He said he was looking for you but you were not in yet and decided to deliver it to me, but I was also out at the time."

"That's odd. I came in about six this morning to catch up on some paperwork and haven't left my desk since."

"Well it's just as well you were not bothered with it. It's an odd cryptic message he heard it on his father's shortwave radio. It's probably some prank. Sometimes people who have nothing better to do like to generate panic on the airwaves. I'm on my way to see the professor about the museum and I will pick his brain with it and see what he thinks it could mean if anything."

O'Reilly hesitates for a moment and then says, "You said he heard the message on his shortwave radio?"

"Yes I did. Why, what are you thinking?"

"Could I see the message?"

"Sure here it is."

Gallagher watches the expression on O'Reilly's face as he reads the message.

"This sounds like a cry for help but it could be from anywhere the radio can receive a signal," declares O'Reilly.

"That was my thinking exactly. With that massive antenna of his father's he has heard conversations as far away as Europe. Nothing right now indicates it's a local concern but I will have Jonathan look into it if you would like."

"That would be great. But do me a favor and keep this on the QT.; no need to arouse an unnecessary panic."

Gallagher hesitates for a moment. "Sure but why do you think Penny Jones was in such a panic?"

"She said Tobey never showed up for class this morning. I called the school and found out two of Tobey's closest friends didn't show up for class either."

Gallagher shakes his head adamantly, showing his disagreement to O'Reilly's remark and says, "Tobey is not the type of kid to play hooky but you know how kids are at times. If he's with his friend Ernie they probably decided to go on some adventure together. They have been known to do that from time to time."

O'Reilly nods and says, "I will have to surrender to your thoughts on the matter because I really don't know Tobey very well. It's going to take me a while to get to know everyone to point where I can tell if what I hear should become a concern of mine. I know in this business there can be a lot of wasted time worrying over nothing."

"You could easily fix that problem. Have your morning coffee at the Village Tavern everyday and in a short period of time you will know everyone and everything that goes on in the valley. In the meantime is there anything I can do to help?"

 O'Reilly hesitates for moment and says, "I don't think there's anything at the moment. I will let you know. I'll have one of my officers patrol the area to see if he can find Tobey."

"While we're talking. How are you coming along with the investigation into Ben's murder?"

"Well I think it's an open and shut case. Little Hands had motive and we have two witnesses."

"From my understanding the two hikers did not witness the murder they just witnessed an argument two hours before finding him."

O'Reilly shows the first signs of being impatient with their conversation and says, "Gallagher, I can understand your thoughts and feelings about it but I think I'm in a better position to be more objective. I know Little Hands is a good friend of yours but the facts reveal a very strong man strangled Ben. Little Hands recently had words with Ben in the Tavern in front of several witnesses. They saw him lift Ben up off the floor by the neck with one hand and throw him across a table."

"I know I heard about it from Gus. But it's still just circumstantial evidence. Look at your hands. I know you have a wrestling background it could have easily been you. Where were you at the time of Ben's demise?"

"I beg your pardon. You think I could've have strangled Ben? I don't even know the man and I'm quite irritated by your allegation."

"Calm down Chief. I'm just trying to make a point. What about the third hiker? Have you made any effort to find out where he is so he can be questioned?"

"He left the two other hikers we talked with and continued on his own way on the AM trail. He could be anywhere by now."

"Was he heading south?"

"I couldn't tell you."

"Lieutenant Perry told me the very same thing and Chief...I don't think that's good enough."

"What are you getting at?"

"I mean you no disrespect but it looks like there's a rush to judgment. I've seen how that can turn out to be a very bad idea."

"The two hikers we talked with said the other hiker just kept to himself and said very little and moved on."

"I'm glad you got at least their names."

O'Reilly looks intently at Gallagher and says, "What are you planning to do right now?"

"Well right now I'm going to see the professor."

An apparent look of relief comes across O'Reilly's face as Gallagher leaves and heads towards the professor's home. A new question comes to Gallagher's mind. What's bothering O'Reilly and what's on his agenda?

***

O'Reilly goes back into his office and reaches for his phone and dials. "This is O'Reilly. We have a problem. Brady is asking questions about Willard's murder."

"That's not all you have to worry about. There has been an accident at the main site," says the man on the other end.

O'Reilly almost chokes from what he had just heard and asks, "Is the project suspended?"

"No. They are not finished. They had to shut down site number one and move to site number two. Call in tomorrow at the same time for an update. Until then keep an eye out. Let me know if Brady starts getting in the way. This can't become public knowledge or it will be a disaster. We already have had two incidences at the airport. One of them I'm afraid had to end tragically. The other one escaped who incidentally happens to be a close friend of Brady's."

"Who was he?"

"Jonathan Henry."

"Do you want us to take care of him?"

"Definitely not. One incident can look like an accident. Two would bring out the dogs."

"I understand. I'll be in touch."

'Click'

***

8

Gallagher arrives at Professor Meridian's home about 1:30. His daughter Louise escorts Gallagher into his library and finds the professor surrounded by the clutter of his many books and periodicals. It was not unusual to see the professor smothered in his never-ending research about anything and everything.

"Gallagher, good to see you. I'm still having a difficult time calling you Gallagher, even after all this time. As soon as you returned to the valley as the adult named Gallagher Brady I could see the young Thomas Blackthorn behind those wire rim glasses."

Gallagher laughs. "I knew you were not fooled for a minute but I had to convince everyone else for a while. I knew I could trust your discretion. That's one of the reasons why I've come by today. First of all, I appreciate the addition you are making to the museum. Your collection of books will enrich the museums Science section tremendously. Secondly I need you to analyze a strange message that young Tobey Jones heard on his father's shortwave radio last night. The man sounded very distressed according to Tobey."

Gallagher hands the note to him and he reads it out loud...*"You have to stop this...found out...I'm sorry...for...happened...called...aricona...basker.....help...quickly...abandon...live...before.............out of hand...come...it's too late."*

The professor looks at Gallagher shaking his head and says, "What do *you* make of it? You're the one who can figure out mysterious messages."

"I don't have a clue, that's why I'm here. I thought you might be able to shed some light on its meaning; particularly the word *aricona*."

"That's your department. You have proved that very clearly in the Thorn Hill Case. It may be nothing and Tobey may have even spelled it wrong. It means nothing to me."

"As far as what happened on Thorn Hill I had a little help from my grandfather from the grave on that one."

"This message is too deficient and could be from anywhere. All I can say is focus your attention on the word you mentioned, 'aricona'. It must mean something important to be included in a distress message. It's the only word I can see which needs further study. It's an anomaly. The word basker only brings to mind the name Baskerville like in the Hound of the Baskervilles."

Gallagher's jaw drops at hearing the Professor's words. He looks at his watch and says, "Thanks professor, it's not much to go on but here we go again. Samuel Hayes leaves a message at my doorstep one night, which leads to an exhausting string of nightmarish events. I can only imagine where this will lead me."

"Before you go what about the books I mentioned to you for the new museum? What do you want me to do with them?"

"I'm sorry professor, I'm a little distracted all of a sudden. I will have one of Harry's men come by and pick them up. I really appreciate your generosity."

"You're the generous one by building such a beautiful addition to the valley both in structure and culture."

The professor then rubs his salt and pepper beard and says, "I know all about being distracted. My appointment with Dr. Dredmeyer was a no-show. He was suppose to see me today regarding the seminar he attended last night Friday night with Dr. Jones. That was to be at 10:00 this morning. I called his home but there was no answer; it's not like Wallace. He's precise and organized to the letter. I fear something has happened to him."

"This is getting more interesting as the day goes on." Gallagher exclaims.

"How do you mean?"

"Oh...nothing. I'm just thinking of my day so far. It's been quite educational."

Gallagher thanks the Professor and finally leaves the professor's home without letting him know about Dr. Philip Jones and how he did not return home from the seminar either. Then the other thing that caught Gallagher's attention was the professor's mentioning of the possibility of the word basker could actual be Baskerville. It was too much to take in all at once and so he headed for Eagle House to see if Helen could make anything out of it all.

***

Jonathan arrives at Eagle house to find Gallagher and Helen sitting on the front porch studying the mysterious radio message.

"Where have you been?" asked Gallagher.

"Where have I been? Well let me see. First thing this morning I took Valerie to breakfast at Molly's Kitchen and then I dropped her off at Mary Ann's. From there I went straight to the office and found a note for me to follow up on a report of a dead bear that was found at Jigger Johnsons campground back on Saturday."

"I heard all about it at the Tavern. I meant to ask you if you could look into it and it slipped my mind. It was the same day I heard about some dead fish floating in the Swift River. Anything else?"

"Anything else? Isn't that enough?"

Gallagher encourages Jonathan to sit and says consolingly, "I don't know how to tell you this other than to be straight forward with you. The State Police found Larry Nelson's body about five miles west of Concord in Penacook Lake. It was an apparent drowning due to a drug overdose. An autopsy is being done and we should know in a day or so."

"That explains a lot."

"Did you know him well? I know you worked for the same paper but did you know him personally? Was he a druggy?"

"He was freelance like me. He wasn't an employee of the newspaper. We sometimes ended up on the same story together. I had a drink with him once after we worked a crime scene. He was sort of a go-getter type and was always interested in getting the exclusive on a story. I wish I had his ambition. But I always thought his aggressive approach might get him in trouble one day; apparently it got him dead. As far as being a druggy I couldn't say but to be an investigative reporter like he was, drugs are not part of the equation to stay on top of a story. It sounds like foul play."

"I know that something like this can hit home. Are you alright?"

Jonathan remains quiet for a moment trying to take it all in. He finally looks up at Gallagher and says, " Yeah, I'm okay but I'll tell you this much; I've had a feeling of dread since I left Concord. I even imagined being followed by someone in a big truck. It made me think about the letter from Anderson. I've been meaning to ask you. Does Helen know about the letter?"

Helen overhears and says, "Gallagher, let me read it. Jonathan, do you think Larry's death may have something to do with what's in this letter?"

"Now that I put the two of them together, I wouldn't be surprised. It has the fifth column group, 'The Cause', written all over it. That whole scene at the airport convinced me something was brewing and certain parties did not want it to be exposed. He must have asked too many questions and wouldn't take no for an answer and paid for it in the end. Now I know it wasn't my imagination. I was followed from Concord."

Gallagher speaks up. "I don't think you should dwell on it right now because at this stage it would only be speculation. You said you only worked with him a few times. Maybe he was a druggy. Some can hide it very well. We need something more concrete to deal with right now. What did you find out about the dead bear?"

"The bear was definitely poisoned. They found an extremely high amount of radiation in the bears liver."

"Any idea how it got poisoned?"

"It had been seen roaming around the Swift River shortly before they found it. The bear was seen several times during the middle of the day at the campsite, which is very unusual. The ranger I talked with said black bears occasionally can be seen in daytime, but they are usually active at night when they are roaming long distances in search of food such as fruit, berries, nuts, roots and honey. They also feed on insects, rodents and other small mammals, stranded fish and even carrion and refuse."

"That explains it. Bill Waters said he has been noticing dead fish floating to the edge of the Swift River for a number of days. You can't get anymore stranded than that!"

"Right now the ranger said they are screening off all streams and brooks that overflow into the lakes and ponds. If it can be isolated they may be able to find the source."

Gallagher thinks for a moment and asks Helen if she would get him a map of the area.

"What's going through your mind?" Jonathan asks showing signs of weariness.

"I think finding where the river's source is will help us determine where the fish may have been exposed to that amount of radiation."

Jonathan rubs his chin and says, "I'm not familiar with any mills or factories along the Swift. Many of them that existed years ago have been shut down and dissolved. They all had to do with the logging industry. That whole area has changed so much since the turn of the century."

After several minutes Helen hands Gallagher the map. "This is all I could find up in the attic."

Gallagher studies it for a few minutes then says, "According to this map the Swift River rises in the township of Livermore on the eastern side of Kancamagus Pass, and flows east into a broad valley, surrounded by the mountains, which we know as the Albany Intervale. Flowing from the Intervale the river enters a narrow gorge passing over two sets of small waterfalls. The river continues east through the town of Albany and joins the Saco River in Conway. Along the way it looks like there are many small streams that feed some of the nearby lakes and ponds."

Jonathan nods, showing his familiarity with the area and says, "It seems pretty clear to me. From Livermore the Swift River runs along the Kanc then eventually into the Saco River at the junction of West Side Road and East Side Road in Conway."

Gallagher continues reading, "According to the map the village of Livermore has an elevation of 1,264 feet. Definitely anything could run down into the streams from that elevation. It's the law of gravity."

"If my memory serves me correct," Helen recalls. "Livermore was briefly inhabited as a logging town in the late 19th and early 20th centuries. Since then it has been abandoned. I had read an article on the history of the region and the fact that the whole town became a virtual ghost town and was officially dissolved in 1951."

Gallagher eyes Jonathan and says, "If you're up to it, how would you like to do some more research on this and find out what you can about the little village of Livermore? See if there's anything suspicious that could cause the poisoning of the fish. If this is not stopped soon, tourism could come to a grinding halt if this becomes public knowledge."

"I'd be happy to. Hopefully it will get my mind off of what happened to poor Larry in the process."

***

9

Tuesday morning ...March 20, 1962

Jonathan headed for Route 302 towards the direction of Crawford's Notch and decided to stop into Daisy's Trading Post on his way. When he walked in he saw a handful of people browsing through the aisles. They looked like your typical tourists with cameras around their necks and holding on to maps and locally made souvenirs. He figured they wouldn't know anything about Livermore so he continued to walk around and spotted an old woman sitting in a rocking chair knitting a sweater. She noticed him right away and said with a smile revealing the absence of some teeth, "Is there something I can do for you young man?"

The woman with her dark complexion reminded Jonathan of an old Indian squaw who could be the wife of some tribal Chief. She had deep-set gray eyes that looked like they had seen too many sunrises. Her hair was jet black defying her age and the skin on her face looked like wrinkled polished leather.

"Yes...I was wondering if you could tell me anything about the town of Livermore."

The woman's eyes lit up at those words and said, "I haven't heard anyone speak of Livermore in many years?"

She put down the sweater she was knitting and said, "Livermore was a company town owned by the Saunders family. At one time a little over two hundred people lived and worked there. It was a logging town that flourished in the late eighteen hundreds and continued for a short time after the turn of the century but eventually died as a town because of over deforestation."

"So no one lives there anymore?"

"That's right...it's what you can call a real ghost town."

"My name is Jonathan Henry and I work for the Jackson Observer as a freelance reporter. I don't believe I have ever seen you in here before. You seem to know a lot about Livermore. Have you always lived around here?"

"My husband Angelo died three months ago. He was the one who always worked in the store. I usually keep to myself and only go into Jackson a couple of times a month for my personal needs. I'm about ready to sell the store because I'm getting too old to run it myself."

"He was the big gentlemen who has waited on me in the past."

"That was my Angelo. I miss him so much."

"I'm sorry about your loss. Do you have any children to help you?"

"My son Mario decided to leave home about five years ago to seek out greener pastures. He never got along with his father and was never interested in working the store. He ended up joining the Army and eventually became part of a Special Forces outfit called the Green Beret. After two years he left the military. He said he was disenchanted with the government's military policies. We have not seen or heard from him since. He doesn't even know about his father's death. I tried to find out where he was stationed to see if they knew of his whereabouts but all they said to me was, it was classified; whatever that means. I thought that was strange if he left the military but my husband said he would come home someday. My daughter Yellow Doe got married three years ago and moved to Maine. Her husband has asked her to stay away from here."

"Why? It seems rather cold and uncaring especially now that you're alone."

"It's not because of me but because of my son. He has a strong dislike for him because of his treatment of Yellow Doe when they were very young. Mario was very abusive to her. I think that's why my husband and Mario did not get along. Angelo said Mario was just a bad seed."

"By your dark complexion are you native Indian?"

"I'm full blooded Abenaki and my husband was a full-blooded Italian right from the old country. My children are half Abenaki and half Italian. Quite a mixture don't you think?"

"I would say so. Do you happen to know John 'Little Hands' Russell?"

"Of course. We are all one big family here. He's my cousin's boy. Mario and John grew up together and they were involved in wrestling competitions in their youth."

"Mario must have had his hands full competing with Little Hands. The size of his hands alone would be enough to scare off the competition."

"You haven't met Mario. He's a large man like his father. He has been known to take on two men at a time and win. It's one of the reasons he fit in with the Special Forces Unit. He won several competitions while in the military. But thinking of Little Hands, he has not been the same since his mother's death. He blames the government for cutting back on her medical benefits. She was released from the hospital too soon because of not having adequate insurance and soon after that she developed pneumonia. Her heart finally gave out. It has soured him toward our government."

"I'm so sorry to hear of such an injustice. Little Hands never spoke about it to me. We are not that close. I only have been in his company a few times with my friend Gallagher Brady."

A smile comes over her face at the mentioning of his name and says, "Gallagher is your friend? Well then you're my friend too. His grandfather Jonas helped my people out when no one else would and Gallagher has continued to do the same."

"You knew Jonas Blackthorn?"

"I sure did. I know, I don't show my age," she said with a big laugh.

Jonathan laughs and says, "I think you remind me of a movie star."

"Now I really know you're my friend but you are a good liar too. Maybe you can answer a question for me. What has been happening up the road off of Rte. 302? The truck traffic has been non-stop for the past six months. Someone mentioned a shopping center was under construction; is that true?"

A customer getting ready to leave overhears the conversation and says, "I only know what I heard in town. They are building a shopping center in Hart's Location about six miles west of here."

The old woman shakes her head and says, "I've learned to mind my own business but I felt comfortable in asking you because you work for the paper. What goes on around here is of little concern to me at my age. I've seen too many changes in the past few years and you get used to it. Skiing has become big around here. Many of the big Inns and Hotels have converted over to offer heat for the winter skiing season. You may not have known this but this valley was for years a summer retreat for people from the big cities."

Jonathan smiles. "I believe I've heard that before."

Jonathan looks at his watch and says, "Thank you Mrs.?"

"Call me Daisy."

"You've been very helpful Daisy. I will have to tell Gallagher I met you."

"Please do and tell him I will be in soon to pick up my usual."

"I will and I wish you the best with selling the Trading Post. I will miss coming in here to buy my coffee."

Jonathan leaves the store very interested by what she said about the truck traffic and continues towards Sawyer River Road. As he approaches the entrance to the road on his left he stops and looks to his right across a large plush meadow which was the center of Harts Location and saw what had the Abenaki's so up in arms about. A large section of land had been cleared and the foundation of the shopping center had already been constructed. Several trucks were coming and going on the newly made road called Willard's Way.

After driving about five miles on Sawyer River Road, which was an old logging road he finally enters the center of the abandoned village of Livermore. Several rundown buildings were scattered along what was once the main street. Jonathan drives very slowly through the disserted town and sees on one side of the street an old icehouse, an engine house and a blacksmith shop. On the other side were the remains of a small grocery store, a boarding house, a school and a large barn. Several foundations of demolished homes were scattered about on roads leading away from the center of the village. They were overgrown with grass and shrubs because the roads were never paved to begin with and nature had an easy time reclaiming them through the many years the town was in disuse.

Jonathan parks his Land Rover behind one of the buildings and proceeds to walk up a small path leading to an old millhouse. It was apparently once used to generate the electricity for the town according to the sign on the front door, which reads Livermore Power Company. What Jonathan found strange was water was flowing down from the upper hills and was turning a large millwheel. Electricity was being generated but no one was around to use it; at least it appeared so to Jonathan.

Jonathan opens the door of the millhouse and to his surprise finds evidence of someone recently having been there. Unspoiled foodstuffs were left on a table and what looked like white medical lab coats were found hanging on hooks by the door. Also on the table was a telephone with a pencil and notebook next to it. Jonathan picks up the receiver and the phone had no dial tone.

After looking around for any sign of life Jonathan goes back outside and carefully scouts out the immediate area but doesn't find any indication of anyone being around. He begins to return to his vehicle, assuming there was nothing else to see, when he notices faint tire tracks leading out from a fenced in area. It looked like they had recently been brushed over. He looks up and notices the telephone line and electrical wires overhead were going from the millhouse to an area on the other side of the fenced in area. The gate to the fence was chained and locked. The gate had a warning sign posted which read 'High Voltage Keep Out'.

Jonathan thinks for a moment and decides to see if he gets any reaction by shutting down the power. He decides to go back to the millhouse and diverts the flow of water away, which was turning the millwheel. After about a half hour goes by, no activity was observed coming from the fenced in area. So he gets back into his Rover and heads back to Jackson forgetting to reconnect the flow of water to the millwheel. As he slowly drives away he couldn't help feel he had been watched the whole time he was there.

***

In the meantime Gallagher and Anna decide to drive over to Jigger Johnson's Campground and see if they could find any revealing evidence of anymore poisoning. While they were poking around the shoreline a police cruiser drives up and Lieutenant Tom Perry gets out of his vehicle with a troubled look on his face.

"Gallagher we have a problem. Tobey Jones and his father are still missing. Also, Professor Meridian called and said Dr. Wallace Dredmeyer was scheduled to meet with him yesterday at 10:00 but did not show up and there is still no answer at his home or his office today. He sounded very upset."

"I know, he told me about Dredmeyer when I saw him yesterday. I guess he didn't feel it was necessary to call the police until today. They are close friends and it's not like Dredmeyer not to call or Jones for that matter. Something is up and it doesn't look good."

"There's even more to it. The professor is worried because lately Dredmeyer has been deeply troubled about something but had refused to discuss it with him when he asked about it. When he called the professor to make the appointment he said he had to get something off his mind that had been bothering him for several months. He said he felt it had to come out before it got out of hand. That's all he said and hung up. That's why the professor is so worried. Dredmeyer is not the type to get flustered or anxious about anything. They witnessed the bomb test at Los Alamos and Dredmeyer didn't even flinch accorded to Meridian. The professor said he had to run to the latrine almost immediately."

Gallagher perks up and says, "Are those Dredmeyer's exact words; *get out of hand?*'"

"That's what Meridian told me."

Gallagher looks at Anna shaking his head showing his frustration. "We seem to be having a buildup of mysterious circumstances leading to questions that none of us can answer at the moment."

"Did Jonathan come back from Livermore yet?" Perry asked.

"I told him to make a quick scan of the town and come back soon as he could. I would expect him back anytime now."

"Well in the meantime we will start a search for Tobey, his father and Dredmeyer. I'm sure it's just a coincidence that they are all missing at the same time."

Gallagher gives Perry a peculiar look and says, "I don't believe in coincidences anymore. I've learned my lesson."

***

Jonathan got back to Jackson by 2:00 p.m. and went straight to the bookshop. Gallagher was on the phone with Professor Meridian.

"Jonathan is back professor. I will call you when I find out more."

'Click'

"Jonathan, what did you find out in Livermore?"

"Something is going on out there for sure. In an old millhouse I found fresh food on a table. Also, electricity was being produced for some reason but no one was around that I could see. So I shut it down to see if anyone would come out of where the electrical lines were connected; they were leading to a fenced in area. There were signs everywhere warning to 'Keep Out' and 'No Trespassing'. I waited but no one showed up but I had the strangest feeling I was being watched the whole time."

Gallagher nods his head and says, "I think there's definitely something going on up there and its not good."

"Something else," Jonathan remembers. "I met your old friend Daisy. She said there's been an increased amount of truck traffic along the stretch of road coming through where Sawyer River Road connects with Rte. 302 for the past six months. The shopping center construction just started recently."

Gallagher seems unfazed by Jonathan words and forms a smile. "So you met good old Daisy Saffron. Isn't she a sweet old lady? You can count on what she says to be right on. She's sharp as a tack. She comes in here at least twice a month to pick up her latest romance novels. She reads them and then she sells them at a discount in her store. She also likes to read a good mystery. Her favorites are Dashiell Hammett novels featuring Sam Spade and also Nick and Nora Charles in the Thin Man series."

"Well I didn't know. Who would have thought? I just know I've never seen her in there before or anywhere else for that matter. I thought she was married to a man named Angelo. Saffron doesn't sound Italian."

"Daisy Saffron is her Abenaki name; it means Yellow Flower. Her husband Angelo never minded her keeping her given name. Angelo Caruso was a decent man and knew my grandfather very well. Helen always said nice things about him."

"How about Daisy? Do you know much about her other than what you told me?"

"She keeps very much to herself and has become somewhat of a recluse since her son Mario left. I never met him because he left the valley in 1957 and I showed up here a year later. When she comes into town she's usually dressed up to conceal her face with a large hat and kerchief. She's definitely an odd duck but I like talking with her. She knew my grandfather and my parents and I've been able to find out more things about them from an outsiders perspective."

"Getting back to what I was saying," Jonathan continues. "What about the increased truck traffic during the past six months?"

Appearing to ignore the question Gallagher hands Jonathan a folder. "We got the autopsy report back on the bear. It died of radiation poisoning. What's even stranger, it was also full of sulfur dioxide. When they cut open the bear it had eaten several pounds of fish which also were contaminated with radiation."

"Sulfur dioxide... Isn't that one of the antidotes for radiation poisoning?"

"That's right! So the question is; what's the source of the radiation and who is responsible for possibly concocting an antidote."

"Not to change the subject," exclaims Jonathan. "Any word on Dredmeyer since I've been gone?"

"Nothing yet. But Dredmeyer is not the only one missing. Tobey's father never came home after a seminar he attended Friday night with Dredmeyer. Professor Meridian was scheduled to meet with

Dredmeyer but he didn't make the appointment and he cannot be reached. He called the police about it today and indicated he's worried about Dredmeyer because it's not like the doctor to be so irresponsible and there was something important Dredmeyer wanted to tell him that has been bothering him for some time."

"Doesn't Tobey's father work at the same research facility as Dredmeyer?"

Gallagher thinks for a moment. "I need to call Penny Jones and find out if you're right. I knew he was involved in research but much of what he did was classified. I don't know if Penny is privy to any details of what he's currently working on and if it involves Dredmeyer but it's a start."

Gallagher is about ready to call Penny Jones when Lieutenant Perry walks into Gallagher's office.

"Gallagher...I've got some great news. Tobey is home safe and sound."

"Where was he all this time?"

"He's on his way over to tell you himself. He told his mother he wanted to talk with you specifically."

"Really!" Gallagher exclaims surprised. "Why me?"

"He said it has something to do with H.G. Wells."

***

10

Tobey Jones walks into the bookshop and is warmly greeted by Anna, Gallagher, Jonathan and Tom Perry.

Gallagher speaks first and says, "Tobey...you put a scare in all of us. Where have you been since yesterday?"

Tobey puts is head down. "I'm sorry if I caused so much worry for everyone. It all happened so fast."

Gallagher invites Tobey to sit and share his experience. "Tobey, you have our undivided attention."

"Yesterday when I heard the message on the radio I didn't tell Anna everything. The frequency the radio was set on was on a list my father had in his notes, which I found on his desk next to the radio. Also, there was a map of Livermore County and a marker indicating the main street of the village. My curiosity got to me and like you already know, I tried to stop in and see you to find out what you thought of the message. I told my mother I was going to see the Chief but I lied. I thought you could figure it out faster."

"Sorry I wasn't here Tobey. I guess you missed me by a few minutes."

"I decided to ride my bike with a couple of my friends to Livermore. It took us a couple of hours but I'm familiar with the ride because Ernie Williams and I ride there often to go the Arethusa Falls. It's also one of the hikes we do in the Scouts. I first went to Ernie's house to see if he would play hooky from school and then we went to Charlie Bates' house and he jumped at the thought of skipping school. He hadn't done his homework and there was going to be a big test and he thought he was going to flunk anyway. I had him get us some food for our trip. He then snuck out of the house with a backpack full of food and we left undetected from his parents."

Gallagher shows extreme interest in Tobey's story and says, "Please continue."

"When we got near the entrance to Sawyer River Road we saw a black car leaving with four men inside. They took a right onto Route 302 and headed towards Jackson. We made our way towards the main street of the village and decided to hide our bikes behind an old millhouse. We could hear water flowing down from the hills and saw it was turning the millwheel. We were a little thirsty from the ride so we walked over to get a drink. We then decided to go inside the millhouse and have something to eat. We were about ready to eat when we heard people talking outside. I looked out the window and saw two more men coming out from a fenced in area that was posted with the sign, 'KEEP OUT'. They locked the chain that went across the entrance and walked over to another building, an old school house, and they stayed inside for the rest of the day. The black car returned with only the driver about an hour later. We decided to stay hidden in the backroom of the millhouse until they all left. I didn't realize they were going to stay the whole night. Eventually I fell asleep."

"What happened then?" Jonathan asks.

"We woke up early this morning to the sound of men arguing. Ernie and Charlie were getting worried and wanted to go home. I told them to cut through the woods so they wouldn't be seen. I told them I would catch up. It started to get very windy

70

and leaves and dust were flying everywhere but I could just about make out two men brushing tire marks away in the road and then I saw one of the men who was a very short man put a blindfold on the other taller man and then tied his hands behind his back. The man who was blindfolded struggled to get away but the other man punched him in the face and forced him into the car and slammed the door then they drove off. I didn't know what to do at that point. I kind of froze. After about a half hour when it all looked quiet I decided to leave. Then I saw a Land Rover driving through the main street moving very slowly. I quickly hid in the backroom of the millhouse in case it was the police or one of them returning. I heard the man get out of his car and start walking towards the millhouse. I remained very still in the backroom."

Jonathan laughs. "So it was your eyes that were watching me."

Tobey looks confused for a moment. "It was you? I didn't recognize you from that distance with the dust and leaves blowing all around. You looked like you were being very cautious because you kept looking on both sides of the street and behind you like you were looking for someone or like you were being followed."

"It's something I've recently learned was a good idea."

"Anyways, I heard you leave and I saw you shut down the millwheel before you left."

"Why didn't you say something?"

"Like I told you I couldn't see very well because of all the dust flying around. If I knew it was you I would've yelled out to you. Thinking it might be the police I didn't want to make things worse for myself. I needed time to come up with some excuse but as you can see, I didn't. What I'm telling you is what I saw."

Gallagher remains very quiet during most of Tobey's recounting of his experience. But then his analytical mind goes to work.

"You mentioned something about H.G. Wells. What's that all about?" Gallagher asked.

"On the map I found by my father's desk of Livermore Village he had scribbled and circled the name 'H.G. Wells' on it. Isn't he the one who wrote War of The World's?"

"Yes he was but it's not the only book he wrote."

Gallagher pulls out the radio message. "This message you heard on the radio spells it out quite well. In the message you wrote the expression 'madness', also the phrase 'out of hand'. Is that exactly what you heard?"

"Yes. For what I could make out I wrote it down just as I heard it."

Gallagher continues, "Granted the message was filled with static where you marked it with dots but what is spoken is enough to place the message as coming from Livermore. The message has the word 'live', which I believe stands for Livermore and the word 'abandon' really is abandoned. I'm now convinced the message came from Dr. Dredmeyer and he may still be at Livermore and needs our help."

"Why do you think he's still there?"

"The whole setup sounds like it could be the place where the message came from."

"What about my father?"

"I don't want to give you any false hopes. He could be there or he could have left in the first black car you saw when you first arrived at Sawyer River Road. We do believe they were working together and went missing together. But I'm convinced it's Dredmeyer who sent the message for two reasons. First he said the expression "something has gotten *out of hand*" to Professor Meridian when he said he wanted to talk to him about something, which had been bothering him for some time. That's the same exact expression in the radio message, '*out of hand*'". Secondly, if there were any scientific experimentation going on having to do with radiation; he would be the one involved. That was his field when he worked for the military back during the war."

"Perry takes the message from Gallagher and reads it out loud...

"You have to stop this...found out...I'm sorry...for...happened...called...aricona...basker..... help...quickly...abandon...live...before.............out of hand...come...it's too late."

"It looks like a lot of gibberish to me but I'm not a cryptologist," Perry declares. "I will get a couple of my officers to go there right away and check it out."

Gallagher interrupts Perry and says respectfully, "I don't mean to disagree with you Tom but I think we need to be very low key on this; other interested parties might be close by and we don't want to scare them off so soon. It would be very advantageous if we could catch them in the act.

From what Tobey has told us it sounds and looks like an illegal business is going on which could be connected to the poisoned fish in the Swift River."

"Would Dredmeyer get involved in something illegal."

"He may have had no choice or was mislead. There may be other interested parties involved."

Perry shrugs his shoulders and says, "Interested parties?"

"It's just a hunch of mine."

Jonathan pats Perry on the shoulder and says with a big grin, "He gets those from time to time."

"Okay I understand it's possible but what about it being an illegal business?"

Gallagher smiles and says, "H.G. Wells."

Jonathan looks at Perry. "Don't worry about it Tom. He won't tell you what's on his mind. He likes to make sure of his facts before he moves in for the kill."

Perry looks at Gallagher and asks, "What's our next move then?"

"We need to see the Chief before we do anything, don't you agree?"

"Well here's the problem; he's gone!"

Gallagher rolls his eyes. "What do you mean he's gone? Gone where?"

"We don't know. He left in the middle of the night. Our night dispatcher said he came into the station about 10:30 last night and said he had a family emergency and he would be back in about a week. He left word for me to cover for him while he was away."

"Just like that? It's a little unprofessional if you ask me. I would think he would have told you about it first. Especially with what's been going on around here lately."

"We need to talk in private." Perry urges.

Perry looks at Tobey while resting a hand on his shoulder and says, "Tobey, you have been a great help and we will work on finding your father. You probably should go home now, your mother is waiting for you."

"Okay Lieutenant, bye everyone. See you in the morning like usual with your newspaper."

Tobey hesitates a moment before leaving and says, "There's one more thing my father wrote down on the map. I don't know if it means anything but he wrote the words 'foot of the sleeping Indian'."

***

Anna walked Tobey out of the bookshop and then returned to waiting on customers with Kathy. Gallagher and Jonathan followed Perry to the police station across the street.

They entered the police station and went inside Perry's office and sat down around his desk. "I didn't want to talk in front of Tobey," Perry admits. "He has a high respect for our men in blue. Gallagher, you mentioned unprofessional to describe O'Reilly's actions; that's only part of it. Since he's been here he has been preoccupied with his own agenda and sometimes he leaves the station without telling anyone where he's going. We tried getting him on the radio on several different occasions but he never picks up. The other officers have been grumbling about it and I'm afraid it's going to become public knowledge."

"Have you tried talking to him about it?" Gallagher asks.

"Once and that was enough. He has a mean temper and he expressed it very clearly to me. "He said it wasn't my place to question him. He said if I didn't like how he does things I should request a transfer."

"Touchy, touchy!" Jonathan exclaims.

Gallagher stands up and says, "You mentioned he had his own agenda. Can you elaborate?"

"One example was when he first started here. He arbitrarily suspended routine surveillance of the old Goodrich Falls Dam. It has been a routine detail for our officers both day and night ever since little Bobby Baker and Billy Clark drowned when they both got too close to the falls and fell over. Chief Peterson immediately initiated a daily detail to drive by the dam at least twice a day so something like that would never happen again."

"Did you tell him the whole story?"

"Gallagher...we all did. He used the excuse of not having enough officers to patrol the high traffic areas of the valley and he also said the department was working way over budget. He said it was his goal to clean up the department and get rid of the waste."

Gallagher thinks for a moment. "Would you be opposed to going to his home and doing a little investigating?"

"Investigate? What do you think we'll find?"

"I'm just thinking of the timing of all this. It has to do with a conversation I had with him about Ben Willard's death the other day. He got rather defensive when I questioned the way the investigation was being handled and that it looked like it was a rush to judgment to accuse Little Hands of Ben's murder."

Perry starts laughing. "I'm surprised you made it out alive. That's exactly what I'm talking about. He marches to a different drum. I wish John Peterson would come out of retirement just long enough so I can get enough hours of experience under a veteran like John so I can qualify for a promotion."

"I agree with you without hesitation. I was really surprised you didn't get promoted to Chief to begin with. So what do you think? Can we pay Mr. O'Reilly a visit?"

"Sure. When do you want to go?"

"How about tonight about 9:00?"

"Meet me here at the station."

"Sounds like a plan."

***

11

Later that night about 9:30...

Gallagher, Jonathan and Tom Perry drove to O'Reilly's home, which is off Hurricane Mountain Road set back deep into the woods. Chances of them being seen was highly unlikely because the driveway extended around to the back of the house.

"He usually keeps his backdoor unlocked, which I find odd," declares Perry as he leads them around the back of the house.

"A little irresponsible if you ask me for a law enforcement guy," exclaims Jonathan.

Perry acknowledges Jonathan's thoughts and says, "He's just renting temporarily and has basically nothing of value inside. It almost looks like he's not planning to stay very long."

"I was afraid of that being a possibility considering his sudden departure," Gallagher declares.

All of them entered the house and Gallagher immediately heads for what looks like O'Reilly's office. After shoveling through some papers on his desk he picks up a small appointment book and starts flipping through the pages and finds what he was looking for on the last written page.

"I found something very interesting," declares Gallagher.

Perry and Jonathan join him in the office and Gallagher hands the appointment book to Perry, "Read the last page."

Perry reads it out load, "March 21st at the sleeping Indian on Wednesday evening at 8:00 p.m. sharp."

Perry looks at Gallagher puzzled, "Tobey said his father scribbled 'sleeping Indian' down on the map he found by his desk. Doesn't the sleeping Indian have something to do with Mount Chocorua? "

Jonathan concurs and says, "There's a legend about it."

"Yeah, my grandfather told me the story when I was about seven years old," recollects Gallagher. "Most around here know the area as the Moat Range but the longtime locals of the valley call it the sleeping Indian; Mount Chocorua being its foot."

"Now that you mention it I do recall reading something about it but I'm a little fuzzy on the details. I know it had to do with some local dispute."

"That's right. It's actually a legend about a native American named Chocorua who lived in the 18th century. The story is that in the year 1720 Chocorua was on friendly terms with settlers and in particular the Campbell family who had a home in the valley now called Tamworth. Chocorua was called away and left his son in the care of the Campbell family. The boy found and drank a poison that Mr. Campbell had made to eliminate troublesome foxes, and Chocorua returned to find his son had died. Chocorua, distraught with grief, pledged revenge on the family. Shortly thereafter, Mr. Campbell returned home one afternoon to find his wife and children had been slain. Campbell suspected Chocorua and pursued him up the mountain that today bears his name. Chocorua was wounded by a shot from Campbell's rifle. Before Campbell could reach him, Chocorua uttered a curse upon the white settlers and their homes, livestock, and crops, and leapt from the summit to his death."

"I'm not sure what connection there is with Jones, O'Reilly and the sleeping Indian but what's revealing is, O'Reilly is going to the sleeping Indian tomorrow night at 8:00 p.m. to meet someone."

"Maybe that's where Jones is hiding," Jonathan adds. "Maybe O'Reilly found out something and is pursuing is own private investigation in Jones' disappearance."

Gallagher rubs his chin and pauses for a moment, "Or it may be a trap."

***

12

9:00 a.m. - Wednesday - March 21, 1962

Lieutenant Perry, Jonathan and Gallagher began working out their plans and it was decided they had two objectives to carry out before time ran out. Jonathan and two officers were to go the Liberty Cabin on the main trail to the summit of Mount Chocorua and Gallagher and two officers would go to Livermore Village. Both plans would be carried out at night, which was risky but it was the best way to go unnoticed.

"We need to hike into Livermore by an unmarked trail off Rte. 302, which I'm very familiar with. It's about a half mile north of Sawyer River Road. The trail was used some years ago by the AMC but they have discontinued clearing the trail."

"Why hike the trail?" Perry asks confused. "We can take the road right up to the doorstep of the millhouse according to Tobey and Jonathan."

"It's a little bold at this early stage. We should be more prudent in our approach. If anyone is still there we can go unnoticed by entering from the back way and especially at night. Taking the road would be like blowing a trumpet before a charge. From Jonathan's description the phone and electrical lines lead to a fenced in area. It must be connected to something that needs a power source. If my assumption is correct we are not going to like what we find there."

Jonathan follows his friends thinking. "Are you thinking about the lab coats in the millhouse?"

"Exactly! Why would lab coats be found in an old millhouse in the middle of nowhere unless the electrical and phone lines are leading to some kind of secret lab facility. It's the perfect location to secretly carry on...." Gallagher hesitates a moment. "Experiments."

Jonathan looks at the Perry and says, "Think about the bear and the fish. The radiation and the sulfur found in each specimen had to come from some kind of experiment that either went bad or is a result of sloppy work."

Gallagher adds, "The location of a facility like a lab could account for the reason the fish ended up dying in the Swift River. We are looking at serious chemical pollution."

Tom Perry reveals a startled look on his face at what Gallagher was saying. "Are you suggesting some kind of animal experimentation?"

"Precisely. H.G. Wells was the tipoff. I rattled my brain thinking if the name had anything to do with this whole scenario; then I remembered. H.G. Wells wrote the book 'The Island of Doctor Moreau'."

"I'm not a dunce when it comes to literature," Perry declares. "His novel of science fiction had to do with experimentation on animals and humans and the disastrous side effects, including grotesque mutations, but as I said, it's science fiction."

"Yes, it is science fiction but if my theory is correct we may discover something that others may not want to be revealed, just like in Well's story; it took place on a secluded island. We have to be very covert about our movements. That's why we need to hike into Livermore the back way and preferably at night."

"Perry starts shaking his head in disbelief and says in a stronger tone, "I'm sorry Gallagher but I'm having a hard time believing what you are saying could be true. It's sounds impossible for something like what you're describing as happening here in our valley."

Gallagher pauses for a moment and then looks at Perry and Jonathan and says calmly, "When you eliminate the impossible, whatever remains, no matter how improbable, must be the truth."

Jonathan, with raised eyes looks at Gallagher and asks, "Where did you get that little gem of wisdom?"

"Jonathan, I'm surprised at you. Sir Arthur Conan Doyle had his alter ego Sherlock quote it many times. Once in the story of The Sign of Four, another time in the case of The Blanched Soldier and still another time in the case of The Beryl Coronet."

82

Jonathan just shrugs his shoulders while looking at Perry and says, "How can you compete with that kind of mind?"

***

Later that afternoon - Mary Ann's Gift Shop

Mary Ann Blair was busy waiting on a customer when a short stocky man dressed in a dark business suit walks over to her and says, "Excuse me for interrupting but I have received some information from a reliable source that you have acquired two rare copies of 'The Hound of the Baskervilles' signed by the author himself. I am a book collector and I would pay handsomely for them; money is no object."

Mary Ann was taken by surprise at the request. "I'm sorry but those books are not for sale. They are not even on display. May I ask who told you about the books?"

The man hesitates for moment. "Oh, it was at some function I attended in Boston having to do with rare and hard to find works of literature. Someone happened to mention it in conversation. I didn't really know who the person was but I took his word for it and decided to travel up here and see for myself."

"I see, well I'm sorry to tell you but they have already been donated to the new Antiquarian Museum, which is in the process of being built in the center of town."

"Oh my... what a shame. I've traveled all the way up here for nothing. Can I at least examine the books? You know how us bibliophiles can be."

"Sure, I can understand being a book collector your desire to see them for yourself. Let me get them for you."

He waits patiently for a few minutes then Mary Ann finally comes out and hands the books to the man. The man reaches for the books and Mary Ann notices he was missing the middle finger of his right hand because of the way he grabbed the books. He begins flipping through the pages very delicately when three customers come in all at once and begin milling around the shop. The man begins showing signs of uneasiness and places the books down and says thank you to Mary Ann and then abruptly leaves without saying another word. Surprised at his sudden departure, Mary Ann quickly goes to the window and sees the man get into a black sedan and drive off with another man behind the wheel. She shrugs her shoulders and returns to wait on the other customers.

***

Later that evening...

Two of Jackson's most qualified officers on the force and Gallagher are ready to face whatever lays ahead on the trail. They are all in top physical condition to handle a hike at night and will have the stamina to move fast on a trail unmarked and seldom traveled. One of the officers is carrying a portable radio in case backup is needed when they arrive at the site. Lieutenant Perry and two members of the State Police will be standing by to move in if necessary.

Gallagher and the police make their way through the heavily overgrown trail and head for the logging village of Livermore. Gallagher is not wasting any time because he has a suspicion they are going to find the missing Dr. Dredmeyer somewhere on the grounds. He is not sure whether he will be alive but is hopeful to find him so. Dredmeyer could be helpful in solving the mysterious contamination of the Swift River.

After hiking about an hour and a half they approach a large brick building from behind. It has a high chain link fence all around with barbed wire at the top. It is doubly secured with a heavy chain and carbon steel lock. It has no windows and has just one entrance in the front. Fresh cement can be seen between the bricks indicating it has recently been restored. The electrical wires attached to it are coming from the direction of the millhouse in the center of the village. One of the officers tests the fence for voltage then proceeds to cut the fence with a chain cutter. They slowly walk around to the front of the building. The door is a solid metal door with two combination locks. Gallagher turns to Officer Taylor and says, "The juice has been cut off so what we may see inside might not be too pretty."

Taylor looks at Gallagher confused and says, "Why do you think so? What are you expecting to find in there?"

"If my reasoning is correct and this facility is being used for animal experimentation like I suspect there will be animals either dead or alive inside and possibly Dr. Dredmeyer."

Taylor is shocked at Gallagher's assumption and says, "This is the first I've heard of it. No one said anything to us about finding the doctor inside. Does Tom Perry know about what you're thinking?"

"Yeah...I told him but he had a hard time believing it but it's only logical because Dredmeyer said something very revealing in a conversation with Professor Meridian that matches the radio message, which Tobey Jones heard on his father's radio."

Taylor shakes his head showing his confusion and questions Gallagher no more. He proceeds to use a sledgehammer and pry bar to break the locks from the metal doorframe. The door opens slowly and they find total darkness inside. Gallagher holds back for a moment while Taylor leads the way in and before he turns on his flashlight he stumbles on something on the floor and falls to his knees. Immediately a strong stench overwhelms him and causes a gag reflex in his throat. He staggers to his feet and says gasping, "Morris, shine your light over here. I've tripped over something on the floor and it's wet and gooey and it stinks."

Officer Morris turns his light on and gazes at what Taylor had fallen on and quickly runs back outside vomiting in the process. Gallagher goes over to him and says, "What did you see in there? Is Taylor aright?"

Morris is overcome with fright and couldn't get a word out of his mouth. Officer Taylor emerges from the building covered in blood and body parts. "Gallagher, you're not going to believe what's in there."

"Believe it or not I was ready for something like this," Gallagher reluctantly admits.

***

In the meantime several miles away off the Kancamagus highway...

Jonathan and two of the officers with him notice the gate to service road to Liberty Cabin was unchained. The drive to the cabin was about a half a mile up the road. As they make the first turn up the drive they immediately see a rolled over Jeep covered in mud.

All of them quickly get out and see what they feared. It's the jeep belonging to James O'Reilly.

Jonathan looks all around and says, "It looks like there was a small mudslide enough to cover the jeep."

Jonathan looks inside and says, "The jeep's empty. O'Reilly might be inside Liberty Cabin."

***

Back at Livermore...

Gallagher takes Taylor's flashlight and makes his way inside the building. From inside Gallagher yells out to Taylor, "Call for backup right away and tell them to get here with medical supplies. Also, have someone divert the water back to the millwheel as soon as they can because we need power right away."

Morris finally recovers and asks, "Why do we need power?"

"We need light to see what's in here and there's a refrigeration unit in the back room that needs to be turned on. I believe Dredmeyer may be trapped inside."

As Gallagher walks further inside he sees what Officer Taylor had stumbled onto. "There's a large dead dog on the floor along with a man's mutilated body. Blowfly maggots are already having a feast on both of them. I believe it's only been about forty-eight hours since their deaths but the lack of air and the excessive warmth in the room has caused a speedup in the decaying process."

Gallagher proceeds towards the refrigeration unit when the lights kick on and he notices the shortwave radio on a table. He concludes it was the one Dredmeyer used to make the distress call. He opens the refrigerator door and after a few minutes he comes out looking pale. "It's what I thought. Dr. Dredmeyer is barely alive and needs medical attention right away. An animal may have attacked him. Most likely it was the dog that's dead on the floor."

Officer Morris gains his composure and asks, "Can the dead man be identified? It may be Dr. Jones."

Gallagher shakes his head. "He has been picked almost clean by the dog. There's very little flesh left on his body. We need to get Dr. Matthews here right away before he's moved."

Twenty minutes later Lieutenant Perry, Dr. Matthews and several officers arrive and tend to the doctor. Gallagher is watching as Matthews bandages the doctor's legs and asks revealing his doubt, "Is he going to make it?"

Matthews finishes and turns to look at Gallagher and says with equal doubt in his voice, "He's suffering from shock and he's lost a considerable amount of blood. When we get him to the hospital I will immediately start him on an intravenous drip of Ringer's lactate solution to restore the volume in his blood vessels."

Dredmeyer is then rolled out on a gurney and rushed to Memorial Hospital in North Conway. Perry tried to question him before he was taken away but he could only mumble the strange word 'aricona' twice before he lost consciousness.

Gallagher had overheard what Dredmeyer mumbled and said to Perry, "Did you make out what he said?"

"It sounded like ari... something. Whatever that means?"

"Did it sound like aricona?"

"Yes...that's it, aricona. Do you know what it means?"

"Not yet but it's the second time the word has come up. It's added proof it was Dredmeyer who sent the radio message."

Perry, showing signs of uneasiness says, "If Jones and Dredmeyer were working together the dead man on the floor could very well be Philip Jones. He went missing the same time as Dredmeyer. Hopefully the dental records will reveal if it's him one way or another. In the meantime the building will be sealed off until we find out."

Gallagher hitches a ride with Tom Perry. Taylor and Morris ride back with the State troopers. Perry is just about to turn onto Rte. 302 when a call comes on his radio, "Lieutenant Perry, can you hear me?..."

"This is Perry,... out."

"It's officer Donahue. We found O'Reilly's jeep. It's buried in mud from an apparent landslide. We are proceeding to go inside Liberty Cabin,... out."

"Ten four."

Gallagher, Jonathan and Perry wade through the mud and rocks and make their way up the road to

Liberty Cabin. Tom Perry takes out his gun and approaches the door, "Chief, are you in there?"

They wait a few seconds but no answer.

Perry points his gun at the door. "I don't like this!"

Gallagher moves in front of him and says, "I'm good at opening doors. With one swift kick the door flies open and Gallagher steps aside to allow Perry to enter first with his gun raised.

After a quick search Perry concludes, "No one seems to be here."

"What about downstairs?" Jonathan asks.

Gallagher descends the stairs, looks around and finds no one, then comes back up to find Perry reading a note, "What did you find?"

"It's a message."

"What does it say?"

"It just says, I'M SORRY!"

Gallagher takes out his flashlight and begin a more thorough search of the cabin. "Oh...what do we have here?" he declares.

Gallagher picks up a pair of muddy hiking boots near the doorway and examines the boots carefully and says, "They are Merrill Hikers!"

He then turns them over and begins scraping the sole of one of the boots with his knife and sees what he was afraid of and says, "The muddy sole has the remnants of red paint."

***

The three of them make their way back down with the evidence. When they reach the jeep Gallagher walks through some of the mud and debris and picks up fragments of a dynamite stick. "It looks like whoever did this knew what he was doing to create a small enough explosion just to cover the jeep and nothing more so it would go unnoticed."

"Our troubles have not ended yet," Perry declares. "If the owner of those boots is Ben Willard's killer; he's gone."

Gallagher looks at the note again. "Whoever he is, is toying with us!"

"Could it be O'Reilly?" Jonathan asks.

Gallagher shrugs his shoulders. "Your guess is as good as mine."

***

13

Next morning...March 22, 1962

Gallagher slept later than usual and finds Helen sitting at the kitchen table reading the newspaper.

"Look who finally woke up this morning." she comments while sipping on her coffee.

"I didn't sleep so well. Yesterday was a horror show and I believe the show carried on in my dreams."

"While you were in dreamland Tom Perry called and would like to see you at the station sometime this morning. He said it had to do with the same

91

horror show. Also, Mary Ann stopped by about an hour ago and said she wanted to talk to you about the Conan Doyle books."

"I think I might want to go back to bed. I'm not ready for this today. I need a break."

"While you're contemplating your escape you might find the latest news very interesting."

Gallagher took a sip of coffee and opens up the paper. His eyes become glued to the headline.

'President Kennedy and Khrushchev have a war of words over the Cuban incident. Khrushchev tells Kennedy of his predecessor's big mistake in meddling in another countries affairs. Khrushchev reminded Kennedy of the imprisonment of Gary Powers for his surveillance mission over the Soviet Union two years ago. On February 10, 1962, Powers was exchanged, along with American student Frederic Pryor, in a well-publicized spy swap at the Glienicke Bridge in Berlin, Germany.'

Gallagher looks up from the newspaper with disgust written all over his face. "Why don't people just stop and smell the roses; they will become so gratified in doing so. They won't care to fight and bicker over things that in themselves mean so little in the bigger scheme of things."

"You sound just like your grandfather. He was an idealist and I believe you are becoming more and more like him. I thought maybe after what happened on Thorn Hill you would have tempered the idea of such a panacea could be possible for the world's ills."

Gallagher gets up and looks out the window to the valley below. "Have you been talking to Jonathan lately? Where is he anyways?"

"He left real early this morning."

"Did he say where he was going?"

"He said he had to address the senior class of the Jackson High School on the current political climate in the world. Maybe you should go and listen. It will further remind you of the world's current state of affairs."

"Oh that's right. I know all about it. He read a portion of it to me a few days ago. He wanted to know what I thought and I said I really thought the students wouldn't get it."

Gallagher then opens to the next page of the newspaper and sees photos of Dr. Philip Jones and Dr. Wallace Dredmeyer. The caption under the photo reads, "Dr. Wallace Dredmeyer pictured here was found barely alive in an old abandoned building in Livermore Village. He had been missing since last Friday. He was taken to Memorial Hospital and is in critical condition. His longtime associate Dr. Philip Jones remains missing at this time."

"I hope young Tobey and his mother are doing okay. Finding Dredmeyer may help us in locating Jones if he regains consciousness," Gallagher declares.

With those words Gallagher kisses Helen on the cheek and says, "I need to talk with Mary Ann so I have to run. I hope you're done with the paper. I want to read the rest of it at work. We temporarily lost our paperboy at the bookshop. He has been grounded for a month."

"You are amazing. I didn't think you even heard me when I told you about Mary Ann's visit. You seemed like you were in a fog."

"It's your wonderful coffee. It should be nicknamed Aunt Helen's Fog Cutter."

***

Gallagher walks into the Jackson police station and finds his old friend John Peterson sitting at his old desk.

"Chief...what a surprise. Did you forget you retired last year?"

Peterson laughs. "Very funny. I would rather be fishing."

"What's this all about?"

"First of all I'm back on a temporary basis until a replacement can be found. Tom is a little overwhelmed with all the happenings in recent weeks. I've been catching up on the latest and I understand his feelings and will do whatever I can to help him get over the hump. We need to make him the next Chief."

Gallagher hears some commotion in the back of the station and Officer Taylor and Tom Perry walk in both looking exhausted.

"Gallagher, we need to tell you what we found at Livermore," exclaims Perry. Your theory about animal experiments was right on."

"What else did you find? You both look like you've just run a marathon."

Perry speaks up first and says, "Gallagher...that's an understatement. We went back to Livermore and with the benefit of daylight we were able to see why the Swift River has been teaming with dead trout. The building where we found Dredmeyer had a drainpipe going from several of what I would call autopsy tables to a holding tank outside. The drainpipe was cut and pulled away from the tank and allowed whatever was on those tables to drain right into the Swift River. The pipe and the tables were tested on the spot and evidence of radiation was present. Also there was a very strong scent of sulfur permeating from the pipe. The dog has been thoroughly examined and the same was found in its bloodstream."

"What about the dead man?"

"Forensics is still working on it. We should know by tomorrow."

"Is that it?"

"No, I'm afraid not. Four government officials from the State Department showed up at the hospital this morning with legitimate documents stating we were to release Dredmeyer to their care. He was flown out by helicopter to an unknown facility where we were assured he would get the best doctors to care for him. We tried to find out where but they said it was classified."

Gallagher, with a troubled look on his face comments with a suspicious tone in his voice. "Government officials! That's interesting. Mary Ann had a visitor yesterday who claimed to be a book collector and was looking to buy some books, which were donated by a very generous man who wanted to remain anonymous."

"I don't follow. What do the books have to do with the government?"

Gallagher reveals a slight smile. "You should know me by now. It's too soon to start guessing."

"I thought I would take the chance and ask just in case you wanted to talk more about what's going through that mind of yours?"

Peterson starts laughing and says, "Tom you might as well get used to it. It's the way Gallagher works. It's frustrating at times but he does get results."

"It's only theory, not fact, but what I do want to know is what else did you find when you went back to Livermore?"

Officer Taylor speaks up. "There were several rooms adjoining the main room with the refrigeration unit. They all had animal cages the type you would find in a kennel but very large."

"Anything else?"

Perry adds. "We searched some metal cabinets and found jars of sulfur dioxide and bottles of a greenish mixture that produced a horrible odor. Also, in further examining the phone system, it was only used as an intercom. The phone system was not hooked to any outside lines. It all makes sense because the phone company would have known of its use if it were on their lines. It also explains why the shortwave radio was used to communicate to the outside. It was a secret operation all the way around."

"Well it definitely appears that Livermore is the source of the dead fish. Hopefully we've ended the contamination."

***

Gallagher left the police station with more questions on his mind as to what went on in Livermore and the reasons behind it. It was too much to absorb after his experience the day before and was curious to find out what brought Mary Ann by so early in the morning. He enters the shop and walks over to her as she's hanging a painting on the wall. "Good morning Mary Ann. Can I help you with that interesting painting?"

"Do you recognize it?"

"Yes, it's the Russell-Colbath House."

"That's right. What an interesting story. Thomas left the family farm to run errands. Thomas never returned that night and his wife never saw him again. Ruth Colbath waited thirty-nine years for her beloved husband to come home. She missed him so much that she left an oil lamp burning in the window every night, hoping for his return."

Gallagher continues, "Ruth Colbath died in 1930, at the age of eighty. Three years after Ruth died, Thomas returned. Thomas offered no explanation for where he had been for the past thirty-nine years. He claimed he wandered away and was too embarrassed to return and admit he was lost."

"Well I have another interesting story for you," declares Mary Ann "Yesterday a man came into my shop and was very interested in buying the two Conan Doyle books. I told him they were not for sale and were being kept for the new museum. He

97

was very let down about it and said he was a book collector and had traveled all the way from Boston to purchase them."

"What's so interesting about it?"

"The whole time he was here he seemed extremely distracted. He asked if he could at least examine the books; so I agreed. As he was looking through one of the books the shop got very busy with customers. He quickly put the books down and left without saying another word."

"Can you describe him?"

"He was very short, kind of stocky, about five feet, four inches tall and I noticed something very interesting; he was missing the middle finger of his right hand."

"Good detective work. I can't say I've ever seen or met anyone who fits that description in the bookshop before. I think I would've if it's true he's really a book collector. Let me know if he returns. To travel all the way up here to buy a couple of books he had not seen before tells me he knows quite a bit about those books."

"I don't know about that because he said he only heard about them in a passing conversation at some event in Boston."

"To me that's very revealing."

"Okay...I will let you know and I will let Valerie know because she's been helping me on weekends."

"Good. While I'm still here have you seen this morning's paper?"

"No... I haven't had a chance to look at it yet."

Gallagher hands her the newspaper already opened to the second page. Mary Ann looks at the photos of the two doctors and a startled look appears on her face. She looks at Gallagher and says, "Dredmeyer was the man who donated the Conan Doyle books."

"You mean you had never met the doctor before?"

"No...I never did. I've heard of him but remember; I'm still very new to this valley and I have yet to meet everyone who lives and works here."

"Are you positive?"

She looks at it more closely. "He's definitely the man. His white beard is missing in this photo but it's absolutely him. I can tell by those deep blue eyes of his. I'm a helpless romantic when it comes to tall distinguished looking men with blue eyes."

***

Gallagher left Mary Ann's shop and headed for the Turning Page. He was expecting Jonathan anytime to fill him in on his experience at the High School.

When Gallagher walked into the bookshop Anna was busy tending to customers so he decided to head for his office and list all that had transpired in the past few weeks in the order they occurred.

First of all Dr. Dredmeyer donates two rare editions of 'The Hound of the Baskervilles' to Mary Ann's gift shop. John 'Little Hands' Russell has an altercation with Ben Willard at the Tavern because he purchased some land at Harts Location. Gus Swenson and Bill Waters inform Gallagher about dead fish floating in the Swift River and a dead bear was found at Jigger Johnson's campground. Ben Willard is found dead by the Swift River shortly after he was heard having an argument with John 'Little Hands' Russell. Paul Anderson sends Gallagher a letter regarding the possibility of further Fifth Column activity from the group named the Cause. A list of names associated with the Cause was found in Chicago, which had the two last names scratched out. The list corresponds to the list found in Echo Lake many months earlier, which had omitted the two names altogether. The question remains; what were the two names? Tobey Jones hears a distress call on his father's shortwave radio pointing to the abandoned town of Livermore. Mary Ann gets a visit from a book collector with a missing finger desiring the Conan Doyle books. O'Reilly's jeep is found at Liberty Cabin. An anonymous note is found inside the cabin along with the muddy boots with evidence of red paint on the sole of one boot. Dr. Dredmeyer is found in critical condition at Livermore while Dr. Jones remains missing. Dredmeyer is identified by Mary Ann as the donor of the Conan Doyle books.

Gallagher was still listing the order of events to try to get some pattern when Jonathan and Valerie walk into the bookshop. They both have smiles on their faces. "What are you doing?" asks Jonathan as he enters Gallagher's office.

"I'm trying to make heads or tails of everything that's been happening lately, but enough about what I'm doing. It's good to see you both. You look as though you have something good to tell me. How did your address go today at the school?"

Valarie pipes in and says, "It went very well. I was very proud of Jonathan's public speaking ability. I used to teach that course in Boston before I taught violin."

Jonathan just smiles. "What else is she going to say, she loves me."

"Speaking of love. Have either one of you thought about tying the knot?"

"You need to talk to your friend, exclaims Valerie. "I think he has cold feet."

"I'll work on it," Jonathan assures her as he holds her tightly to his side.

They all laugh together then Anna says to Valerie, "Come and let me show you some patterns I have picked out for my wedding dress."

While they were busy talking wedding, Jonathan follows Gallagher into his office and notices he is lost in thought and says, "What's going through that computer you have attached to your shoulders?"

Gallagher smiles. "It's good to see Valerie, it's been awhile."

"Yes it has. She's been busy with the Boston Symphony and will be performing in concert soon and is getting us front row seats."

Gallagher and Jonathan catch up on the latest events with each other but what took Gallagher by surprise was what Jonathan heard while he was at the school.

***

Gallagher's curiosity was aroused and quickly responded to Jonathan's remark. "Don't leave me in suspense. What did you hear at the school?"

"When I left the High School and walked by the Jackson Elementary when classes were being let out for the day and Tobey Jones saw me and ran over and said he had heard from his father by phone. He said he had been abducted by some men but was able to escape and was hiding from them."

"Did he say where he was?"

"No because he didn't want to drag Tobey and anyone else into it. He told Tobey he and Dr. Dredmeyer had been involved in a secret project set up by a special military unit and they were not able to speak about it to anyone; not even family. He said after a while they both didn't like what was going on and whom they were working with and decided to no longer cooperate. An accident took place and a wild dog attacked a fellow scientist and Dr. Dredmeyer. Philip said he wasn't allowed to help and was taken away and beaten. They eventually took him away blindfolded from Livermore to an unknown destination. He estimated it was about ten miles away. He did say he could hear rushing water near where he was taken. He was able to get free and hide in one of their vans at night when all was quiet. Early the next morning the van he was hiding in drove off and eventually stopped at a local gas station and he was able to jump out the back while the driver was paying the attendant."

"Is that it?"

"No, he said his father said to look inside one of the books Dredmeyer donated to Mary Ann's gift shop. He wanted to say more but suddenly the line went dead."

"Well then our next move is to get the books and without delay. There are others who are also interested in those books."

Jonathan looks at Gallagher surprised and asks, "Who?"

"Someone claiming to be a book collector. Mary Ann never saw him before but noticed he was missing his middle finger. He was very discreet and appeared distracted according to her. It's possible he may be from the government. The timing is about right when the government officials took Dredmeyer away."

"Should we let the powers that be know?"

"I don't want to shake things up right now by pursuing the government on this incident. Something is not right and I think time will be our best friend to flush out what this is all about. The Jones family is in danger and apparently the government or some other group are more interested in getting those books then they are with Philip Jones' welfare. We need to find out what all the interest is in those books for ourselves first. We have no time to waste."

***

Gallagher and Jonathan arrive at Mary Ann's gift shop and notice her sorting through some jewelry and rare coins in her display case.

"It looks like you found a buried treasure," Gallagher says showing his curiosity.

"You might say that because it comes from an old Spanish galleon, which was discovered off the coast of Portugal. A dealer was in here this morning and I couldn't pass up the deal he offered me."

"Apparently it's not the only treasure you seem to possess."

"You must mean the Conan Doyle books."

"That's right. We need to examine them."

Mary Ann laughs. "That's exactly what the man said to me yesterday. He used the same exact word; examine. He didn't say look or see but he said examine. I thought it was odd. What's there to examine?""

The three of them went into her backroom and she pulled out both copies from her safe and placed them on the counter. "Here they are, ready for your examination."

Gallagher thoughtfully says, "We don't know what we are going to find but for your own safety it would be best if you don't know what this is all about. There may be an opportunity in the future for certain people to force it out of you if you came to have knowledge of what we may find. You already had a strange visitor wanting to buy the books. I will take the books with me and eventually store them in the vault at the new museum. We don't know if he will be back or any others who may be interested."

"Good idea. I'll feel better if you do."

They both left Mary Ann's and walked over to the new museum. Harry Fuller had recently finished Gallagher's office, which included a state of the art high security vault.

Jonathan took one book and Gallagher the other and they carefully scrutinized each book from top to bottom. After a few minutes Jonathan gives up and puts the book down. "I can't find anything. I flipped through almost every page and I don't see anything out of the ordinary."

Gallagher is not so quick and meticulously feels around the edges of each cover. He remembers the words Dredmeyer said when he donated the books to Mary Ann. "There are books of which the backs and covers are by far the best parts."

After a few minutes Gallagher exclaims, "I think I found something?"

Gallagher takes the blade of his Swiss army knife and carefully splits the top corner of the back cover. "Eureka! It looks like some type of film; microfiche to be precise."

Gallagher pulls out a long piece of film and holds it up to the light. "It appears to be some kind of formula. Chemistry was not my favorite in school but it's no doubt a formula and is partially written in German. It has that odd word again that was in Dredmeyer's radio message; aricona."

Jonathan takes a look and says, "I'm sure Professor Meridian will know how to decipher it. We need to see him right away."

They wasted no time and drove over to Professor August Meridian's home and found a note attached to his door. Gallagher takes it and reads it aloud, "I've gone fishing and will be back tomorrow. If it's urgent contact my daughter Louise."

Jonathan is perplexed and says, "What do we do now? We have this formula in our hands and no way to know what it says or means. Maybe we should let Louise know it's urgent."

Gallagher shakes his head showing he's not in full agreement with his good friend and says respectfully, "I think the best thing to do is to hold on to it for now. It might be wise not to drag the professor into something we have no idea what the implications could be. A so-called book collector was looking for it and it might draw him and others out again. I think the best place right now is to keep it here. There are around-the-clock security guards on duty in case anyone tries to walk off with any building materials from the site. The formula couldn't be safer if it were in a bank."

***

PART TWO

Fowl Play

14

Sunday morning - April 1, 1962

Gallagher and Helen are enjoying their breakfast together when Jonathan arrives with the latest news.

Gallagher looks at Jonathan and says, "What got you out of bed so early this morning?"

"I had to deliver my report in time for the final edition."

"What report would that be?"

"Bad news I'm afraid. Evidence was found at Liberty Cabin revealing the muddy boots are a size fourteen; the same size that Little Hands wears. He will remain behind bars for the foreseeable future until more evidence is found that will clear him. Forensics also verified the red paint on the hiking boots was the same color paint that was dumped by the Saco River. Theirs is a bit of good news to report. The dental records of the dead man found at Livermore did not match Dr. Jones's."

"Oh that's great. I'm sure Penny and Tobey are relieved."

"Only a little because he's still missing. Ever since he made that phone call to Tobey he has not been heard of since. As far as Little Hands is concerned, we need to clear him somehow."

Gallagher is quiet for a moment and starts rubbing his chin. Jonathan notices it and asks, "What are you thinking now?"

"I was thinking of Paul Anderson's letter. I believe now is the time to call him for his help. I think what has recently happened here fits the need. After all he's the one who told us about James O'Reilly and how he was highly qualified to take John Peterson's place. I think he might find it rather enlightening to hear how O'Reilly isn't all he is cracked up to be."

***

Gallagher dials the phone number Anderson had given him. A voice comes on the other line. "You have reached the headquarters of the Federal Bureau of Investigation. All calls are monitored for security reasons. How may I direct your call?"

"Please connect me to agent Paul Anderson's office."

"Just one moment."

"Paul Anderson's office. This call is being recorded. May I ask who's calling?"

"Gallagher Brady from Jackson, New Hampshire."

"Is he expecting your call?"

"No, but it's urgent that I speak with him right away. The code word is Echo."

There was a pause for about thirty seconds then Paul Anderson comes on the line, "Gallagher, good to hear from you...my secretary said it was urgent. What's happening?"

"It's urgent but I'm not sure why. We have some funny business going on up here and it looks like our government may be involved."

"Let me switch to a secure line; just a minute."

Gallagher waits patiently while all kinds of thoughts are going through his head.

Anderson returns and asks, "What kind of funny business?"

"It looks like we have a situation where there's a real possibility of some kind animal experimentation going on at an old abandoned logging village called Livermore. We have been finding dead fish in the Swift River, which runs through the village and the evidence indicates they have been poisoned by radiation exposure. As a result other wildlife, which feed on the fish, are also dying. It has gotten to the point where bears are dropping dead in front of campers."

"You're positive it's radiation poisoning?"

"The fish and the bear were examined in our Health Department's lab and it was confirmed. But there's another significant thing they found in both the fish and the bear; evidence of sulfur dioxide. Sulfur has been used as an antidote for radiation poisoning in lab studies."

"Okay, where does the government fit into this?"

"It's complicated but trust me on this; I'm not jumping to conclusions. I'm not outright accusing our government of performing some illegal top-secret experiments on animals but I guess I've learned to check out all things, which appear out of the ordinary. One of our leading scientists named

Dr. Wallace Dredmeyer was found critically injured at the site in Livermore. Also a colleague of his, Dr. Philip Jones had disappeared at the very same time. We were attempting to question Dredmeyer when he was well enough but men from the State Department extracted him from our hospital before he regained consciousness. I believe our government had fears he would talk. That's why I decided it was time to call you."

Anderson pauses for a moment. "You must keep this out of the press."

"It's a little late for that. There was a small clip in this morning's paper about finding Dredmeyer in Livermore Village and it described him as being in critical condition."

"Oh boy...do you remember the letter I sent you warning about the possibility of two members of the Cause who have not been identified yet? They might be working in your area?"

"Yeah...how could I forget? It's the other reason why I called."

"I'm not at liberty to tell you much at this time for security reasons. To further investigate this situation I'm going to have to keep looking over my shoulder. Our director is starting to act a little funny lately. He seems preoccupied with spying on the first family. He and the President do not get along very well. The President's brother, our Attorney General, may have contributed to the tension that's between the two of them. The Director and Bobby have some bad blood between them but in any case I will look into this without broadcasting it all over the bureau. We have had some chatter about the CIA poking their noses where they are not authorized. I will have to come and go like a shadow in the dark and get back to

110

you. I will call you at....let me see...the number I have is your home number at Eagle House. Is that still the best number to reach you?"

"We have recently added another line, which is connected to the carriage house. It will be best if you call that number."

"It's okay to give it to me. This line is totally secure and is not being recorded."

Gallagher gives him the number and says, "I will let you know if I hear or see anything else."

"Good enough."

'Click'

***

Paul Anderson quickly calls agents Drew and Foster and assigns them to Jackson Village without delay. They take the next flight out of Dulles two hours later with a copy of the brief explaining their mission.

***

15

Next day...April 2, 1962

Gallagher was relieved that Agent Anderson was now working on the case. He felt he could finally get some quality time with Anna. Two things were on their agenda. One was to take in a movie and then the following day take a trip to Maine to make arrangements for their upcoming wedding in October. Anna wanted the wedding to take place outside by the ocean and the reception at the Cliff House.

Anna arrived at Eagle House about 5:00 p.m. and had dinner with Gallagher and Helen. Anna asked Helen if she would go with them to Maine and she jumped at the idea.

After a delicious meal Anna and Gallagher arrive at the Majestic Theatre in Conway for the nine o'clock showing of West Side Story. Gallagher has wanted to see the movie especially because Leonard Bernstein had written the musical score. As far as the story goes, he isn't interested in watching two gangs fight it out in New York but he figured his ears could hear the music and his eyes could be on Anna.

***

The movie was over at 11:30 and Gallagher is driving Anna home by way of West Side Road, which is the roundabout way to get to her home. The locals in the valley always take the road to avoid the heavier traffic on Rte. 16. Gallagher isn't quite ready to end the evening so a slow leisurely drive back is his plan. The stars are out and the crescent moon is shining brightly on a perfect April night. Gallagher turns onto Rte. 302 in Bartlett and heads for Jackson Village when two cruisers are spotted blocking the road at the junction of Rtes. 16 and 302. Officer Morris approaches Gallagher's Rover and says softly, "Gallagher, there's been a horrible accident. We are in the process of identifying the driver and his passenger but it's going to take some time. They both were blown out of their car upon impact so I have to tell you to take an alternate route."

"Blown out! You're not talking about a bomb are you?"

"Morris looks both ways and puts his head further into the Rover. "It had to be a bomb to do that much damage. Chief Peterson wants this out of the news until further notice."

"Does Jonathan know about this?"

"Yes...he was here a few minutes ago. He understands the Chiefs concerns about it getting out in the press."

"What getting out?"

"They both are wearing belt badges. They are FBI agents."

"Where is the Chief now?"

"He went back to the station. He was looking for you when he got here but Jonathan told him you were on a date with Anna."

"I *was* on a date, but apparently not anymore."

Anna grabs Gallagher's arm tightly. "Let's go back to Eagle House. I want to stay in your guest room for the night; I'm a little scared."

They left the scene of the accident and Gallagher was lost in thought during the whole drive home. As he's parking the car Anna looks at him and asks, "Who do you think could be responsible for such a tragedy?"

Gallagher shakes his head and says somberly, "Paul Anderson must have sent them out after my conversation with him. I shouldn't have..."

Anna interrupts him knowing he's feeling responsible for the tragedy. "Gallagher let it rest till tomorrow. It's too late to do anything about it now. Anderson knew the risks and so did the agents."

"You're right. Tomorrow is another day."

Anna smiles and says, "That would make a great line in a movie."

Gallagher laughs. "I hope Scarlet O'Hara will forgive me for my plagiarism. I'm really glad you're with me tonight. I need your refreshing outlook on things. I get so wrapped up in what happens in this valley I lose all perspective. My grandfather was so concerned about what could affect the happiness of the people in this town. I'm glad he's asleep and untouched by what's going on."

Anna shows a little confusion on what he has just said and asks, "Don't you think he can see what's going on in heaven?"

Gallagher shakes his head. "That's what many believe but I believe he's just asleep waiting for a better day to come back to the valley where he belongs and had loved so much."

***

Early the next morning...April 3, 1962

Gallagher wakes up from a restless night's sleep and looks out his window and notices the sun filtering through the trees creating golden rays spreading through the valley. The sky is clear and birds are chirping. He looks at his watch and is now very upset for wasting his favorite part of the day. He cleans up and goes downstairs and enters the kitchen looking for Anna. Helen is cooking breakfast for Jonathan while he is waiting patiently at the table.

"What's happening this morning? You two look like you have been up for awhile."

Gallagher then looks around and asks, "Where's Anna? I was looking forward to seeing my girl this morning."

Helen speaks up and says, "She had to leave early to help her parents at the grocery store. They had to pack up some dairy products that had gone bad."

"You want to know what else is happening this morning?" Jonathan says with an apparent disgust in his voice. "First I found out from the police who the two men were in that car last night. They were FBI agents sent by Paul Anderson."

"What's Anderson going to do now?"

"Anderson told Peterson to have us continue our work here because they still haven't found out who the mole is at the Bureau. Only his office knew about the two agents and their mission. He said he would be in touch soon. He also said to keep whatever we find strictly confidential. Do you think the government has some secret agenda that the FBI is not privy to? Philip Jones said Livermore was a military operation."

"I believe Anderson thinks so. He mentioned the CIA. It seems the government has agencies checking up on other agencies. It's well known that the FBI checks up on the CIA making sure their activities are outside US borders. I believe they are trying to hush-up the operation because they took Dredmeyer away before he could talk to any of us."

"That would explain Dr. Jones' abduction. He was working with Dredmeyer."

"You may have something there. If the government is behind Philip's abduction and Dredmeyer's extraction; something went drastically wrong besides just a freak accident; if that's really what happened. Maybe the operation at Livermore is legitimate and someone had infiltrated the site and sabotaged it. We never did find out about the identity of the dead man we found at Livermore."

Jonathan looks at his watch. "The medical examiner must be in by now; we need to call him. In all the confusion I forgot all about it. His identity might help us find where Dredmeyer was taken."

***

"Examiner's office. Can I help you?"

"Barbara...this is Jonathan Henry from the Jackson Observer; I need some information regarding the body that was found at Livermore a few days ago. You know the one that was picked clean by a wild animal. Sorry to be so graphic!"

"Hello Jonathan. I think I know whom you mean. We don't get many in that condition. Let me see what Dr. Matthews has on file; just a moment."

After a few minutes Barbara returns to the phone. "He's a John Doe. Dr. Matthews was not able to get any definitive information about him. There are no fingerprint or dental records on file for him. He had no identification on him but there is one thing Dr. Matthews has in his notes. He has a small tattoo on his lower back right above the buttocks but it has been mostly eaten away by the dog so it's hard to make out exactly what it is."

"Are we allowed to see the body?"

116

"If you are involved in the investigation, most definitely. "The body is in the morgue under refrigeration until it can be identified by next of kin."

"We will be right down."

"Just to let you know we have a new employee named Gerald. He will assist you in whatever you need."

"Thanks Barbara."

Jonathan hangs up and reluctantly says to Gallagher, "We definitely need to go to the morgue. There may be a glue in the form of a tattoo on the victim's lower back."

Jonathan then hesitates for a moment. "I really could think of a lot more enjoyable things to do right now than looking at the rear end of a mutilated body but we must do what we must do."

Gallagher thinks for a moment then says, "Show me a man with a tattoo and I'll show you a man with an interesting past."

"What are you talking about?" Jonathan asks stumped by Gallagher's remark.

"Oh,...just quoting the author Jack London who was known to have said that one time. Interesting phrase don't you think under the circumstances?"

***

One hour later...

Gallagher and Jonathan arrive at the North Conway morgue. The recently hired morgue attendant

117

escorts them into the refrigeration area and pulls out the draw marked 'John Doe'.

The attendant looks at them both, "We were not expecting any visitors from outside the family until he was identified by next of kin. This is a little unusual."

"This is an unusual circumstance because we are looking at the possibility of unintentional manslaughter. This man may be a victim of a bizarre experiment gone bad. We have to find out whoever or whatever is responsible for his death."

"I need some help lifting him up on the examining table."

The three of them lift the body up and lay it flat on the table. Gallagher addresses the attendant and says, "We have a problem. The body needs to be rolled over so we can see his lower back area right above the buttocks."

"Sure...no problem. As you can see the body is in a heavy gage plastic bag. The body has been kept between 14 °F and minus 58 °F so it should roll over fairly easy. He's not a very big man."

The three of them roll the body over. Looking at the attendant Gallagher now says, "Because this is police business we need for you to step out of the room while we make our examination."

"Whatever you say sir."

Reluctantly the attendant leaves the room but remains just in earshot by the door, which he slightly leaves ajar.

Gallagher takes out his magnifying glass and discreetly examines the tattoo. He shakes his head and says in a whisper, "Most of the flesh has been eaten away around the tattoo. Hand me your camera. We can analyze the photo when we get back to Eagle House. I don't want to draw any more attention than we have to."

They leave the room and meet the attendant who had walked into the main lobby. The attendant asks, "Did you find what you were looking for?"

Gallagher reveals a slight grin and says, "It would only be a guess and guesses lead to mistakes so I don't want to put my assumptions in anyone's mind until I am positive. I will let Chief Peterson know what we found and he can let everyone else know; those who need to know I mean."

The attendant looks disgruntled. "Why all the secrecy? Do you have some idea who this person is?"

Gallagher starts showing signs of being annoyed with him and says, "What's your name?"

The attendant starts to squirm. He realizes he has pushed Gallagher too far with his questions. "My name is Gerald."

"How long have you worked here Gerald?"

"I just started working here four days ago."

Gallagher looks him squarely in the eye, "That's right. We were told you were new here so it seems to me you're not quite sure how things work in a police investigation. Gerald, there's one thing you need to learn about your job. You attend and

119

attend only and leave the investigation to the experts. No more questions."

"Where's Rudy?" Jonathan asks.

"He quit suddenly about a week ago. That's all I know."

***

Gallagher and Jonathan leave without saying goodbye. Gerald quickly reaches for the phone and dials. "It's Gerald. They just left the morgue. They took a picture of Boris' tattoo. I don't think they know what it is. I questioned them on it and I could see they were frustrated and Brady became quite upset at my questions."

"You were told to observe, not to question. I think your usefulness to us is over. We will contact you soon to compensate you for your work."

"How will you find me?"

"Don't worry. We are good at finding people when we want to. Just sit tight and don't tell anyone what you saw or heard today."

'Click'

***

Gallagher and Jonathan arrive back at Eagle House and go immediately to Gallagher's study. Gallagher takes the film into his darkroom and begins developing the photo. After ten minutes he comes out and places the photo on his desk. They both examine it more carefully.

120

Gallagher's wheels start to turning. "I think I know what this is and I'm not liking what I'm seeing."

Jonathan looks carefully and still is at a loss. "You got me. It looks like the dog ate the best parts."

Gallagher soberly says, "It's the Soviet symbol of the hammer and sickle. It can be found in the upper left corner of the Soviet flag. The dead man must be a Soviet scientist who was working with Dredmeyer and Jones."

"Why would Dredmeyer and Jones work with a communist scientist?" Jonathan asks perplexed.

"They most likely didn't know or he was a defector. They would've had to take his pants off to know," Gallagher says with a slight laugh.

"What about a Russian accent? They would have caught that I'm sure."

"Easy enough to hide. I've heard the Soviets have schools to teach Russians how to be Americans for the purpose of spying in this country. They teach them how to speak, how to act and how to simply blend into our society. Ian Fleming even wrote about a spy who was trained to be an Englishman so he could fool James Bond in order to kill him."

Jonathan laughs. "I know the one you mean. He ordered Chianti "the red kind" as he put it with his fish. But you are talking fiction not reality."

"Oscar Wilde said in his essay 'The Decay of Lying, 'Life imitates art.'"

"Okay, so what are we talking about here?"

"Think about it. Scientific experiments are being performed where radiation is being used to poison animals then they are given an antidote to see if they can survive the radiation. To top that off, government agents are lurking around every tree. Something is coming down the pike and they are using our backyard as their laboratory."

Jonathan thinks for a moment. "That's if we are talking about *our* government."

"What are you thinking?"

"Oh no...two can play your game. I don't want to say anymore until I have all the facts."

Gallagher smiles at his friend and says, "Fair enough."

***

16

Later that afternoon ...Saco, Maine - Camp Ellis

Gallagher, Anna and Helen arrive at Camp Ellis on the Maine coast about 2:00 in the afternoon. After checking in at the Ellis Beach Resort, Anna and Gallagher take a walk along the beach while Helen drives into Old Orchard to do some shopping. The sky is clear and a cool ocean breeze is lightly blowing soft sand across the shoreline. Off in the distance several fishing boats are spotted along the horizon. Some fishermen are trolling back and forth hoping to pull in a day's catch of striped bass and bluefish while others are checking their lobster traps.

Gallagher takes a deep breath sucking in the fresh ocean air and says with a tone of absolute approval in his voice, "It's good to get away for a few days. I needed this time to unwind."

Anna holds Gallagher close and says, "I'm glad Kathy was able to run the bookshop on such short notice while we are away. I finally asked her to be my maid of honor and she accepted."

"I'm not a bit surprised. You two grew up together in the valley and she has been close to your family ever since she worked in your parents store when you were both in high school. I know Scott has designs on her."

"Did he tell you that?"

"Sometimes we men talk about things like that."

"Oh,...I see."

They walked for about an hour along the shoreline and as they were making their way towards the river Gallagher stops and points to the jetty. "Let's go over and sit on the rocks and watch the seagulls; it looks like they're playing. You can see them diving for the fish in the water. The blue fish must be chasing the small bait fish into shore."

As they are getting closer, Anna takes a better look and starts shaking her head and says, "They're not diving for the fish. They're falling dead in the water."

Gallagher begins running towards the jetty, which separates the ocean side from the river. He is about ready to climb up on the rocks when he notices the entire area is cordoned off with yellow tape and two official looking white vans are parked along the riverbank near the jetty. Four men dressed in scuba gear are dragging large nets through the water. Gallagher holds back from going any closer pretending not to notice them and makes his way back to Anna. Not knowing what was going on she asks, "What's the matter? Who are those guys?"

Gallagher points to the vans. "Look at the seal on their license plates."

"State Department!" Anna exclaimes. "What's going on here?"

Gallagher studies their movements in the water for a few minutes then declares, "They're retrieving dead seagulls and scooping up dead fish with their nets."

"Why don't we ask them what they are doing?"

"I don't think so. My guess is they're trying to cover up something they don't want the general public to know about; we shouldn't butt in."

"What do you mean?"

"My experience tells me asking too many questions can get you in a lot of trouble. I think of Larry Nelson and how he ended up."

"You really believe it was foul play?"

"What would Larry be doing in a lake five miles away from where he was working that morning in early March when he was supposed to be on an assignment at the Airport? He wasn't fishing that's for sure; especially because they found him naked."

"I suppose your right. I didn't hear all the details."

"I try to spare you from hearing and seeing all that I experience for your own good."

"Well right now I'm seeing what you're seeing so how are you going to spare me?"

"I guess you're in on this one like I am...so think about what we know so far. The Swift River at some point connects with the Saco, which eventually ends up here. It means the contamination we found in Livermore may have reached all the way to the ocean. It's hard to grasp it could happen but I think it's what we're seeing."

"Anna grabs onto Gallagher's arm and reveals her sudden feeling of anxiety. "I don't want to see anymore. Let's go back to the Inn."

They are about ready to leave when Gallagher sees a lone seagull barely walking along the shore on the ocean side of the jetty with a fish hanging from its mouth. He looks at Anna and says in a whisper, "I have to catch this one to be sure of my thinking."

Gallagher approaches the seagull, which is no longer able to fly and picks it up easily and covers it with his jacket. He looks to see if he was spotted by the scuba team and feels sure he has gone undetected and quickly walks away from the scene with the seagull tucked under his jacket .

"What are you going to do now?" Anna asks revealing her uneasiness.

"I have to call the Jackson Police and find out if any more fish have died since Livermore was shut down. In the meantime I need to put the gull and the fish on ice until we get back to Jackson."

They return to the Inn and Gallagher places the seagull in his cooler and then notices something odd about the fish. "This fish is not a brook trout like the others found in the Swift; it's a tagged brood Atlantic salmon."

"What's the difference?"

"The difference is we have a bigger problem on our hands."

Gallagher immediately calls the Jackson Police. "Chief...this is Gallagher. I'm calling from Saco, Maine. Have there been any new reports of dead fish in the river?"

"Gallagher! I'm glad you called. We got a report late this morning from a group of white water rafters. About a mile south of the center of Conway they spotted about a dozen dead salmon washed up on shore. Also a dead moose was found lying on the side of the road on Rte. 16 with no indications of being hit by a vehicle just like the bear."

***

Later that evening...

Gallagher, Anna and Helen had finished dinner at the Inn and decided to return to their rooms. They walked out onto the beach to enjoy the clear night sky, which was filled with a myriad of stars when an old man approaches them and asks, "I saw what you did at the jetty earlier today. I hope you can stop them."

Gallagher scrutinizes the old man who has the appearance of an 'old salt' who has lived and breathed the sea air all his life. He has a thick white beard and is wearing a weatherworn sea captain's cap.

"Stop who?" Gallagher asks innocently.

"The men over by the jetty in their scuba gear claiming to be from our government. We have been seeing these guys every day for several months now. They always come by twice a day when the tide starts going out to collect dead fish and seagulls that have gathered by the rocks. The other fishermen and myself are a little troubled by their presence. We were told fishing off the jetty was temporarily suspended until further notice."

"Why are you telling me this?"

"Because we tried to find out what they were doing with the fish and we paid for it. Two of our fishing boats were drilled full of holes and sunk. It was a warning for us to stay away."

"Why do you believe they're not from our government? They have the State Department's seal on their plates."

The man reveals a look of self-assurance and says, "Trust me on this one. I wasn't always a fisherman; I will leave it at that for now."

"Did you call the authorities?"

"We called the harbor police and they said to go along with their request to stay away. He said they were from the government and are performing ecological tests."

"What kind of ecological tests?"

"I asked him the same question and he said it was none of my business. I told him some of us have been fishing on this river before he was born and it was our business by right of birth. He just laughed at us and said if we didn't cooperate he would have to fine us and suspend our fishing licenses."

"I can see your dilemma. There goes your livelihood."

"It's already gone; Atlantic salmon spawn up river in November and December. The adults with their smolt return to the ocean between March and June. We harvest the smolt or those in their juvenile stages for further growth in controlled environments and sell the adults to markets. So the salmon are plentiful and we make most of our income for the year during this time."

"What about the seagulls?"

"We just noticed that recently and the policeman said they were being thinned out because of over population. They are feeding them whole corn laced with a poison that affects their nervous system. A few will die but most of them will be spooked and fly off. What you took from the beach hopefully has gone unnoticed."

Gallagher is a little unnerved at being seen removing the gull. "Thank you Mr...."

"Call me Ishmael."

Gallagher was taken aback and says with a slight grin, "You're kidding me, right?"

"I wouldn't kid about a thing like that; I've had to live with that name all my life."

Gallagher realizes he is serious and says, "Well Ishmael, thank you for the information and the warning. I hope this gets resolved quickly so you can get on with your fishing."

Gallagher, Anna and Helen leave the old fisherman and head back to the Inn with more questions in their minds than before.

***

Helen and Anna had an adjoining room to Gallagher's and they all planned on having a nightcap on the balcony overlooking the beach. The air was unusually warm for April and they wanted to take advantage of the clear night sky. Gallagher approaches the door of his room and finds the lock has been tampered with and he easily pushes the door open. He quickly surmises what has happened and looks for the cooler with the seagull and the fish inside. The cooler is gone.

***

17

The next morning - Wednesday – April 4, 1962

Gallagher regretfully had to leave Anna and Helen in Saco and was picked up by Jonathan to travel back to Jackson. The trip usually takes about ninety minutes on a weekday.

Gallagher is remaining very quiet has they drive back Jackson and Jonathan is filled with all kinds of questions and finally breaks the silence and asks, "Was Anna upset with you leaving?"

"That's an understatement. Helen was able to cool her down; a little psychology helped. She told Anna

129

it was best for them to make the arrangements at the Cliff House without me. The wedding planner doesn't need a man to complicate things. You *know* how men only complicate things. I couldn't have agreed more."

"So what did you find in Saco. You were vague on the phone."

"Poisoned Atlantic brood salmon and seagulls were found dead at the mouth of the river. We have obviously another source where experimentation is taking place causing the contamination."

"Are you positive?"

"I'm positive but the evidence was stolen from my room."

"What are you going to do now?"

"We need to find out where the contamination is coming from and quickly."

"Any ideas?"

"Just one. I had a conversation with Tom Perry right after O'Reilly went missing. He told me about some things O'Reilly did without consulting with him. They were police details, which were put in place for public safety reasons. One in particular was the routine surveillance of Goodrich Falls Dam. He suspended it because of budget and manpower problems. I know the dam was used back at the turn of the century to power the ski lift at Black Mountain. In the late forties the power was no longer generated from the dam and was put off line by Conway Power Utilities."

"I see what you're saying. It's out of the way and it's capable of generating its own power and can go unnoticed by being off the power grid. I know the road to the dam well and it's closed off. Through the years trees and shrubs have overtaken the area making it invisible from the main road. At one time there was a gorgeous covered bridge crossing the Ellis River on what is now Rte. 16."

"That's right and the Ellis River flows into the Saco River in Jackson and then the Saco River eventually meets with the Swift River right in Conway. From there it flows all the way to Maine and then out into the ocean."

"I guess that will be our next adventure but first I have to tell you what I did while you were chasing seagulls. I got a call from the Jackson Observer and my editor told me they had the results of the autopsy on Larry Nelson. He was poisoned with an acute dose of radiation. It was not drugs!"

'Wow! This is getting creepier by the minute."

"I know you said we should keep the professor out of it for his safety but this put me over the edge and I had to show him the formula. I was able to track down Harry Fuller and he let me into the museum and thankfully you had not changed the original combination so he was able to open it."

"I understand. I think I would have done the same thing under the circumstances. What did you find out?"

"The professor was able to decipher most of the formula. It's the ingredients for an antidote and an analysis of the effect of radiation poisoning determined by time and distance. The antidote is a combination of amino acids, an unknown herbal mixture written in some kind of code and sulfur dioxide. It definitely has to do with what was found in the fish and in the dog found at Livermore."

"But it was only sulfur the health department found in the fish."

"I asked Meridian about that and he said the amino acids and the herbal mixture would have quickly dissolved in fast running water. He said during the Spring's snow meltdown from the mountains it would make the solution virtually untraceable."

"What about the source of the radiation?"

"It was not included on the microfilm. Meridian said there have been thousands of scientific experiments performed to study acute radiation syndrome in animals. He called it ionizing radiation. The radiation causes cellular breakdown due to the destruction of the cellular walls and other key molecular structures within the body such as the cells mitochondria; this breakdown in turn causes eventual death if not treated in time."

"We are talking mutations," Gallagher concludes.

"Yes and the word Aricona is the actual name of the project for developing the antidote."

Gallagher pauses for a moment. "The word Aricona was exactly what came out of Dredmeyer's mouth before he slipped into unconsciousness. It was also in the cryptic message that Tobey heard on the shortwave radio. Another bit of evidence proving it was Dredmeyer who transmitted the radio message."

"That's right and I still wonder who was he hoping would hear the message if Jones was with him?"

"In desperate situations there is no place for logical thinking, only instinct. Dredmeyer's knee-jerk reaction was to send the message on the frequency used to communicate regularly with Dr. Jones with the hope that maybe Tobey or Penny would know what to do with the message if they heard it. It was a chance he took in desperation."

"It was good Tobey was right there to hear it."

"My only guess on that one would be Jones and Dredmeyer, being colleagues, would have known each other's habits and possible intimate family details. Philip may have told Dredmeyer of Tobey's fascination with the shortwave radio and even the times he would be at the radio."

Gallagher thinks for a moment before continuing. "Getting back to what we know, it's been a few days since shutting down Livermore. The fish found in the Saco had to have been in contact with the poison very recently, which proves we are looking at another possible source."

Jonathan's eyes widen. "What are you saying?"

"I'm saying Goodrich Falls Dam may still be in operation. I remember Tobey saying his father told him, after he was blindfolded, he was taken about ten miles away and he could hear rushing water."

Jonathan, revealing his mounting frustration says, "Who's behind all this and what's it all for? Why are they experimenting with dogs and who knows what else. Is something big going to happen that we are not aware of? Another thing; why are they doing it here and not in some official government clinic or laboratory? Why the seclusion? Why the secrecy?"

"That my friend is what we have to find out. Whoever is behind these experiments are performing them here believing it would go unnoticed in our backwoods. That's why they picked an abandoned place such as Livermore; how perfect. Goodrich Falls is another secluded place we have to investigate."

"If we are dealing with educated men such as scientists who can work with radiation why would they allow contaminated materials to drain out into our rivers? It would expose them. Rather unprofessional and stupid if you ask me."

"Unless Jones and Dredmeyer, who are respectable men of science, were misled and got themselves involved in an illegal operation instead of a government sanctioned one. Officer Taylor said the pipe had been cut and diverted to the river. Maybe it was one of them yelling for help."

"You mean by allowing fish to be contaminated in the river would be a great way to alert anyone on the outside to what was going on in secret."

"Exactly."

***

18

Later the same day...

Anna and Helen decided to cut their vacation short in Saco and came home early. Anna still wanted Gallagher to be involved in planning their special day and put the meeting with the wedding planner on hold until they could make it back to the Cliff House.

Gallagher was in his study at Eagle House looking over a map of where the Saco River connects to other rivers in the area when Helen arrives back home. As he thought, the location is right in Jackson. Helen walks in with a cup of tea and asks, "What have you found?"

Gallagher relates to Helen what he and Jonathan had concluded and what they have to do next.

***

Later that evening...

Gallagher was able to get the help of Officer Taylor and Officer Morris again and they said the road leading to the dam had been off the regular police patrol list for more than six months.

The Goodrich Hydro Electric Dam is located off Goodrich Falls Road. After driving on the road for about three hundred yards they come to Fallsview Road, which comes to a dead end at the far end of the dam. The access road has been closed off once the plant was no longer in use. Gallagher parks by the entrance of Fallsview Road and notices the gate across the road has been opened recently. Overgrown shrubs and young saplings had been cut down and were placed across the entrance to serve as camouflage. Gallagher pulls some of the shrubbery away and finds fresh tire tracks leading down to the dam. Gallagher looks at Officer Taylor and says, "It looks like a hike is no longer needed. The road appears passable."

They drive down slowly and notice the main building to the dam is quiet and no lights are on. There are no vehicles parked anywhere near the building. All things look innocent as they approach the entrance to the plant. They decide to walk around the outside of the building and examine

135

anything suspicious before they attempt to go inside. Gallagher immediately spots a drainpipe coming out of the back of the building connected to a holding tank just like the one described at Livermore. Instead of the pipe being cut, a large hole was made in the tank, which allowed all the wastewater to end up in the Ellis River.

"I think we are going to find the same scenario as we found inside Livermore," admits Gallagher.

"You mean animal experiments?"

Gallagher looks at Taylor knowing how he feels about the situation and says, "Yes, so we need back up right away before we do anything."

An expression of relief comes across Taylor's face. "Great idea! I'm not ready for another dance with the dead."

Within fifteen minutes Lieutenant Perry, and to Gallagher's surprise, Chief Peterson get out of their cruiser and approach Gallagher as he waits by the door.

As they got closer Gallagher remarks, "Chief I didn't expect to see you here, you're really getting back into the work."

"After the tragedy the other night I decided to come myself and see what this is all about first hand. I'm getting tired of surprises."

Peterson hesitates and looks away for a moment then says, "I called Anderson myself and he told me about the mole at the Bureau so for now his hands are tied so we are on our own. He called Quantico and they are conducting an internal investigation. He told them he needed to take a leave of absence but his request was denied. They told him the mole had to be found first."

"Does he have a clue as to who it could be?"

"Yes, but you're not going to believe it. He believes it's Agent Stephen Harmon, who we all know from our experiences last year, was his partner on the Thorn Hill Case. Supposedly he's currently on a special assignment in California. Anderson called the Deputy Director and told him of his suspicions. The Director told Anderson there was going to be exhaustive search for evidence leading to Harmon's activities. There are a number of government agencies working out of Quantico and something is bound to leak out. He gave him your number in case he needs to reach you personally."

"Why would Harmon turn against the Bureau?"

"I asked him the same question and he said it wasn't the Bureau he was turning against, it was him."

"Really! Did he say why?"

"He said it had something to do with his honest and unbiased assessment of Harmon's abilities in the field after the investigation in the Thorn Hill Case. I believe the phrase was 'too green for the field'."

Gallagher thought to himself how cold and unfeeling Federal agents must become after so many years in the field. Gallagher then looks back at the entrance to the hydro plant and asks, "Are we ready to go in Lieutenant?"

"Let's go and get this over with; I don't like this place."

Peterson emphatically nods his head showing he's in complete agreement with Perry and say's, "I definitely would rather be fishing."

They all enter a very large room and find several long examining tables resembling equipment found in autopsy rooms; just like in Livermore. They all have drains leading to one main drainage pipe. It's the same pipe connected to the containment tank Gallagher noticed outside. Perry and Peterson enter another room, which had empty cages varying in size. There's straw on the floor to absorb what smells like animal feces and urine.

Perry took a reluctant sniff. "They must have evacuated recently because the stench in here is very strong."

Gallagher and Taylor enter a back room and come face to face with three large German Shepherds who are caged up and foaming at the mouth, revealing their teeth. Gallagher gets closer to the cage and all three started growling and then one of them suddenly turns on the other two and starts clawing and biting the flesh off their backsides.

Lieutenant Perry hearing the commotion walks into the room and draws his gun. Gallagher quickly raises his hand up and says, "Hold it Tom. We better leave one alive; the aggressive one. It might help us in determining the cause of their rabid appearance and overall condition."

Perry starts shaking his head revealing how disgusted he is with the whole situation and says, "How in the world could this have gone on without us knowing about it? The idea to stop routine surveillance of the dam was very foolish and irresponsible. I told you I wasn't even involved in O'Reilly's decision."

"I think we found out why," Gallagher declares. "He was up to no good and he no doubt was in league with whoever murdered Ben Willard."

Gallagher turns to Peterson. "Have you been able to find out more about O'Reilly from Anderson?"

"He found out he was in the Army during the Korean War and he had been reprimanded on three occasions for dishonorable conduct and probably would have been discharged if the war hadn't come to an end. His enlistment was up and they let him go. They said he was suffering from Post Traumatic Stress Syndrome ever since he saw his closest friend blown out of his boots by a mortar explosion."

"So it looks like O'Reilly had been a ticking time bomb ever since he arrived in the valley," Gallagher exclaims. "With his background in martial arts and his several wrestling titles and to top off the list, having Post Traumatic Stress Syndrome; he's been one dangerous man. How did he ever get on the list to replace you with that kind of record?"

"I asked Anderson the same question and all he could say was he had little say on his appointment. The decision came from his superiors. If our government is behind these experiments it's for a purpose that has to remain secret. These out of the way places fit perfectly to achieve their goals. But if it's not their operation we have to find out who's behind it and quickly."

"Philip Jones told Tobey it was a classified military operation," Gallagher remembers. "But there's one big problem. The Russians are also involved. We found a tattoo in the shape of a hammer and sickle on the dead man we found in Livermore. It was strategically place on his lower back right above his buttocks. We believe he was a Soviet scientist working with Jones and Dredmeyer. He had been attacked and eaten by a large dog that had obviously been used in an experiment. An unexpected mutation took place and the experiment went drastically wrong. It's something out of an H.G. Wells horror story.

"Have you told anyone else about what you found?"

"No, but two things I didn't tell you was we found an interesting note at Liberty Cabin. It said in bold letters 'I'M SORRY'. Also, tucked away in a corner we found a pair of muddy boots with remnants of red paint which fits the description of the boots belonging to the person who may have strangled Ben Willard."

"Perry filled me in on those interesting details. Well it looks like this nightmare is just getting started. Anderson told me their labs were able to extract a small portion of one of the names on the Chicago list. He sent it to me yesterday by special delivery. What do you make of it? Question marks are where they found the letters missing."

Gallagher pulls the photo out and scans it with his magnifying glass.

[?an???p? ?or??n]

***

19

The next day – Thursday - April 5, 1962

Gallagher and Jonathan decided to drive back to Saco and find the old fisherman named Ishmael and see if anything else was happening at the mouth of the Saco River. It was a beautiful Thursday morning for a trip to the beach. Anna wanted to go but Gallagher said it was a working trip and not a vacation in the sun. They arrived about 11:00 a.m. and found Ishmael and his buddies rigging up a boat near the jetty.

Pointing to the river Gallagher declares, "There he is over there by the jetty."

"Oh my! He's what I pictured; Hemingway's 'Old Man and the Sea'."

"Ishmael, it looks like you got the go ahead to fish again," Gallagher says as he reaches for his hand.

"Yes sir! It was a funny thing. As soon as you left the area the ban was lifted and we could carry on in our work. This morning the tide was going out at 7:00 a.m. and for the first time in months the frogmen didn't show up; they were like clockwork before. Every time the tide started to go out they would arrive and quickly go to work. Come to think of it, we haven't seen any more seagulls falling into the water either."

"What a coincidence," Gallagher says with a grin.

"What brings you back so soon?" Ishmael asks out of curiosity but revealing a troubled look on his face.

"I wanted to find out exactly what you just told us. I had a suspicion something suspicious was going on and we found the source back in Jackson and shut it down. But there's another thing in particular I wanted to find out. Where can we find the harbor policeman you have been dealing with all this time? I want to know if he could tell us anything about the frogmen."

Ishmael hesitates for a moment. "After he came by and lifted the ban he said he had to go into town to meet with the Mayor at 10:00 and he wouldn't be back until late that afternoon."

"You look concerned Ishmael," Gallagher observes. "What's bothering you?"

"Yeah, I guess I am. I called the Town Hall later that afternoon and asked to see if Andy was still there and they said he had not been in all day. They were as puzzled as I was. It was supposed to be an important meeting he was to attend."

Gallagher turns to Jonathan and says, "Interesting turn of events."

Gallagher looks back at Ishmael. "How long has this Andy been working here as a harbor policeman."

Ishmael rubs his beard and hesitates again before answering. "I would guess about six months. The policeman who was here before him was named Buddy. He had been the harbor policeman for fifteen years and all of a sudden he gets up and leaves without giving any notice to anyone."

Gallagher starts to think about everything Ishmael has told him and it's not sitting well in his mind. Gallagher then asks, "What kind of car does Andy drive?"

Ishmael's brow raises upon hearing the question. "A white late model Chevy station wagon. I think it's an Impala. Why?"

"Just curious. Thank you for the information. I'd like to come by again and go out on the high seas with you someday soon. I've always wanted to catch myself a striped bass."

Ishmael reveals a slight smile and says, "It would be a pleasure. We really appreciate what you did for us. Where are you headed now?"

Gallagher returns a smile and says, "Just like a fisherman I test the wind and observe the current and then I proceed where the fish can be found."

Ishmael watches the both of them as they head back to their car. He immediately heads for an old fishing shack and picks up a phone and begins dialing.

"It's Ishmael...Gallagher and his friend have left the beach. They are curious and looking into Andy's disappearance, which we were warned could happen. Do not interfere. The job was done quickly and they shouldn't suspect anything. No harm is to come to them; understand?"

"Understand!"

'Click'

***

Gallagher and Jonathan left Camp Ellis around 3:00 p.m. and headed back to Jackson. They took Rte. 117 out of Saco and then will connect to Rte. 113 then eventually Rtes. 302 and 16. It's about an hour and half trip from Saco. They both were trying to piece everything together now that Livermore and the Goodrich Fall sites had been shut down. They concluded the seagulls in Saco were dying from eating the poisoned salmon that floated down the Saco River and eventually the ocean. The harbor policeman's sudden disappearance was troubling Gallagher. As they were driving on Rte. 113 they drove by an abandoned white Chevy Impala station wagon on the side of the road. The State Police were examining the car and curiosity got the best of Gallagher and decided to pull over and check it out. Jonathan walks over to the State trooper and flashes his ID.

"You're a little out of your neck of the woods Mr. Henry. This is Maine not New Hampshire," remarks the trooper with a laugh.

"We have to go where the news is, and right now it seems we found some."

"Really? We see cars left on the side of the highway all the time. He probably ran out of gas and hasn't returned yet. Fryeburg is about mile up the road. He probably went to get some gas."

Jonathan went over to the car and says, "There's an orange sticker on the car. It's dated last night. One of your officers must have already tagged it."

"We have no record of any of our officers marking the vehicle. We just ran the plates through our system and found out the car is unregistered. We're waiting for a wrecker to tow it away."

Gallagher decides to get down to business and walks over and says, "Excuse me officer my name is Gallagher Brady."

The officer perks up and says, "You're the guy who cracked that big case a little over a year ago in Jackson. Well I'll be darn. What do you think of that Billy? We have a real celebrity here."

Jonathan smiles. "He's the one and I'm the one who wrote about it."

Gallagher just shakes his head and tries not to burst out laughing. "Do you mind if I walk a little distance into the woods and look around?"

"No, not at all. What do you expect to find out?"

"We just came from Camp Ellis in Saco and we found out their harbor policeman vanished without giving notice a day ago and our information leads us to believe foul play is involved. This car fits the description of his vehicle."

The trooper opens the car door. "There's been no evidence of a struggle. There's no blood or any other signs of violence."

"I wouldn't think there would be if it was a professional job. It would be clean and efficient."

The trooper's eyes widen and says, "I don't know what you're getting at but I can call for more backup if needed."

Gallagher shakes head adamantly and says, "What we find here, if anything, can't be leaked to the press right now."

"I don't understand. I thought Mr. Henry is an investigative reporter."

"That's true but we have strict orders from a higher source to keep everything we find on the QT for now. We may be dealing with a foreign entity that may be up to something that could have serious implications regarding the health and welfare of our country. We must find out what that is before it's too late."

"Foreign entity. You mean alien?"

Gallagher rolls his eyes and says, "We could be talking Russian spies."

The trooper looks puzzled and is overwhelmed by Gallagher's remark. Jonathan catches his look and says, "Don't feel bad if he shocked you. I'm used to being shocked most of the time these days. He makes perfect sense as long as you don't try to figure it out."

"Okay whatever you say...how can we be of help?"

Gallagher points towards the side of the road. "I noticed drag marks leading into the woods. I suggest we check it out."

They all heads for the woods. Gallagher notices broken branches on the ground and decides to checkout wherever he sees them. The trooper being curious asks Jonathan, "It looks like he knows where he's going."

"No...he really don't but he's an avid hiker and mountain climber and can read signs in the woods of there's any evidence of man or beast. I swear he's part Abenaki."

They eventually come to the edge of a cliff with a drop to the bottom of about two hundred feet. Gallagher looks down and notices more broken tree limbs, which are protruding out from the wall of the cliff.

146

"Something or someone has been thrown off this cliff. My guess it's the harbor policeman we are looking for."

"The trooper looks down and says, "I don't see a body but I'll take your word for it and call for a copter to lower one of our men down and see what we can find."

"I don't think that will keep this on the QT. A copter lowering a man off a busy highway will not go unnoticed. Our best option is to remove the car and come back tonight and I will climb down with one of your officers to investigate."

"I will call this into headquarters and explain what's happening. We have climbing equipment at our barracks. We can meet you here at 9:00 p.m.; how does that sound?"

Gallagher nods and says, "Sounds like a plan. We will drive into Fryeburg and get something to eat and see you back here at 9:00. Remember to tell your superiors it's not to go to the press."

***

Gallagher and Jonathan stop at a small diner in the center of Fryeburg. Jonathan orders some food while Gallagher makes a call to Helen.

"Helen, I'm calling from a phone booth outside a diner in Fryeburg. We found out some interesting things and probably will find out more tonight. We have to investigate a possible homicide."

"What do you mean... a possible homicide? Don't you know for certain?"

"Well, not really. I will explain when we get back but I just wanted you and Anna to know we are all right and we will be back late tonight. "

***

Gallagher and Jonathan meet with the State police at 9:00 p.m. Officers Walker and Talbot along with Gallagher descend down the rocky cliff without difficulty. The body of a man is quickly discovered lying in some thick bushes. After the police are sure he is dead they pull him out and lay him flat on the ground. Gallagher spots the Harbor Police insignia on the sleeve of his shirt. "It's him alright," Gallagher says pointing to the insignia.

"We will hoist him up to the top," Walker says while preparing to wrap the man in a body sling.

Gallagher quickly responds and says, "Before you do that, I'm just a little curious. Could you please unbuckle his belt and unzip his pants. Then would you please roll him over on his stomach?"

The two officers look at each other puzzled at his request but do as he asks without any questions. Gallagher kneels down next to the body and pulls the man's pants down revealing his lower back right above the buttocks.

"We don't do that sort of thing here in Maine," one of the officers declares."

It was Jonathan's turn to hold back a laugh and says, "It's a new investigative procedure we adopted in New Hampshire."

"Just what I was afraid of," Gallagher declares.

The two officers take a look and see a chunk of flesh cut away right above the buttocks. They look at each other again dumbfounded but say nothing not wanting to appear unprofessional.

Jonathan stoops down and examines the man's backside. The two officers slowly walk over and see nothing but a bare patch on the man's backside. One of them speaks up and says, "I don't see a thing?"

Jonathan looks at the officer with a slight grin and says, "Oh... we do and it is most enlightening."

***

Gallagher's head is filled with all kinds of questions as they drive back to Jackson. Jonathan is remaining quiet as he drives to allow Gallagher time to think. He has learned when Gallagher is beyond reach in conversation he is working out things in his analytical brain. How to proceed forward is the big question. If the United States Government is involved; it's a highly classified military project. If the government's intentions and designs are to protect the American people it's best for it to be left alone. But if the Russians have spies working right under the government's nose and their intentions are to harm the American people they have to be stopped. The questions going through Gallagher's mind are numerous and difficult to answer. Why the animal experiments? Why the antidote for radiation poisoning? What do the Russians have to do with what's been going on? Where did they take Dr. Wallace Dredmeyer and who really are they? Were they really from the government? Is Dredmeyer still alive? Where is Dr. Philip Jones and is he still alive? Who killed the harbor policeman? What is the missing name on the Chicago list?

"Jonathan, pull over to the side of the road for a minute," Gallagher urges.

Gallagher takes out the photograph Peterson had given him of the partially legible name that was on the Chicago list.

[?an???p? ?or??n]

After several minutes Gallagher finally speaks up and says, "I've got it. The missing name is Randolph Morgan."

***

20

Jonathan became the quiet one after Gallagher revealed whom he thought was the missing name on the list. After much thought Jonathan says, "I'm looking at the missing letters and I will agree Randolph Morgan does fit perfectly but we are talking about Jane Willard's father here. How can he be on that list?"

"I realize what I'm saying but think about it. We have never met the man. In itself that's very odd considering the fact he's Jane's father and both Jane and Ben have lived in the valley for several years now and are very much a part of the community. Through those years they have purchased a considerable amount of land throughout the valley. From my understanding much of their buying power has come from her father."

"Okay that does seem odd but what are you thinking here? Are you thinking there's a connection with what has been going on around here and Morgan?"

Gallagher nods his head and says, "All I'm saying is; let's keep an open mind about it and see what our investigation further reveals."

***

Gallagher and Jonathan finally arrive back in Jackson and approach the entrance gate at the beginning of the long winding driveway leading to Eagle House. Jonathan passes his key card through the card reader to open the electric gate and nothing happens. Gallagher quickly gets out of the Rover and examines the gate.

"Someone has bypassed the security system. The wires have been cut at the junction box."

Gallagher then opens the gate by hand and they proceed to drive up to Eagle House. As they are about to go around the last turn they spot an unmarked white van parked on the side of the road out of view of the surveillance camera.

"What's going on here?" Gallagher exclaims.

Jonathan parks right behind the van and notices the license plate on the van is missing. "We got trouble," Jonathan declares. "Our visitors want to stay anonymous."

"With the wires being cut by our anonymous guests we need to be careful not to draw any attention to our arrival," Gallagher declares.

"Fortunately for us the surveillance camera has been disconnected as well," adds Jonathan.

They both get out of the Rover and walk stealthily towards the back of the house. Gallagher leads the way and suggests, "We better go in through the back entrance of the carriage house and enter the main house from the tunnel. My grandfather was wise to have this tunnel built during the war. I never thought we would ever need its use today."

"Great idea."

They are about ready to enter the carriage house when a voice calls out to them in a whisper. "Gallagher!"

Gallagher stops in his tracks and asks, "Who's there?"

"It's Tom Perry."

Gallagher turns around and looks into the woods and sees Helen and Tom Perry huddled behind some high bushes. In a whisper Gallagher says, "What's going on in there? Who are they?"

Helen speaks up and says, "We don't know. I called the police when I realized we had visitors who don't bother to knock before entering. Tom came up the back road, which our visitors apparently don't know about and came in through the carriage house to meet me."

"I was thinking of Helen's safety so we bolted for the woods. We have been here for about an hour waiting for your return."

Gallagher, a little puzzled asks, "Tom, why didn't you call for backup?"

"I did but the Chief said to wait it out in case they decided to handle the situation like they did with the two FBI agents."

"I can understand his concern but I'm so tired of all this clandestine maneuvering. I really don't care who these guys are. I'm going inside to find out."

"I wouldn't recommend it. They are the type who shoot and ask questions later."

"I'll take my chances."

Perry reaches into his belt and hands Gallagher his gun. "You may want this. The Chief said not to debate you on this because I would lose."

"He's right. I don't need it. I'm not a fan of using guns to get my way through life's difficult moments."

Jonathan rolls his eyes revealing his exasperation with his friend and says, "I wouldn't exactly call this one of life's difficult moments; I would call it downright scary and foolhardy if you go in their without some protection. If they are the Russians, remember we are not on their favorite people list. The cold war hasn't begun to thaw out yet."

Gallagher ignores his friends concern and enters the tunnel. After walking about thirty yards he reaches the door, which opened to the basement. He slowly opens it and ascends the stairs. At the top of the stairs the door opens to the back hall off the kitchen. He makes his way inside and walks carefully towards the living room where he can see the entrance to his library. He hides himself from view and spots two men looking through his many books that line the back wall. Without hesitation he boldly steps right into view and asks with complete calmness, "Do you have a search warrant gentlemen?"

One of the men reaches for his gun and asks, "Are you Gallagher Brady?"

"Who else would I be? This is my home and you are here without an invitation."

The man lowers his gun and says, "Sorry Mr. Brady. We had to do it this way."

'What are you talking about? First of all who are you?"

"We are with the FBI. We are working with Paul Anderson."

Gallagher is about ready to ask for some identification when he hears a voice from behind him. "Agent Grimes and McClouskey, good work he's still in one piece."

Gallagher turns around. "Who are you?"

"I'm agent Don Myers. These two gentlemen with me are also agents with the FBI. They are two of the best agents we have in the Bureau; handpicked by Anderson himself. Lieutenant Perry and Chief Peterson were very cooperative in going along with our little exercise."

Gallagher's wheels start to turn. "Why the game?"

"It's no game Gallagher, believe me," declares Myers. "We had to test you out first, if you are to continue in this operation. You have become quite valuable to the Bureau and we had to make sure you had the nerve and determination to continue in helping us in this very deadly business."

Jonathan and Helen walks into the room and Jonathan having overheard Myers says strongly, "I don't know why you would even have to question Gallagher's nerve. If what he did last year in exposing the Fifth Column group, the Cause, and what he did in exposing the District Attorney and his crooked brother in their web of corruption doesn't convince you; I don't know what would."

Myers nods his head in recognition of Jonathan's words and says, "The whole Bureau heard about it right up to Hoover himself. I read the brief on Gallagher before we got here. The reason for the test is simple. On the Thorn Hill Case Gallagher was working from passion and conviction. Fear was unable to make inroads in his quest to find the reason why his parents were killed in that plane crash. This case however has no attachment to his heart. Fear can work its way in but as we just observed, I was wrong. The Bureau can actually use the both of you in a limited capacity but I have to warn you. Because of a rift in the Bureau it may be difficult to know who the bad guys are. That's the reason why we were picked to work on this case. We go way back together with Anderson when Hoover became the first Director in 1935. We have been growing older and wiser together."

Gallagher is not buying his story; it didn't sound like Anderson's methods to him. "Are you here because of what happened the other night with two of your agents?"

Myers clears his throat and says, "It seems our government is split on the prime objective. I can't go into more detail than that but there's a mole in the department whose acting with the understanding he's working for the benefit of the current administration. He can't be culpable of treason because he has not been kept in the loop by design. I really can't say anymore."

Gallagher, not wanting Myers to know what he had found out about agent Harmon from Anderson nods and says, "This mole you're talking about is working for the welfare of this country but because he does not have the full picture he will try to stop anyone who appears to be going contrary to their official agenda?"

Myers nods and says, "You've got the picture."

Jonathan showing his frustration says, "Are you saying the two agents who were blown out of their car was a misunderstanding due to a lack of someone in the Bureau not being in the loop as you say?"

"I'm afraid so. It's the price some of us have to pay."

Gallagher, being annoyed at what he was hearing just shakes his head and looks at Helen. "Did you know about this game?"

"Yes I did. I thought it was a good idea after they explained their reasoning."

"What if I took up his offer about the gun? I could have gone in here, and as you put it Tom, shoot and ask questions later."

Perry hands Gallagher the gun. "I'm no fool. As you can see the gun is not loaded."

Gallagher rolls the chamber and sees it's true. He hands back the gun and sits down showing his exhaustion. "This has been some day."

***

21

Later that evening...

Chief Peterson was invited over for dinner along with Anna, Jonathan and Tom Perry to review the situation that has caused so much chaos in the valley. Myers and the two agents with him left Eagle House and said they would be close by. Before discussing what to do next they all enjoyed Helen's special roast beef dinner with all the trimmings. After dinner they reclined in the living room for dessert and coffee.

Gallagher directs his attention to Peterson and says, "Chief, I'm so happy you are back at the helm and we could share this meal together before discussing what our next move should be. It seems like old times."

"I just wish it was under better circumstances but anyways, this is what I know. The Bureau has been aware of a paramilitary group who have been undermining the research sites in other parts of the country. They have not been able to expose their leaders in the act. What has happened in Livermore and Goodrich Falls has been the biggest breakthrough so far thanks to you and Jonathan."

Jonathan interrupts and says, "Wait a minute. It sounds like Anderson has been aware of what has been going on in Livermore and Goodrich Falls all along?"

"No, it's not what I'm saying at all. Paul sent Gallagher the letter so he would be aware of the possibility of unusual activity in the area. They still have some missing pieces and if we are not careful this major sting operation will fail."

"I believe we have found one of the pieces." Gallagher declares as he pull out the photo. "I figured out the partial name you gave me. It's Randolph Morgan."

Peterson's eyes light up and says, "How does he fit?"

"Randolph Morgan is Ben Willard's father-in-law and he coerced Ben into purchasing the plot of land at Harts Location with the presumed intentions of building a shopping center in the middle of nowhere. Not a fiscally responsible move."

"Why didn't he buy the land himself?"

"He technically did because it was his money that backed the purchase of the land but his name is not on any legal documents having to do with the sale of the land; it was his daughter Jane. He basically used her as a screen to keep his hands clean and out of the picture."

Peterson interrupts. "For what purpose?"

"To create a diversion right in Livermore's backyard. All the truck traffic up Rte. 302 was being attributed to the construction of the shopping center. No one would suspect anything going on in Livermore."

"Very clever." Peterson exclaims.

"There's more to it. I believe Randolph Morgan and possibly O'Reilly were working together to silence Ben. Also, whoever was the one wearing the size fourteen Merrill hiking boots is the one who carried out the deed. Ben and O'Reilly were liabilities to Morgan. He simply didn't trust either of them. I believe Morgan wanted the formula and did all he could to protect the Aricona Project from failing so he could get his hands on it. Regarding Little Hands, he was just a victim of being in the wrong place at the wrong time and was used as a convenient scapegoat."

Lieutenant Perry remained quiet during the interchange between Gallagher and Peterson and finally decides to ask one simple question. "Chief, where do we go from here? This whole thing has my head spinning."

Peterson laughs and says, "Welcome to Gallagher's world."

Perry looks at Gallagher and shrugs his shoulders. "What's he talking about?"

"Yeah Chief, what are you talking about?"

"Never mind. It's out of our hands now. It's now a Federal issue because the State of Maine has been involved. Our work here is only to be the eyes and ears for them out in the field. Whatever we hear in the streets or in the taverns or restaurants needs to be accessed as being credible and passed on to them."

Jonathan doesn't like what he's hearing and speaks up. "You're telling us we just sit here and wait to hear something? You're telling us to go about our everyday business like nothing has happened here?"

Peterson paused for a moment understanding what he had just told them was hard to swallow. He then directs his next question to Gallagher. "Is there any reason to believe Randolph Morgan suspects he's been linked to Livermore?"

Gallagher thinks for a moment. "I don't believe so. He has cleverly stayed behind the scenes and most likely he will remain there."

***

22

Two days later - Saturday morning – April 7, 1962

Gallagher's involvement in the investigation didn't allow him much time to see how the work was progressing at the museum site so he decides it was time to concentrate on his agenda for a change.

Gallagher enters the museum and notices Harry Fuller studying some of the sketches Gallagher had given him on the interior of the main entrance to the building. "Harry...it's looking great. I can't believe the exterior is almost complete."

"Once you okayed the final drafts of the layout it was full steam ahead. We have a deadline by this November before the heavy snows fly. While I have you here I wanted to mention something to you, which has been bothering me. There's been a stranger seen poking around the site on a number of occasions. One of my men approached him and asked him if he was looking for someone but he just walked away without answering."

"What did he look like?"

"He was a well dressed man. He's short with a stocky build and balding on top. I would say he's in his late sixties."

"Did anything else stand out?"

Harry starts to laugh. "Just one thing. I felt like calling him the Little Corporal because he wouldn't take his right hand out of the breast of his suit coat."

***

Gallagher leaves the museum and walks toward the Tavern consumed by what Harry had just told him. Anna was waiting at the counter looking lovely as usual. Gallagher sits next to her and gives her a long lingering kiss. Gus Swenson comes over wearing his usual smile and says, "god middag...how are you two love birds doing today?"

"Good afternoon Gus," Gallagher replies. "We are doing just fine as you can see on this gorgeous Spring day."

"Are you two getting ready for a climb this time?" Lars asks as he walks over to join the conversation.

"No, nothing planned but we need some lunch before we do anything today."

"Any investigating today?" Lars asks hoping to hear some news.

"Well Lars if I was I couldn't tell you," Gallagher replies with a laugh.

Lars smiles and says, "I suppose your right. But I know when most of the folks around here see you these days, it's what their thinking. You have developed quite a reputation."

"Thinking is okay but knowing is another matter."

Gallagher orders their food and then make their way over to a table towards the back so they can talk in private.

"Why the seclusion?" Anna asks.

"First of all the book collector has been snooping around the museum."

"How do you know that for sure?"

"Harry described him to me and he fits the description I got from Mary Ann. Also Harry said something peculiar."

"What?"

"He kept his right hand inside the breast of his coat like he was hiding something."

"You mean like a missing finger?"

"Exactly."

"Did you tell Harry to let you know if he sees him again?"

"No because I want the book collector to show his hand; no pun intended. In the meantime lets look over the radio message again and break it down and see if we missed any clues."

..."*You have to stop this...found out...I'm sorry...for...happened...called...aricona...basker..... help...quickly...abandon...live...before............out of hand...come...it's too late.*"

"So far we know what aricona stands for."

"We do?"

"Yes but I would rather keep you free from that knowledge for now. Trust me on this one."

"Whatever you say. I know you're looking out for me but sometimes your elusiveness on details can be very exasperating."

"That's funny. Jonathan feels the same way. Getting back to the message. We know 'live' is the abbreviated word for Livermore. There has to be something else we're missing."

"I don't know what could be missing?" Anna asks perplexed. "The only other things you said Tobey mentioned was something to do with H.G. Wells and there was one other thing if I remember correctly. He said it was something his father scribbled it on the Livermore map. What was it?"

Gallagher's eyes light up. "The sleeping Indian."

Anna looks at Gallagher with an expression of bewilderment. "Right! What's that suppose to mean? Do you think Phillip is in league with the likes of O'Reilly and Morgan? It seems suspicious to me that he had the sleeping Indian scribbled on his map and it was the rendezvous location for O'Reilly and our nameless assassin."

"I don't know. There's one way to find out. Let's visit Penny Jones."

***

The Jones's home is located on Hurricane Mountain Road and is only a few minutes' drive from the Tavern. Tobey came to the door and showed his relief at seeing Gallagher with hopes he had some news about his father.

"Please come in. I'll get my mother."

After a few minutes Penny walks into the living room where Gallagher and Anna are already sitting on the couch and asks, "Have you brought us some good news?"

Gallagher speaks up and says, "We were hoping you did."

"Tobey has been staying by the radio almost around the clock. I've kept him out of school for the time being and I've been housebound waiting by the phone for any word from Philip."

Gallagher stands up and walks over to the fireplace and picks up a photograph on the mantle of Philip and Penny on their wedding day. "I must admit I haven't really been able to get to know the both you since I moved back to the valley. If it wasn't for Tobey I wonder if we would ever have gotten to meet you. If you've visited my bookshop at anytime I may have been out."

Anna pipes up and says with a smile, "I know Penny has been in the bookshop a number of times. You were just not around."

"I never seem to be able to spend the amount of time I would like at the bookshop. It's always been a great way for me to be in touch with the folks in town. Lately I have to go to the Tavern and get the latest on what's happening."

Penny expresses a rare smile and says, "We all know how valuable you are to the local police and we understand how precious your time is."

Looking at the photograph Gallagher asks, "Where was this photo taken?"

"Philip and I met at Caltech in the spring of 1948. He was teaching a course and I was a post grad student who quickly developed a huge crush on him. We only dated for three months then we got married."

"Was this taken in California?"

"No. Philip wanted to have his family attend the wedding so we flew back to his hometown right outside of Dresden, Germany. All that was left to my immediate family was my sister and she was able to come and be my maid of honor."

"Did your parents died young?"

"My parents divorced when I was three and I never saw my father after the divorce then he was killed fighting in the Pacific. My mother died a year before our wedding from lung cancer."

Anna can see the discomfort on Gallagher's face for bringing up such a painful memory and decides to change the direction of the questioning. "How long have you lived in the valley? I've lived here all my life and it seems I only know of you because of Tobey."

"Because of the nature of Philips research we have stayed very much to ourselves and have tried to stay out of the public's eye. It's the reason we moved here in the first place."

Gallagher is appreciating the new direction of the conversation and asks, "How long has Philip known Wallace Dredmeyer?"

"They met in Berlin right after the war. They both were sent there to examine how close Hitler was to developing an atomic bomb. The V-1 rocket was originally designed to carry a more destructive explosive and the Germans were only months away from succeeding."

"I see. What were your husband's feelings about the war being a citizen of Germany?"

Penny looking uneasy at the question says, "He's a scientist and he abhors the thought of man destroying life for any reason. Let me show you something in his office. He was thinking of donating his set of the Lord of The Rings to your museum. It's his favorite set because Tolkien himself signed it. Even though Tolkien denies the work as being a denunciation against Hitler and his war machine my husband strongly believes it was and thinks everyone on this planet should know of the horrors of war and maniacs like Hitler."

"I didn't mean to imply anything. We are trying to find who would want to harm your husband."

"I know. I guess I'm a little sensitive when it comes to the war because of Philip being raised in Hitler's backyard. But I can tell you this much about his disdain for war; he rejected the recruitment of becoming a part of the Hitler Youth League which cost his family considerable hardship. His father lost his job and his mother was forced to clean floors to help support Philip and his two sisters."

Tobey, overhearing the conversation asks, "Do you think my father is still alive?"

"Tobey, I don't want to give you and your mother any false hopes but I really believe whoever abducted him, needs him alive for his knowledge."

Anna, trying to remain focused on why they wanted to see Penny asks, "Has Philip ever mentioned to you anything about the sleeping Indian?"

"Why do you ask?"

"It was circled on a map Tobey found in Philip's office."

"I really never look through his papers because of what he gets involved in with his work. I never heard him speak of it until the other day when he was talking to someone on the phone. I didn't know who but my guess it was a fellow scientist."

Gallagher perks up and says, "Can you remember the gist of the conversation?"

"The only thing that stands out was something about a government installation. Would that have anything to do with it?"

"I'm not really sure. I want to thank you for being so frank. You have given us a lot to work with and I promise you we will do our best in finding Philip."

Gallagher and Anna leave about an hour later after having a more positive conversation with Penny and Tobey over tea and cake. As they are driving back to Eagle House, Anna is overwhelmed with questions in her mind. She looks at Gallagher and notices he was smiling. "What are you smiling about?

Gallagher thinks for a moment before answering. "I think what we just heard is an example of the typical problems that arise when trying to figure out a puzzle."

"What's that?"

"We can't see the forest for the trees."

"What do you mean? What are we not seeing?"

"I guess if I knew we would not be having this conversation. But speaking of not seeing the forest for the trees. There's something I need to do right away. I will drop you off back at the bookshop if you don't mind."

"What could be so urgent?"

"My life."

"What's that suppose to mean?"

"I can't get into it right now but it's real important to me that I drive to Boston tonight. Would you close up the bookshop for me?"

"I can go with you. Boston is a long drive. I can have Kathy close it up. She's planning on working till closing anyways."

Gallagher hesitates and moment then says, "I have to go alone."

Anna just shakes her head. "There are things about you that really puzzle me!"

Gallagher doesn't say anymore about it and drops her off at the bookshop. Before she gets out of the car he kisses her like he has never kissed her before and then drives away.

Anna walks into the bookshop and sees Kathy who is waiting on a customer at the counter. The customer abruptly leaves upon seeing Anna.

"What was that all about?"

"He was asking a lot of questions about the town and about Gallagher," she replies. "I didn't give him any information. He wouldn't give me his name he just said he was a book collector."

***

23

Sunday – April 8, 1962

Gallagher slept in late, which was very unusual for him. He had arrived back late the night before from Boston and spent most of the day secluded in his study, which of late was also very unusual for him. Helen offered to make him a late breakfast, which is his favorite meal of the day but he told her he wasn't very hungry; another unusual thing.

***

Later in the evening...

Gallagher gets into his Rover and heads for Anna's home. Something has been stirring inside him for weeks and he can't go on any longer. He wants Anna for himself and he's not going to let the troubles of this crazy world interfere with his happiness. It seems to be one hurdle after another he has to clear before he can satisfy his own needs, but not anymore.

Gallagher pulls into the driveway and knocks on the door. Tom Rawlings opens it and warmly greets Gallagher with open arms. "Gallagher... what a surprise. What brings you by tonight?"

"I have a surprise for Anna. Is she home?"

"Well yes come in and make yourself at home. She's in the kitchen with Mary."

"Is Scott and Stephen here too?"

"Yes they are. We are having a late Sunday dinner together and you are welcome to join us."

"That's great and I would love to but first I need to talk with Anna in private; it's real important."

Tom reveals a big smile and says, "Sure I'll get her."

After a few anxious minutes go by Anna comes into the room and quickly runs over and kisses Gallagher. "What a surprise. I didn't expect to see you tonight. The way you were acting last night I didn't know when I would see you. I called the house and Helen said you were not to be disturbed. I know there's been a lot on your mind."

"Well yes there has been but it was a sudden urge that drove me to Boston last night and eventually here tonight."

"Is there anything the matter?"

Gallagher releases her and says, "There's a lot that's the matter. Please sit down so I can get this out."

Anna sits down on the couch and looks up at Gallagher as he continues to speak in a very low tone, "We can't go on like this any longer; it's not working."

Anna becomes startled at his words and asks, "What do you mean? Are you breaking off our engagement?"

Gallagher kneels down and takes her hand and says, "Yes, I have to."

Tears start to run down her face. "Why...I thought you loved me?"

Gallagher starts to choke on his own tears and says, "I do that's why with all that's been going on I need you to be my wife without further delay. I can't wait till October."

Anna starts to break down with tears of joy and rushes into his arms. "I don't want to wait till October either. I will marry you tonight if you want."

They hold each other for several minutes until they both realize they had family to tell of their new plans. They both enter the kitchen where Tom and Mary are busy preparing the Sunday dinner. Scott and Stephen come in through the back door after chopping some wood and join them in the kitchen.

Anna, unable to hold back says, "Mom...Dad...we have something to announce. Gallagher and I want to get married right away."

Mary reaches out and holds Tom's hand and says, "Anna...you're not...?"

"Ma...no it's not what you think. You know us better than to think we would do such a thing. We both just can't go on any longer. I've felt this way for awhile and..."

Gallagher interrupts, "I have loved your daughter...I think all my life. I don't want to go on any longer being without her wondering where she is or what she's doing all the time. It leaves me empty and alone. I hope we have your blessing."

Mary reaches for Gallagher and says, "Tom and I have loved you as our own son since you were a little boy."

Scott and Stephen look at each other showing their surprise at her words. "Ma, how long have you known Gallagher?" Scott asks.

"It was before you two were born. Gallagher and Anna were schoolmates and they had a crush on each other way back then. When Gallagher or maybe I should say Thomas was taken away when he was only eight years old his life drastically changed. The trauma of losing his parents and grandfather all in one night affected him deeply to the point where he erased almost all of his childhood memories."

Mary looks at Gallagher and smiles. "Helen always kept in touch with me during the years you lived in England. She even mentioned how you wrote a poem about Anna. I still have a copy of it. Helen sent it to me. She knew it was about Anna."

Gallagher's eyes open wider and says, "Do you still have the poem?"

"Oh yes, let me get it."

Anna with a surprise look on her face says, "Ma...you never told me."

"I didn't want to cause you any hurt in case you never saw him again. Now is the right time."

Mary returns after a few minutes and hands the poem to Gallagher and says, "You may want to read it to her now. We will leave you two alone."

Gallagher raises his hand and says, "No, please stay. I want to share this with my family."

Gallagher begins reading it aloud;

I Never Said Goodbye

We played together and we laughed together.
We were innocent and we were young.
A dark day came and I was taken away from you.
Will you remember me?
I never said goodbye.

I daydream and I wonder.
Will I ever see you again?
My heart aches for you.
Will you remember me?
I never said goodbye.

My feelings are just flying in the wind.
They may never land on your heart.
Where are you now?
Do you remember me?
I never said goodbye.

Gallagher raises his eyes and sees tears flowing down Anna's face. She runs into his arms and says, "I never forgot you. My heart trembled when I walked into the bookshop that morning. I didn't know what to expect. Would you remember me was all I could think about and once I knew I was going to walk through that door and face you my heart trembled."

Scott shows a big smile says to Gallagher, "I remember asking you about your feelings for Anna when we met at the trailhead at Tuckerman's Ravine last year when we began our climb to rescue her. I remember asking you how long did you have feelings for my sister and you said it was the first time you laid eyes on her in the bookshop but now I know it was years before that day."

Gallagher clears his throat before saying, "Remember Scott, I was only known to you as Gallagher at that time. My true identity was only known to a very few. What else could I say to you?

173

It was the truth. It was the first time I laid eyes on her as Gallagher Brady."

Gallagher looks at Scott and Stephen. "When your sister came into the bookshop looking for employment it triggered a repressed memory and it all came back to me. I don't want to lose what I almost lost so many years ago. Do we have your blessing too?"

Scott approaches Gallagher and says, "Ever since the night of the Tuckerman climb during that Nor'easter I have been waiting for this day to come. I knew your love for Anna was something special. You were driven and nothing was going to get in your way. You risked your life for her. I will never forget what you did and I will always look up to you as a brother and friend. Welcome to our family."

Stephen nodding in agreement adds, "I couldn't express it any better. I look forward to many wonderful times together."

All of them enjoyed the rest of the day planning for the big event over a family dinner. Helen, Jonathan and Valerie came by later in the evening and they all celebrated together.

***

24

Saturday – April 14, 1962

Sunrise was a welcome sight to Gallagher as he woke up in anticipation of their wedding. The whole village was invited to witness the outside ceremony, which was to take place in the village common. Gallagher asked Jonathan to be his best man, which was no surprise to anyone, as the two of them in four short years had become the closest of friends. Jonathan was as nervous as if he were the groom himself. Kathy from the bookshop, who has been Anna's closest friend since childhood, was asked to be her maid of honor. During the day Gallagher made final arrangements for their honeymoon in Colorado. Before he could leave everything behind for a week he thought it would be wise to meet with Harry Fuller on some last minute details regarding the museum.

Gallagher leaves Eagle House about 10:30 and drives over to the museum and as he approaches the parking lot he notices a black sedan parked one street over with the motor running but he couldn't see anyone inside.

Gallagher begin looking for Harry and finds him ducking under one of the big windows facing the back entry. "Anything interesting Harry?"

Harry turns around and whispers, "Our visitor is back and he's with a very large gentleman who looks like he could play for the New York Giants."

Gallagher hunches under the window to get a better look. "I don't believe I've ever seen him around here before. I see what you mean about being large. I would say he has definitely had some specialized physical training."

"You mean military?"

"Exactly."

"I don't know what you're getting at but the other one seems to be calling the shots."

"Why do you say that?"

"The giant was about ready to enter the back door of the museum, which I had left open so I could take some equipment to my truck, when I overheard the short guy, you know, the Little Corporal, yell out to him and commanded him to return just as you were pulling into the parking lot."

Gallagher's mind begins to race. "I think I'm going to ask Peterson to step-up security while I'm away. Even though the books that the book collector is looking for are no longer here; it's best to keep him guessing. I'm starting to get a clearer picture in my mind as to what's going on here."

"I don't want to know," declares Harry.

"I wasn't going to spoil your day. I will see you at the wedding right?"

"I wouldn't miss it."

***

Later the same day at the Village Common...

The wedding ceremony began at 6:00 p.m. and was being officiated by John Peterson who had held onto his license to marry couples even after his retirement. Several hundred of the local residents attended along with many who did not know the couple but were in the village shopping and decided to witness the wedding.

When Gallagher saw Anna walking towards him on the flower covered bridle path he was overwhelmed by her beauty that had always captivated him.

By the generous gift offered by Vince and Maria Corelli the reception was held at the Woodland's Inn. Besides family, Gallagher and Anna's closest friends were invited to the reception including Gus and Lars Swenson, Bill Waters, John Peterson, Tom Perry, Mary Ann and Valerie Blair and many others. Anna's family in Colorado, on her father's side, were unable to make it but offered their summer home in Aspen as a honeymoon gift.

As the day came to a close and the sun was setting in the western sky, Gallagher and Anna planned leaving the happy gathering and spending the night in the Bridal Suite at the Woodlands. Jonathan and Valerie said their goodbyes holding each other very close both wishing in their heart it was the two of them who were off on their honeymoon. Jonathan on several occasions thought of springing the question to Valerie but each time it ended with him losing his nerve. He had lost a love once before and was so hesitant on giving his heart completely to another but Valerie was slowly breaking down that solid wall he had built up in his heart. It was just a matter of a little more time.

**

PART THREE

25

Ambush

Monday morning - April 16, 1962

Gallagher and Anna were in eager anticipation of their honeymoon escape to Colorado. Gallagher had never been to the Rocky Mountains and was eager to hike and take in the wonders of the Midwest. Anna's cousins were excited to see them since they were unable to attend the wedding on such short notice. Anna's uncle Arnold and aunt Sophia offered their summer chalet in Aspen to them for as long as they wanted to stay. Anna's three cousins, Christine, Donna and Jeffrey offered to be their tour guides if they wanted some company. For Gallagher it really was an escape but in the back of his mind another possibility was lurking just around the corner. He had finally seen the forest in spite of the trees.

A limousine picked them up and drove them to Logan Airport. The flight out of Boston was scheduled for 10:00 a.m. Anna had called her cousins in Colorado and let them know everything was on schedule and for them to be picked up at the Stapletone International Airport in Denver.

The plane was starting to turn around towards runway 4 when Gallagher looks out the window and sees what started to cause a sickening feeling in his stomach. Across the tarmac a black sedan was parked. The same black sedan he saw at the museum the day before. His mind started recalling what he had learned about what had happened to his parents so many years ago. Were they going to be the next victims, he wondered? It was a thought he couldn't contemplate.

178

The plane lifted off runway 4 and disappeared above the clouds. The weather had been pristine for their departure and after an hour into their flight a slight overcast sky began to greet them as they continued west. Gallagher seemed restless and was fidgeting in his seat. Anna put her hand on Gallagher's arm and says; "I've never seen you like this before. You usually have nerves of steel. What's going through your mind?"

Gallagher looks out the window. "I feel this is too good to be true. Finally I'm able to leave all my troubles behind and spend time with you without interruption and yet I'm feeling vulnerable all of a sudden. The circumstances surrounding the Livermore and Goodrich Falls experiences has got me questioning everything. Who is behind it all? Is it the government? Is it the Russians? Could it be just some homeland corruption involving the FBI or the CIA? Can Harmon really be the mole? My head is spinning with all kinds of thoughts."

"You have gone from a sincere idealist to an insincere cynic."

Gallagher stunned by Anna's perception says, "You really know me, don't you?"

"I do and it's because of how well I know you is the reason why I want to spend the rest of my life with you. But I must admit there's a side of you that is still so mysterious."

Gallagher holds her hand and says, "Even if I might be dragging you down into a volcano that's ready to erupt?"

"See! That's what I mean; mysterious."

"Well think about what has transpired in the last two months. There is the disappearance and abduction of Dr. Jones and the attack and abduction of Dr. Dredmeyer. We have dead fish floating in two of our rivers caused from some unknown radiation contamination. Then to top it off we have two men who have been found dead, who may be Russian spies connected to the mysterious dead fish mystery. What's going to happen next?"

Just as Anna was about ready to comment a loud roar surrounds the plane outside. Two Air Force Fighter Jets come up alongside of the Boeing 707 and directs the pilot by radio to follow the lead jet and not to make anymore radio contact or the plane would be shot down.

Gallagher was anticipating something to happen but was surprised at how soon and how overt. From their wedding day to the time they stepped onto the plane everything had gone off too smoothly. Anna was prepared in her mind and heart for whatever was to take place and was secure in knowing that Gallagher was with her.

Three hours later the plane lands at Moffett Federal Airfield at the southern end of San Francisco Bay. As soon as the plane comes to a stop four heavily armed soldiers board the plane and approach Gallagher.

"Mr. Brady...you need to come with us right way."

Gallagher looks at them and then at Anna. "What about my wife? "

"We will see to her needs and you will be joined with her shortly. Please come now. We haven't much time."

Gallagher kisses Anna goodbye and gives her a wink assuring her everything would be all right. She smiles as he is escorted off the plane by armed guards but inside she knows everything is not going to be all right.

A Lincoln Continental pulls up and Gallagher is directed to get inside. He is seated between two armed men dressed in military fatigues. They drive off the base and after about five miles they come to a gate with an armed guard blocking the way. The driver shows the guard his pass and the gate opens. They continue for about another ten minutes along a heavily tree lined drive and eventually come to another gate. The driver again shows the guard his pass and was about to continue on when a large truck comes out of nowhere and smashes directly into the driver's side of the Lincoln knocking the driver unconscious. Two men get out of the truck and point their guns at the two men sitting with Gallagher in the back seat. Another man pulls Gallagher out of the car and helps him into the truck. Gallagher is bleeding profusely from the back of his head. The truck leaves rubber behind and drives away with excessive speed down several streets crisscrossing back and forth then comes to a stop when another car pulls up and Gallagher, who had now passed out, is taken away.

***

Three days later - April 19, 1962

Gallagher opens his eyes and to his horror he finds himself in a hospital bed hooked up to an intravenous bottle. He attempts to sit up but his head begins to pound and he quickly lays back down. By his side is a buzzer and he presses it to get some assistance. Thirty seconds later a nurse walks in. "Good morning Mr. Brady. Happy to see you're finally coming to life."

Gallagher eyes the nurse and asks, "Where am I?"

"You are at a safe house medical facility in Oregon. You had a nasty crack on the head from the accident."

"Who brought me here?"

"I did," Agent Stephen Harmon says as he walks into the room.

Gallagher doesn't know how to react at seeing the alleged FBI mole. Putting an evident panic feeling aside he says, "Agent Harmon…what happened?"

"I hope you're ready to swallow what I'm about to tell you."

Harmon looks at the nurse and says, "Can we talk for awhile?"

"He's suffering from a mild concussion. As long as you make it brief. He needs his rest."

Gallagher speaks up and says, "I will take the risk."

The nurse leaves the room and Harmon sits in a chair beside Gallagher's bed. "It all goes back to November of last year. I was given the assignment to accompany Paul Anderson to investigate the activity of the Fifth Column group that had emerged in your area. Hopefully the knock on your head didn't wipe out that memory."

Gallagher rolls his eyes. "Nothing could wipe that horror show out of my mind."

"Well I first thought it strange that Paul Anderson was assigned to the case because he had been settled in at a desk job for the past ten years. The activity of the Fifth Column had been his baby some years earlier and when he heard of their resurgence he felt he was the best qualified to head up the investigation. Of course being fairly new to the bureau I was relieved that someone of his abilities and experience was taking charge."

Harmon stops and looks at Gallagher carefully and asks, "Are you still with me?"

Gallagher reveals a slight smile. "You haven't said anything I didn't already know."

Harmon doesn't return a smile and says, "Anderson is the mole."

Gallagher's eyes widen revealing his total surprise. "That's very interesting. He believes you're the mole."

"It doesn't surprise me. When I was assigned to go back to the Academy at Quantico I was receiving special training for this kind of situation. To put it simply; to catch a mole."

Gallagher starts to think about everything that has happened since finding out about the poisoned fish and everything connected with Livermore and Goodrich Falls. Gallagher starts nodding his head acknowledging what Harmon is saying and says, "He gave me his card when you both left after the Thorn Hill Case was closed. He said if I needed anything to call him. In itself, I didn't think much of it at the time but now I see what he was doing. He knew I would call him if I caught wind of the experimentation that has been going on and it would be his tip off to organize things."

Harmon finally smiles. "I knew you would finally get it."

"Now that I think about it. He sends two FBI agents out immediately after I called him about some strange goings on in the valley and they are quickly eliminated. It had to be a professional job for sure."

"They were intended to silence you. We intervened just like we did three days ago when your plane was forced down by Anderson."

"That was you. What about the strange test I was given at Eagle House by Myers, Grimes and McClouskey? They were sent by Anderson."

"They were not sent by Anderson. That's what we wanted you to think at the time."

"Who sent them then and why the silly test?"

"I sent them and the test was an assurance that you could help us in revealing Anderson's secret agenda."

"Do you know about the letter he sent me?"

Harmon shows uneasiness at the question. "Yes I'm aware of the letter."

Gallagher could tell Harmon was lying but thought it best to let it slide and go along with the way the conversation was going. Harmon's story was not ringing true but he was not in a position to argue the point. He then stops thinking about Harmon and the reality of his current situation was becoming evident. "Where's my wife?"

Harmon sees the stress in Gallagher's face as he asked the question.

"We are not sure where she was taken. Anderson knew everything about your trip to Colorado. He was able to arrange a military escort forcing you to land at Moffett Federal Airfield. We were monitoring everything because two can play their game. We also have a mole that was able to tip us off about Anderson's intentions to hijack the plane and abduct you and Anna upon landing. It was my task force who rammed the limousine with a box truck. You were injured badly at the scene when your head hit the gun barrel belonging to the soldier sitting next to you. We are sorry about that but it was the only way to get you out of there quickly; it was a risk we had to take. We were able to get away before they could regroup and catch us. As far as Anna is concerned, we are searching for her right now."

Harmon stops for a moment to allow Gallagher to swallow everything he had just heard. "I was wondering; is there anything about Colorado that would have prompted Anderson to intercept your arrival in Denver?"

Gallagher realizes he needs to be judicious in his answers. "I mentioned nothing about the Colorado trip. Anna has family there and they offered us their summer home in Aspen as a honeymoon gift. Our wedding was planned for October but we both decided to move it up sooner and the honeymoon trip was a surprise. We had no time to really talk about it to anyone outside our immediate family and friends."

"You mean that's why you were flying to Colorado because you were on your honeymoon? No other reason?"

"Yeah...what other reason could there be?"

Harmon hesitates then says, "Just curious."

185

"Everything was on the spur of the moment like I said, the wedding and the trip to Colorado. Speaking of that I have to get out of here. I need to find my wife right away."

"Wait a minute," Harmon says as he grabs Gallagher's arm. "You can't leave right now."

"Why's that?"

"Right now we have gone undetected. Any movements could signal Anderson and his team."

Gallagher starting to lose his patience says strongly, "Wait a minute. Who's in control here? Are you legitimate or are you a rogue group working off the grid? I can't tell anymore. Just call your superiors if you're on the up and up."

"If we were working outside the Bureau's jurisdiction do you really believe you would be alive right now? Certain high level officials who knew what you were able to discover and disrupt these past few weeks would definitely want you out of the way."

"You mean our government," Gallagher replies without wavering.

"I don't think we should go there. Our conversation is being recorded."

"So I'm being held prisoner?"

"I would like to use the word detained; at least for the time being. We are only thinking of your protection."

"You can't keep me here! I have to find Anna."

186

"I'm sorry Gallagher but we can and we are and it's for own your safety and ours."

"I don't get it. Why don't you come clean with me? What are you not telling me?"

"If you don't know then it's best if it stays that way. There has been a big mistake and I'm very sorry."

"You can say that again. Am I allowed to make a phone call?"

"Go ahead but know this; your call will be monitored. It will be on a five second delay. If we find you are saying anything to reveal where you are we will disconnect the call."

"I know... for my protection."

* * *

Three hours later...

Jonathan was about ready to leave Eagle House when the phone rings in the carriage house. Jonathan picks up the receiver. "Hello, who's calling?"

"Jonathan... it's Anna...is Gallagher there?"

"Anna, I'm so glad you're alright. We have been worried sick. Your family in Colorado called and said you never arrived."

"Is Gallagher there?" she repeats revealing her obvious distress.

Jonathan, looking for the right words says, "He's in unknown some safe house somewhere on the West coast. He was badly hurt in an accident. He's with..." Jonathan thought for a moment. "Are you where you can talk?"

"I was being held at the airfield where we landed in a heavily guarded room. They pumped me full of questions but I remained silent."

"Who are they?"

"The ones that questioned me claimed to be from Military Intelligence. They wanted to know what I knew of the Aricona Project. I told them nothing."

"Did they buy it?"

"Not at all. They injected me with Scopolamine but they found out I was telling the truth and stopped questioning me. They finally released me."

"You mean in all this time Gallagher never mentioned to you about the Aricona Project being the name of the research to develop an antidote for radiation poisoning?"

"I only remember seeing the word aricona in the message from Dredmeyer, that's all. You know how Gallagher is; he doesn't giveaway much unless he's completely convinced of something."

"Well... Gallagher keeping you in the dark may have saved your life."

"He's good that way."

"Where are you now?"

"I was able to fly out of there on the first available flight to Colorado. I flew to Denver as originally planned. My cousins Christine and Donna picked me up and I'm staying with them but I have to talk with Gallagher right away. I found out something he needs to know from my cousins. Is there any way to reach him?"

"I'm afraid that's out of the question right now. He couldn't tell me much because the call was being monitored. Leave me your phone number and I will have him call you when I hear from him again. He's under heavy surveillance right now."

"Why? He's no criminal. I'm no criminal. Why are they treating us like this?"

"I don't really know what this is all about but I do know he's in FBI custody and they are afraid he might flee. They know Gallagher well enough and know his capabilities."

"I thought the FBI was on our side. What's this all about Jonathan? Are you sure you don't know. You and Gallagher have a tendency to keep things close to your vests during your investigations. Aricona is a perfect example."

"My guess is; there is one side of our government that's being kept in the dark from the activities of the other side of our government and the Russians are somewhere in the middle taking advantage of the confusion."

Anna remains silent for a moment then whispers, "I have to go to the sleeping Indian at Owl Mountain"

"Sleeping Indian! What are you talking about? You're in Colorado."

"I know and that's what's so strange. I told my cousins all about what was happening back home and particularly Gallagher's experience with Dredmeyer, Jones and O'Reilly. When I mentioned the sleeping Indian they perked up and said they have their own sleeping Indian at Owl Mountain. Either it's a fantastic coincidence or it's the real place Jones was referring to when he jotted it down on his map. I know it sounds impossible but I know Gallagher would want me to look into it. It's want I need to tell him."

Jonathan thinks for a moment. "When you eliminate the impossible, whatever remains, no matter how improbable, must be the truth."

"What's that supposed to mean?"

"I will explain it when I see you but right now I wouldn't go to Owl Mountain if I were you. You will be shot on sight if my thinking is correct. They must have thought your trip to Colorado was to go to the sleeping Indian at Owl Mountain. That explains the hijacking. They had no idea it was an innocent honeymoon trip to your cousins home in Aspen. It all makes sense to me now."

Nothing was going to change Anna's mind and ignores Jonathan's warning and changes the subject and asks, "What about Helen; is she doing okay?"

"Eagle House has an army around it watching every move Helen and I make. I suppose we should be thankful because we can still come and go but with an agent trailing us at all times."

"So are you stuck there until this thing comes to some kind of conclusion?"

"Well I'm going to have them think so but I plan on using the tunnel and leave by the back way. on foot. They are watching the house down by the gate. They won't see me when I leave tonight. The forecast calls for a moonless night. Darkness should cover the valley like a shroud."

"What are you planning to do?"

"I'm going to get in touch with Professor Meridian. He knows where Dredmeyer lives. I'm told it's in a virtually secluded area on Mirror Lake. The two of us may get some answers by going through his personal things. We should find something about what he's been up to; particularly the Aricona Project."

"Now that you mention it. What is the Aricona Project?"

"At this point all we know is; it's the name of the research project for developing an antidote for radiation poisoning."

"Well please be careful Jonathan. Like you said, someone is watching every move we make."

***

Later the same day...

Jonathan and the professor make their way through the many narrow and twisting tree lined roads on their way to Dredmeyer's house. The house is set way back in the woods only offering a narrow view of Mirror Lake from the large wraparound front porch.

"Did Dredmeyer ever marry?" Jonathan asks.

"No, he's been a confirmed bachelor all his life. We met at Harvard and he was always the bashful introverted type. He said he never had time for a relationship."

They make their way up to the front porch and the professor lifts up the front door mat and looks for a key. "That's odd; the key is missing. He has me check on his house whenever he's away on one of his research projects. The key is always here. It was here a week ago."

Jonathan turns the doorknob on the front door. "The door's not locked."

Meridian hesitates and says, "Something's not right here. I know I locked it the last time I was here."

Jonathan opens the door and yells out but there is no return answer. As they enter the main room they quickly notice the furniture has been knocked over and books are laying all over the floor. The professor scratches his head and says, "This looks like my place, that's the way I am but not Wallace; he's as neat as a pin. Something is definitely wrong here."

Jonathan looks at all the books and some of the titles. "Did Wallace ever work for the government?"

"Yes, he was one of the scientists that worked on the Manhattan Project back in the forties."

"That's the project that worked on the first atomic bomb."

"That's right. You can see why he was possibly involved in developing an antidote, but I know Wallace better than anyone; he would never get involved in a project that was not in the best interests of this country."

"Gallagher and I figured that out right away. The men who took him away from Livermore may have been Russian agents dressed up to look like officials from our government. The same was with the frogmen in Saco who pulled up in those vans. Finding the harbor policeman proved that for sure."

The professor, not one for getting into investigative hypothesis, turns to look at Jonathan. "I am of the strong opinion that this whole experimentation with the purpose of developing an antidote is the work of our government, not the Russians. Our government took Wallace away to suppress any knowledge of the Aricona Project. The frogmen at Saco may have been doing the same; they are covering their tracks."

"Those are rather strong words coming from you professor. I feel more comfortable blaming the Russians."

"I know it sounds like treason but there must be something very big in the wind for this kind of covert activity to take place in our backyard. Our government is up to something and they are using innocent citizens as pawns for their purpose. What that purpose is I can't say for sure but I believe Gallagher will find it out if he's not silenced first."

They are about ready to leave when Jonathan thinks to check one more place. He walks into Dredmeyer's bedroom and goes right to his nightstand. A small notebook is by the phone. He begins flipping through the pages when he finds what he was looking for; the word **ARICONA** in large bold letters. He keeps turning the pages and comes to another group of words that stand out in large bold letters; **SLEEPING INDIAN at OWL MOUNTAIN**.

"Professor...Anna was right. The sleeping Indian that was written on Philip's map was referring to Owl Mountain in Colorado."

Meridian ponders for a moment. "If my memory serves me correct Wallace recently had taken a trip to Colorado. He said it had to do with a research paper he wrote some years ago and was to speak about it at the University of Colorado. Maybe it has to do with that visit."

Jonathan starts putting things together. "It now starts to make sense."

"What makes sense?"

"It's too bizarre to even imagine but there's something connected with Livermore and Goodrich Dam in Colorado. It explains why Gallagher and Anna were brought down before they reached Colorado."

"How do you figure?"

"I recently investigated some unusual traffic at the Concord Airport. Cargo planes supposedly carrying medicine were flying out to the west coast according to the manifest. I believe Colorado was the true destination."

Meridian quickly responds to Jonathan's words. "Wallace and I witnessed the detonation of the atomic bomb in Los Alamos, New Mexico. I remember some chatter about a secret facility being built in the mountains of Colorado."

"Do you remember anything at all Dredmeyer could have said to you, which would reveal what he was involved in?"

"Wallace is very closed-mouthed when it comes to his work. Many of his projects are from the government and most of the details are classified."

After doing a further search of the house Jonathan and the professor decide to leave being satisfied they at least found some crucial evidence when Jonathan hears a voice coming from the cellar. "Professor...did you hear a voice? It sounds muffled but I think it came from the cellar."

"My hearing is not what it used to be. Let's take a look."

Jonathan looks everywhere for the cellar door but comes up empty. "Access to the cellar must be from the outside." Jonathan declares.

They both walk around to the back and Jonathan sees the bulkhead. "That's odd! The house has a bulkhead but not a door going to the cellar from inside the house."

Jonathan pulls on the handle of the bulkhead and as he thought, it was locked. Jonathan starts banging on the bulkhead.

"I heard it again." Jonathan declares. "It's definitely a woman's voice."

Jonathan runs back into the house and searches again for a door, but still no door to the cellar is found. In frustration Jonathan runs back outside and goes to his Land Rover and pulls out a heavy one and a half inch gage hemp rope and attaches it to the back bumper of the Rover. He takes the other end and ties it to the handle of the bulkhead. He starts the Rover up and slowly drives forward and pulls the entire bulkhead off its foundation. They quickly enter the cellar and find Penny Jones tied to a support beam by the stairway. She's gagged and sobbing when they get to her. Jonathan removes the gag and she screams out, "He took Tobey."

"Who took Tobey?"

Penny wipes the tears from her eyes. "Philip took Tobey away. Something is wrong with him. It's like he's gone mad."

"Tell me what happened," Jonathan asks as he holds onto her trembling hands.

"What day is today? I'm all twisted around and confused."

"It's Thursday."

"Three days ago, Philip returned home and told us we had to leave immediately. He said to take any clothes we needed because we would not be returning for some time. He took his shortwave radio and some of his clothes. He also smashed the window in the back door so it would look like there was a break-in. We came directly here and he told us not to leave under any circumstances."

Jonathan was filled with many questions but waited for Penny to prepare herself. All of them made their way back into the main part of the house. She told them she had been tied to the post for about two days and hadn't eaten or drank anything the whole time. Jonathan brought her some water and some crackers and cheese. After an hour she was ready to talk.

Penny starts to cry as she begins telling her story. "Philip was a different man when he came home. He was cold and calculating in his speech and movements. I tried to get through to him but he had this glaze over his eyes like he had been drugged. I asked him questions about where he had been but he said only distorted answers that didn't make any sense. He would mumble to himself and I would ask him what he was saying and he would get angry at me so I stopped asking questions."

Professor Meridian reaches for Penny's hand and asks, "Did he mention Dr. Dredmeyer at all?"

"Tears continue to flow down Penny's face. "Philip threw a chair across the room in anger and said he's probably dead by now."

***

In the meantime in Colorado...

Anna and her two cousins collected the needed equipment preparing themselves for their trip to Owl Mountain. Her cousins are well-conditioned mountain climbers and know the terrain very well. Anna was not sure what they are going to find but somehow in the back of her mind she has a feeling Gallagher is making his way there too. She realizes it's only a feeling but it's a strong one.

***

26

Friday evening at a safe house somewhere in Oregon...

Gallagher's watch reads 9:45. He has been carefully observing the timing and routine of the changing of the guard at the safe house where he is not feeling so safe anymore after his encounter with Harmon.

Something is not right in his mind about the whole abduction scenario and the claim that Anderson was the mole.

Gallagher has been allowed full access to the house but has never gone down to the basement level to check it out. His bedroom is the closest to the cellar door and he observes the agent on duty is absorbed in the book he's reading so Gallagher quietly opens the cellar door and descends the stairs. He looks around and there are no bars or locks on the cellar windows, which is common if a safe house is to blend in with the neighborhood. The windows are about twelve feet from the floor, which is unusually high. Two of the windows face the back of the house. If he is to make his move it has to be at the point when the guards change shifts. He has noticed the agents would shoot the breeze when relieving each other for several minutes not paying any attention to where he is at the time. The next change was at 10:00 p.m.

***

Golden, Colorado about 11:00 p.m.

Anna, Christine and Donna drive west on Rte. 40 then turn onto Rte. 125 north and have to drive for several more hours until they reach the base road of Owl Mountain. The time is getting close to midnight and they decide to make camp and start their hike at the crack of dawn. A cold wind is starting to kick up making the ordeal more difficult but Anna's adrenalin is flowing and the hope that Gallagher may be close is keeping her warm under the circumstances.

***

Safe House somewhere in Oregon...

Gallagher finds a small stepstool and is able to reach up to one of the windows and opens it and then holds it there with an eyehook. He then hoists himself up and pulls himself through the window. He rolls onto the grass and then makes his way to a nearby tree and quickly climbs up and hides there among the thick foliage.

Several minutes later he hears a familiar voice coming towards the front of the house. It's the voice of Agent Harmon. It didn't take long when two unmarked cars take off from the safe house and two men on foot start searching the immediate area. Harmon appears deeply stressed and starts shouting at the other agents. "Find him and if you have to, kill him. He can't get away or this whole operation is a bust and they will have our heads."

Gallagher spends the rest of the night in the deepest part of the woods high up in a tree and knows he will have to make a run for it before daylight. The first thing he needs to do is get to a phone and call Jonathan. He's feels he's the only one he can trust besides Anna, Helen and Chief Peterson. As far as Anderson is concerned, he's justifiably confused. He believes Harmon on the other hand is a pawn for either the government or a rebel faction of the government. Gallagher is convinced he made the best move to get out of there as quick as possible.

Gallagher begins to think about everything that has happened and the danger he has put Anna in by getting her involved in the whole Dredmeyer fiasco. He realizes it's going to be a long night. One problem he realizes he has to deal with is Eagle House's phone system. All the lines are being monitored; even the one in the carriage house.

Then he thinks of his good friend, Bill Waters. He's another one he has come to trust.

**

27

Early Saturday morning before sunrise – April 21, 1962

Gallagher finally wakes up from his temporary bed in the tree and climbs down and immediately looks to see if anyone is outside the safe house. To his surprise there is no sign of life. He slowly makes his way over to the far side of the house and peaks inside one of the windows. The house is empty. He immediately begins looking for a phone to call Bill Waters. After walking several blocks he comes to a busy intersection where he finds a phone booth outside an all-night convenience store. He first goes inside and walks over to the magazine section and looks for a map of the Colorado area. After studying the map for a few minutes he finds out what he was looking for and makes his way back outside to the phone booth. Someone is talking on the phone so he has to wait several minutes. While he is waiting a police cruiser is slowly driving towards him. He quickly goes back into the store and pretends to be looking for something to buy when two policemen enter the store and start talking to the storekeeper. After a few minutes the policemen start laughing with the storekeeper and leave with donuts and coffee. Gallagher takes a deep breath and makes his way over to the window and sees they have left the area. He looks at his watch and it's almost 6:00 in the morning. He has to make that call to Bill. As he is about to leave the storekeeper comes over to him and asks, "Is there something you are looking for? You have been in here twice in the past few minutes and you have bought nothing."

Gallagher quickly answers back, "Yeah, coffee sounds good about now. I like it black. Also maybe you could answer a question for me. Is there a place around here where I can rent a car?"

The storekeeper gives him the needed information and Gallagher goes to the phone, which is now free and after calling directory assistance he gets Bill's number and calls.

To Gallagher's surprise Bill answers. "Bill...this is Gallagher."

"Gallagher, where are you? What's happened? Helen is worried sick."

"It's too long of a story to tell you right now over the phone but I need your help. Eagle House's phones have been tapped. The phone calls are being monitored so I can't call Helen or Jonathan directly. I'm a little suspicious of Agent Anderson right now and I don't want the police involved yet. I need for you to go up the back way of Eagle House after sunset and enter through the back door of the carriage house. The key is hanging on a hook under the overhang on the right side. There's a long tunnel which leads to the basement door. Let yourself in and tell Jonathan or Helen I'm trying to find a way to get to Owl Mountain in Colorado."

"What's at Owl Mountain?"

"I don't know how much Helen or Jonathan has told you about what we have been involved in lately but it all started with the poisoned fish you had mentioned to me at the Tavern. Not only the Swift River has been contaminated but also the Saco. The disappearance of Dr. Dredmeyer and Dr. Philip Jones has something to do with it and a lot more."

Bill remained quiet trying to digest everything Gallagher was saying and finally says, "What's this about Owl Mountain? Helen is going to want to know. You know how she gets."

Gallagher manages a laugh. "You know her already."

"She's a fine lady. Anyways, what were you going to say?"

"Philip Jones had the words sleeping Indian written on a map next to his ham radio in his office at home. We thought at the time it had to do with a rendezvous point where O'Reilly and Ben Willard's assassin were to meet..."

Bill notices the long pause on the other end and asks concerned, "Gallagher are you still there? You were saying something about the sleeping Indian."

"Oh yeah, sorry. My mind began to wander. The sleeping Indian Jones was referring to circled on his map must be the one in Colorado. It explains why fighter jets forced us down on our way to Colorado because I think whoever is behind it thought we were heading for the sleeping Indian in Colorado and wanted to stop us."

"Wait a minute; you're losing me." Bill interjects.

"Don't worry about understanding anything I'm telling you right now. As I was about to say, we had no thoughts of going there because we didn't make the connection there was another sleeping Indian. I've had time to think about it and I remember reading about a military installation there and how it was built as a result of the insurgence of the cold war."

"You just lost me again. But that's okay I'm use to it by now. I'm beginning to see what Jonathan talks about when referring to your diagnostic mind. In any case whatever you're talking about sounds like an impossible coincidence. You were just going on your honeymoon."

"When you eliminate the impossible, whatever remains, no matter how improbable, must be the truth."

"What?"

"I'll explain what my mentor Sherlock said some day but right now you need to leave Helen and Jonathan a note if they're not there in the carriage house. Our own village of Jackson was obviously the main experimentation center for producing an antidote along with Livermore Village and that antidote has been shipped to Colorado, we believe right out of our own Concord Airport."

"Okay, I will pass this on to Jonathan. My biggest concern right now is hiking up to Eagle House. That's why I'm still at home. My gout is kicking up again."

"If it helps, the back way is only half as long as the front."

Bill laughs and says, "I guess you never suffered from gout."

***

Bill Waters made his way up the back way to Eagle House as soon as the sun had set. Being the cautious type, he carried his trusty shotgun not knowing whom he might bump into and it also served as a cane to help him in the hike.

He easily finds the key and lets himself in and with flashlight in hand he walks the fairly long tunnel as quiet as an Indian on a turkey shoot. He comes to the door leading to the basement and opens it slowly. He comes to the stairway leading up to the kitchen. He reaches the door to the kitchen. He enters the kitchen and is quickly greeted by Helen who is holding a rolling pin in her hand. Bill drops his gun and instinctively covers his head with his hands. "Don't hit me it's just me, Bill Waters!"

Helen lowers her arm and shouts out, "Bill...what on earth are you doing here? Don't you believe in ringing the bell? You had me scared out of my wits."

Ben regains his composure and calmly says, "I'm not quite sure of all the elaborate details but I got a call from Gallagher and he's trying to find a way to get to Howl Mountain and wants Jonathan's help."

Helen thinks for a moment scratching her head and says, "You must mean Owl Mountain in Colorado."

"That's it; Owl Mountain. How did you know?"

"I started to think about their trip and how they both love to climb mountains and I remembered learning about Owl Mountain in school. Geography was my favorite subject next to English."

"Well he's headed there right now. I guess it runs in the family."

"What does?"

"The way you both think out things."

"What are you talking about? What's there to think out?"

"The sleeping Indian!"

Helen swallows and says, "Oh my, I didn't even connect the two. Is that what Philip Jones was referring to on his map?"

"It's what Gallagher is thinking. There's a lot more to tell you but I could never repeat it. There's more to it than just a connection."

Bill looks directly at Helen revealing his pain and asks, "Can I sit down before I fall down? This whole thing has got me dizzy and sore."

"Oh Bill...I'm so sorry. Please come into the living room and let me get you some ice tea or some freshly made lemonade. You look like you could use some refreshment."

After some refreshments, Bill her in on all the details he could remember Gallagher had revealed to him and what he was up to.

"I had a bad feeling all along about their trip but I didn't want to spoil their honeymoon by saying anything."

"What were you concerned about?"

"All the things that have been going on around here lately with the FBI and the tragic end of Ben Willard. Also, there's a letter Gallagher received from Paul Anderson indicating there's still Fifth Column activity in our neck of the woods. It may have a lot to do with the disappearance of Dr. Dredmeyer and Dr. Jones."

"Really?"

"Right now Jonathan is with Professor Meridian investigating Dr. Dredmeyer's home to see if Philip Jones is hiding out there. His wife and son have disappeared and may be with him."

***

Jonathan and Penny Jones made their way back to Eagle House after dropping off the professor who was grief stricken after learning of his friends possible death. Penny had also told them Philip had taken Tobey away with him with the threat he would harm him if anyone tried to find him. After hearing what had happened Helen took Penny to the guest room and told her she should get some rest.

Helen returns to the kitchen where Jonathan is and she fills him in on what Bill Waters had told her.

"It sounds like Anna and Gallagher are on a collision course headed for Owl Mountain," Jonathan concludes. "Gallagher doesn't know of Anna's plans to go with her cousins to the sleeping Indian and she doesn't know about Gallagher also figuring it out and heading there too."

"What can we do?" Helen asks having a sudden loss for words.

Jonathan thinks for a moment and says, "I'm going to take the chance and get a hold of Paul Anderson. I don't believe he's the mole. He has to be on the up and up. He's our only hope in all this confusion."

"What about our phones being tapped? Why did those other agents tap our lines if they were working with Anderson? Doesn't it seem a little odd if he's on our side?"

"That's right I forgot. Odd is the right word for it. I will sneak out the back way and make my way over to the Tavern and make the call from there. I will take my chances on Anderson. If I'm correct on my thinking Myers and his gang are really working with Harmon who is the mole."

After about twenty minutes Jonathan enters through the back door of the Tavern and is greeted by Gus Swenson and his brother Lars who are working in the kitchen. With a big smile Gus says in his hearty voice, "Jonathan...you must be involved in another one your investigations with Gallagher. We always know because you both always enter through the back door when you are up to something."

Jonathan smiles and says, "You're half right. My partner right now is several hundred miles away looking for an Owl. Can I use your phone in your office?"

They both nodded yes and then looked at each other while shrugging their shoulders. Lars finally says to his brother, "Why so far away? We have owls in our own woods." They continued cooking and asked no more questions.

Jonathan picks up the phone and calls the number Anderson had provided Gallagher. After much delay Anderson gets on the phone. "Jonathan,...am I happy to hear from you. Do you know where Gallagher is right now?"

"I was hoping you knew."

"It's a complicated mess and an unfortunate one. Stephen Harmon thinks he's working for our government but in reality he's working for a rebel faction who are trying to undermine the current administration. If they succeed it could mean political chaos. We now know Harmon's the mole. He caught wind of Gallagher's trip to Colorado and hijacked the plane."

"I know that much because Anna has been in touch and she is on her way to Owl Mountain."

"What are you talking about?"

"Gallagher got a hold of Bill Waters and told him he had escaped from a safe house somewhere in Oregon."

"Go on!" Anderson urges.

"He figured out about the sleeping Indian and he's on his way to Owl Mountain."

"We have to intercept Gallagher before it's too late. If he shows up at Owl Mountain he's a dead man."

Anderson hangs up the phone in completely frustrated.

***

28

Sunday morning – April 22, 1962

Sleeping Indian at Owl Mountain Colorado...

Anna and her two cousins had slept all night in a cave about a half a mile away from the foot of the sleeping Indian. They had found a good vantage point in the rocky cliffs to observe any activity at the entrance of one of the lower caverns. Anna suspects it's being used for the purpose of storing the antidote. The knowledge of several cargo planes leaving Concord Airport a few weeks earlier and flying to a destination out west along with finding the map in Dr. Jones office listing the sleeping Indian has Anna convinced they are in the right place.

According to what Donna and Christine heard around town, the military fenced off the entire area back in January. The local paper said it was for military exercises. Several cargo planes were seen since then landing in open fields throughout the enclosed area.

***

Gallagher uses his American Express card to rent a car so he can get to Owl Mountain by morning. At this time Gallagher has no clue that Anna is tucked away in a cave close to the sleeping Indian.

***

FBI Headquarters Midwest Sector...

"Agent Myers, this is Deputy Director Robert Osgood from Washington. We have a situation involving one of our top agents, Paul Anderson. He's been involved in a covert mission authorized by the Attorney General's office. He is working with a man by the name of Gallagher Brady. He's a bookshop owner from Jackson, New Hampshire and is also a part-time investigator. He's somewhat of a Sherlock Holmes in the way he thinks. He's the one who unraveled the Fifth Column organization 'The Cause' last year in the northeast. Anderson has been working with him for some time now. He

209

has become an important asset in providing us with valuable intelligence but now it appears he has stumbled into a very dangerous area. Agent Stephen Harmon, under the direction of our Director, forced him and his wife down from the sky with the understanding he was going to the Owl Mountain's Military Installation, which as you know is off limits to civilians. We found out later the Brady's were just on their honeymoon and nothing more. Harmon was assigned to keep tabs on his activity and he was the one who ordered the plane down. Anderson caught wind of the hijacking and beat Harmon to the plane and was able to secure Brady off the plane. Harmon and his agents then intercepted Brady and was taken to a safe house in Oregon. Brady since then has given Harmon the slip."

"It sounds like the Bureau is working at cross purposes."

"That's an understatement."

"What are my orders?"

"You must find and stop Gallagher Brady before he finds out what really exists at Owl Mountain."

"Sir. If you don't mind telling me, what does exist at Owl Mountain?"

"It's classified. That's all I can tell you."

Meyers remains silent trying to take it all in without showing any signs of his previous encounter with Brady.

"Agent Meyers, are you still on the line?"

"Yes sir. I will get on this right away. Gallagher Brady will be stopped before another day goes by."

"And I will get in touch with Anderson through special channels. He has a friend that can help."

***

29

The next morning... April 23, 1962

Without being too obvious Gallagher was able to find a specialty store and pick up the needed supplies for the hike to Owl Mountain. Colorado is filled with many shops dealing with hunting, hiking and camping gear. He dressed in a hunters camouflage outfit equipped with binoculars, various ropes, pitons, karabiners, a hammer, a flare gun and a Swiss Army knife.

***

Agent Myers and four of his men travel the quickest route to Owl Mountain; time was not on their side. One of the things he learned from the brief on Gallagher Brady was his climbing ability and his physical condition. The agents with him were not in the best shape so they were at a disadvantage from the start.

***

Gallagher is determined to get to Owl Mountain before it's too late. Gallagher parks in a secluded area off the main road and begins the long trek to the foot of the sleeping Indian. His thoughts of Anna consumes his mind for a time then it shifts to Paul Anderson. He cannot grasp the fact he is the mole. It didn't make any sense. He's a veteran of the Bureau and a trusted friend of the Attorney General of the United States. He thought long and hard and concluded in his mind that Anderson was being made to look like the mole. It's what the individuals behind this elaborate cover-up want him to think. They made his ace in the hole to look like just another joker.

Gallagher stops for a moment to have a drink of water and resigns himself to continue to put faith in Anderson and take whatever comes as a result.

Gallagher continues towards what is sometimes referred to as the Devil's Head. The spring has been dryer than usual and the wind is starting to blow sand around causing Gallagher to have limited visibility and what's making it worse; the sun is going down.

Meanwhile Anna and her cousins had begun their descent from their mountain perch. The three of them are equipped with cameras to expose what activity is secretly going on in the caverns below.

***

The Deputy Director contacted Paul Anderson at a secure location. He informed him of the situation and suggested he get his good and trusted friend at Langley to help. Anderson then informs the CIA agent of the situation with Gallagher. In turn the agent fills in the gaps so Anderson would know the complete plan by the Attorney General including the purpose of the Aricona Project, which he had been purposely left in the dark about for security reasons.

"Does this come all the way from the top?" Anderson asks.

"It almost goes all the way to the top; notice I said almost. I can't stress enough the need to keep this confidential or our trap won't work."

"What kind of a trap?"

"We have intelligence that points to some paramilitary activity that has been going on for some time throughout the country. It's a result of the tension that has arisen due to the cold war and was escalated by the Bay of Pigs incident. There are some very misguided patriots planning some type of military operation not sanctioned by our government. Because we have been aware of their intentions the Aricona Project was designed to lure their interest in developing and acquiring a formula to cure acute radiation poisoning due to an surprise nuclear attack. Dr. Wallace Dredmeyer and Dr. Philip Jones were recruited to work on the project."

Anderson interrupts. "Were the doctors aware of the trap?"

"No. It would have leaked out somehow and we thought it best to have them assume it was for our countries best interests to have a formula in case of a nuclear event."

"If the Aricona Project is a trap like you say and we suspect it has been compromised how can it still be a trap?"

"One of the scientists working with Dredmeyer and Jones was to our chagrin a double agent. He goes by the name of Boris. He found out it was a trap and sabotaged the project by causing contaminates to flow into the Swift and Saco rivers. Mr. Brady was quickly involved and proceeded to investigate the reasons for the pollution but unfortunately has found himself in the middle of the trap."

"I understand it now and I may have helped in providing Gallagher with the intelligence alerting him of the possibility of illegal activity in his neck of the woods. But how can it still be a trap if both sites have been shut down?"

"All I can tell you at this point in time is; they want the formula and they will keep trying to get it. By keeping our distance we may catch them in the act and uncover the whole illegal operation."

"Whom are we talking about? Is it the Russians or is it Fifth Column?"

"Take your pick. They are working together. So what we have arising here is a situation where Mr. Brady is on the verge of spoiling the trap. He has to be stopped before he does and before he is eliminated by your own agents who are heading there to intercept him and silence him. We don't know what Gallagher knows but by his activity he knows a lot more than he should. Agent Myers is on his way to intercept him but he might be too late."

"Where is there?"

"The sleeping Indian at Owl Mountain in Colorado."

"Could you at least give me more to go on?"

"It's no mystery that we placed Jupiter Missiles in Turkey in 1959. That led to the mistrust the Soviet Union has for us and was more recently escalated by the Bay of Pigs fiasco. We have acquired recent intelligence that the Soviet Union is now sleeping with the government of Cuba and may be in the planning stages of constructing missile bays along the Cuban coast. Gallagher is about to expose a secret installation at Owl Mountain in Colorado.

Our government is in anticipation of a possible interchange with the Russians. It's a national security issue; he has to be stopped. Whatever he thinks is going on there I can only imagine. I'm amazed he's figured out as much as he has."

"Whatever reason Gallagher is pursuing this quest to get to Owl Mountain tells me he knows more than we do and has been unable to tell us because of his lack of trust in everyone, including me. He would never deliberately get involved in an activity that could spoil our national security. He must know something and he hasn't been able to tell us because of that lack of trust."

"You know I can't help. It's off limits to us at Langley. But I know someone who can and he will be willing to handle it because he owes me a favor. The only problem is he's living at Alcatraz at the moment."

Anderson's wheels start to turn and starts to laugh. "That won't be a problem. I know the warden and he owes me a favor. I got him his job."

"Well you better get on it right away. If Gallagher knows something that will help us, time is not on our side. Something is going down and it could be disastrous."

* * *

9:00 o'clock Monday night...

Anna and her cousins are making their way to the foot of the sleeping Indian and unknown to them; Gallagher is only five hundred yards behind them. The overcast skies and the windblown sand are making the trek three times longer than usual.

***

After hanging up with his friend at Langley, Anderson gets on the phone and talks to Preston Stone, the warden at Alcatraz. After explaining the situation he agrees to release Frank 'The Snake' Margetti. His time is almost up and is due for parole in two months. The plan is to have a chopper pick up Margetti and then travel to Owl Mountain before Gallagher ruins the government's authorized operation.

***

11:00 the same evening...

The pickup is smooth at Alcatraz and the chopper is heading to Miramar Airbase in San Diego to transfer Margetti to a fighter jet enabling him to reach Gallagher in as little as forty minutes. The plan from there is for Margetti to parachute down and intercept Gallagher. Margetti was an air force pilot in the Korean War and was decorated for his courage in the line of fire with the enemy. He was shot down and severely injured, which led to his life of crime when the war was over. His military pension was not enough to satisfy his exotic tastes in fast cars and women. He became an accomplished thief who excelled by stealth; thus the nickname, 'The Snake'.

***

The sky begins to clear and Margetti is set to jump. Gallagher and Anna are only about a hundred yards apart but they are still unaware of each other's presence. Margetti is catapulted out of the plane and safely lands in an open area about one hundred a fifty yards from the entrance to the caverns. Gallagher spots Margetti and being ignorant of his mission has the noble intention of knocking Margetti's lights out. It's not in Gallagher's nature to inflict harm on another human but being highly motivated because of the circumstances he is faced with is very surprised when he wakes up ten minutes later with a pounding headache from the blow Margetti had inflicted on him. As he begins to focus he sees Margetti standing over him with Anna and her two cousins.

Anna reaches down and holds him in her arms and explains what happened. Margetti is apologetic but makes no excuses about knocking Gallagher out because he had heard Gallagher was not one to fool around with so being cautious he struck first. After being fully briefed about the operation that was going on Gallagher, Anna and her two cousins waited patiently for a chopper to come and take them to Denver's International Airport. When they arrived Christine and Donna said their goodbyes to Anna and Gallagher and thanked Margetti for their rescue. They immediately headed for Boston's Logan Airport where a private jet was waiting for them. From there they planned to rent a car and drive to Intervale and stay with Valerie until they could plan their next move.

Agent Myers witnessed the whole extraction from a safe distance so as not to be seen. He immediately drives to Fort Collins, which is the closest military base and makes a phone call.

"Extension 3 please."

"Harmon speaking."

"It's Myers. Someone got to Brady before we could. It looked like it came from the top. A military chopper picked him up along with three women and another man."

"How close were you?"

"About fifty yards away hidden behind some tall brush."

"Could you identify the other man?"

"You're going to think I'm crazy but he looked like Frank Margetti but I know it can't be him; he's locked up at Alcatraz."

A long pause on the other line...

"Harmon!"

"I'm still here. We better pull back and regroup. I don't like what's happening."

"Do you think Anderson is on to you?"

"He has been for some time. I don't know who he's working for but it's not for the Director of the Bureau and our government."

***

30

Tuesday at noontime – April 24, 1962

Anna and Gallagher arrive in Intervale where Valerie is waiting anxiously. Gallagher had phoned ahead and told her not to tell Jonathan of their arrival because of the phone situation at Eagle House. Frank Margetti was already on the move to take care of that situation. Margetti had been incarcerated at Alcatraz for almost seven years and during that time he became well conditioned by very disciplined workouts in the weight room. He

218

also was a long distance runner sometimes spending four hours at a time on the track.

Margetti approaches Eagle House and sees two FBI agents sitting in a car at the foot of the long driveway leading up to the house. In stealth like movements he is able to disconnect the phone system and rewire it, bypassing the tap connection to the junction box. The next thing he has to do is go to the Jackson police to explain his activity to John Peterson who was informed in advance of his arrival. Peterson then calls Jonathan at Eagle House and tells him of Anna and Gallagher's arrival at Valerie's and that the phone lines are now safe.

The next problem facing Jonathan and Helen is leaving Eagle House undetected in the daytime. This was where Frank Margetti came in handy again. He approached the car at the foot of Eagle House's driveway and crawled underneath attaching a heavy gage rope to the rear axle and then tying the other end to a tree.

At 6:00 o'clock the agents change shifts and quickly chaos erupts. During the confusion Jonathan and Helen make their way to a waiting Jackson Police cruiser, which is parked fifty yards away from the agents line of sight. The get-a-way is a success creating much aggravation to the agents.

They all gather at Valerie's and assess the current state of affairs as Gallagher and Anna explain what had transpired in the last several days. Before Gallagher had joined them he called Paul Anderson and updated him on what happened and thanked him for his help. Anderson had relocated and setup his office in a secret bunker provided by his friend at Langley.

At this time Gallagher and Jonathan are no longer the only ones with the knowledge that Russian spies had infiltrated the Aricona Project.

***

31

Two weeks later early Monday morning at Eagle House – May 7, 1962

Gallagher woke up early and appreciated a leisurely breakfast enjoying the long awaited quiet time in his life after all the excitement he had gone through several days before. In all that time he had lost track of the local goings on in the valley and the progress of his museum. Helen finally comes into the room and sits at the table and says, "Well...you're up early this morning. What are your plans for the day?"

"Anna and I are due for a climb today at Cathedral Ledge. It will definitely help me to unwind. He looks at his watch. "It's almost 5:00 o'clock. Anna should be getting up about now."

Gallagher pauses for a moment and smiles. Helen picked up on it and asks, "What's going through your mind?"

"It just came to me. With all the excitement I really haven't been able to allow the fact that we are finally husband and wife and I no longer have to wait for her arrival from her parents home. She's only a room away."

Gallagher is about ready to get up from the table when Jonathan comes through the back door. "Gallagher! You're not going to believe who they found at the bottom of Arethusa Falls."

220

"Try me," Gallagher replies with a half smile.

"Our friend Gerald from the morgue."

Gallagher looks at Helen. "In all the confusion we didn't get the opportunity to tell you. This Gerald was an employee at the North Conway Morgue. We suspected him of being a plant."

Helen shifts in her chair and says, "What kind of a plant?"

"Russian."

Helen rolls her eyes and replies, "How do you know that for certain?"

Jonathan interrupts. "We didn't but we do now."

Gallagher looks surprised at Jonathan's words. "What did they find?"

"They found nothing but I saw what was missing."

Helen shakes her head and rolls her eyes again and asks, "What in the world is that supposed to mean?"

"I got the call from my office to get to the scene as soon as I could. A man who was hiking the Frankenstein Cliff Trail found Gerald at the bottom of Arethusa Falls crushed against some rocks. I asked to look at his lower back right above the buttocks and a perfectly cut patch of skin had been removed."

Gallagher smiles and adds, "The hammer and sickle tattoo."

"Those were my thoughts exactly."

Helen's eyes widen. "Are you really talking Russians?"

"We might as well tell you what we found. The dead man at Livermore had the tattoo in the same place, which explains why Gerald was conveniently working at the morgue. He was to observe anyone who would notice the tattoo besides Dr. Matthews. We also saw the same patch of skin cut away on the harbor policeman we found at the bottom of a cliff in Maine. We now know the Russians have infiltrated into the governments authorized program called the Aricona Project."

"Who knows about this program?" Helen asks showing her weariness of it all.

"As far as we know, Dredmeyer and Jones because of their involvement in the research. Professor Meridian knows because we asked him about the formula we found in the Conan Doyle books. The only other one is Paul Anderson because of his friend at Langley. We have yet to talk about it with Anderson personally because for a while we weren't sure whose side he was on. So he really doesn't know all we know and he doesn't know about the tattoos. We have to get that information to him now that we know about a third victim."

Helen gets up from the table and asks, "What are you going to do with this information once you fill in Anderson on everything?"

Gallagher reveals a big smile. "Sit on it! There's no reason to pursue it any further if the CIA and Anderson are on it. It's out of our league anyways. I done with investigating this horror show."

Helen couldn't help but laugh. "I've heard that one before."

"The agents have cleared out of the valley. O'Reilly is gone and our friend Peterson is back at the helm. Fish are swimming again in the Swift and Saco Rivers. I think life is getting back to normal."

***

Later the same morning...

Anna and Gallagher start hiking to the base of Cathedral Ledge when Anna stops and holds Gallagher's hand and says, "I was thinking. We never found out what was at Owl Mountain. The CIA and the FBI maneuvered things very fast to get us out of there in a hurry. I wonder what's really there."

Gallagher shakes his head and says, "I hope I never have to find out."

Anna starts laughing. "My dear husband I'm afraid I just know you too well. You won't let this sit until you find out everything."

"Oh no! Look what it got me into the last time I opened up Pandora's box."

***

32

Wednesday... May 9, 1962

Gallagher and Jonathan booked a flight to Washington as soon as Gallagher got off the phone with Paul Anderson. They filled Anderson in on their knowledge of the dead man found at Livermore, the harbor policeman and Gerald the morgue attendant. At Anderson's urgings they were requested to meet with him and some higher officials at a closed-door hearing at Quantico.

An unmarked sedan picked them up at Dulles Airport and drove them to Virginia. Gallagher was to use the word "hammer" as a password so the driver would be sure he was picking up the right package. Gallagher had gone over in his mind how much he would reveal what he knows at the hearing. He realizes he would know best what to say when the time comes, especially when he finds out who the other officials will be attending the hearing. Gallagher asked Jonathan to be very judicious in answering any questions that was asked of him as a journalist. Gallagher thought it was best to let them tell their side of the story first before providing any missing pieces.

The meeting is being held in one of the interrogation rooms at Quantico. First impressions would make anyone a little timid but Gallagher is calm and unnerved by his environment. Jonathan on the other hand is quite uncomfortable and wishes he was back in Jackson.

A highly decorated military officer escorts them to their seats. Gallagher's eyes roam the room and he notices paintings hanging from every wall of every president who has ever held the office. The room has United States Government written all over it. Facing them, sitting at a long table, are seven men and two women. Pitchers of water are placed along the table making Gallagher think it's going to be a long meeting.

The meeting comes to order and the man sitting in the center speake first. "Mr. Gallagher Brady and Mr. Jonathan Henry, please take your seats. My name is Bradford Alexander. I'm with National Security. I want to thank you for coming and I promise this will go quick and smooth if you cooperate. We are being joined by two agents of the FBI, Agent Myers to my right and Agent Harmon on my left. Also with me are six of our Senators who make up a special committee designed to oversee special military operations. They will introduce themselves if they need to before asking any questions. Agent Paul Anderson will not be attending this meeting due to extenuating circumstances."

Gallagher looks at Jonathan and slightly shakes his head hoping he would get the hint not say anything about their knowledge of Harmon's rogue activity.

Gallagher looks across the table before speaking. "Mr. Alexander, I was hoping Agent Anderson could be here for this. It was my understanding he would be."

Alexander looks straight at Gallagher and says, "As I said... extenuating circumstances. Be that as it may, my first question to you is why were you interested in Owl Mountain?"

Gallagher unfazed by the direct question says with equal directness, "We were not interested in Owl Mountain. My wife's cousins live in Colorado and we were going there on our honeymoon. It was their gift to us. We add no intentions of going to Owl mountain because we had no knowledge of its significance until you brought that to light by your overt display in bringing us down by military jet fighters."

"You're telling this panel that you had no prior knowledge of the military facility at the sleeping Indian at the foot of Owl Mountain?"

"That's correct sir."

"We find that hard to believe Mr. Brady."

Gallagher took the pitcher of water in front of him and poured himself a glass before he continuing. "Why are you having a hard time believing? Please enlighten Jonathan and myself."

At that moment Jonathan wakes up out of his stupor caused from his acute anxiety and sat straight up in his chair and turned toward Gallagher with a look of bewilderment on his face. Alexander noticing his abrupt movement asks, "Is there something you would like to add to this conversation Mr. Henry?"

Jonathan sits back in his chair and says, "No sir."

"Are you sure?"

"Yes, I'm sure."

Looking again at Gallagher he asks, "So you're telling this panel your interest in hiking Owl Mountain was only after we brought its attention to you."

Gallagher thinks before he speaks, holding back his anger and says, "That's correct. We decided to climb Owl Mountain while we were there; that's what we do. We climb mountains. Is there anything wrong with that Mr. Alexander?"

"Mr. Brady...I will ask the questions here."

Gallagher stands up and says, "I realize we are in one of your interrogation rooms but I wasn't under the impression we were to be interrogated. This meeting was actually my idea. I feel like asking you the questions."

Alexander forms a half smile and replies, "It seems we have gotten off to a bad start. Let me rephrase the question. "Was there something of interest in Owl Mountain that made you want to climb it other than, as you put it; it's what you do?"

"I want to know what would even lead you to that suspicion?"

"We were given a brief describing your abilities as an investigator and a number of others talents you possess such as mountain climbing. Owl Mountain is a walk in the park compared to what you are used to in the northeast. The elevation at the trailhead of Owl Mountain is 9,280 feet and the elevated climb from there is only 610 feet. Your own Cathedral and White Horse Ledges are more challenging in vertical height; not even having to mention the mountains in the Presidential Range such as Monroe and Jefferson."

Gallagher remains quiet not showing any signs of backing down. Jonathan fidgets in his seat and says after a long sigh, "Mr. Alexander, I suggest you cut to the chase because you are definitely beating around the bush. The interest in Owl Mountain is not at the top, it's underneath."

"I don't quite follow."

Gallagher smiles at his friend then faces Alexander and says, "What we have come to know by the unfolding of much evidence, which we have been able sort out because of the systematic events that now have been brought to light at this very meeting, needs to be told to a much larger audience; like the American people."

"I'm afraid that's out of the question. Our countries national security is at stake."

"We are well aware of that fact and that's why you need to hear what we have to say but before we tell you anything; tell us where you are keeping Dr. Dredmeyer."

Alexander, with a look of bewilderment written across his face looks directly at Agent Myers and Agent Harmon. Both of them maintain a stoic expression on their face. Alexander shifts in his seat indicating his embarrassment says, "It appears you have us at a loss. We don't know of any Dr. Dredmeyer."

"Does a Dr. Philip Jones ring a bell?" Gallagher asks while eyeing Alexander and the two agents carefully.

Alexander shakes his head. "Not at all."

Gallagher looks at all them in disgust. "I think we are done here."

Alexander then presses a button under the table and immediately two armed men walk into the room.

Alexander, without flinching says, "I'm sorry but you are not done here. We will have to detain you until you cooperate with us. Until then you pose a threat to our national security. Officers, take them to Quarantine."

"Quarantine!" Jonathan exclaimsd. "What have we done?"

"Until we find out exactly what you know you will be treated as though you have a deadly contagious disease; that's what we do here. Take them away."

***

33

Ten days later... Saturday morning – May 19th, 1962

For several days Anna and Helen tried to reach Paul Anderson but he never returned their calls. Chief Peterson was informed of Gallagher and Jonathan's disappearance and tried to reach Anderson himself but was given the runaround by the Bureau.

 Anna sits down in the living room and accepts a cup of tea from Helen. "Thanks Helen...what are we going to do? I'm at my wits end. They are supposed to be in a safe place. What could have happened? Where could they be? I don't understand why Paul Anderson is not returning our calls. Maybe he was the mole after all."

Helen sitting across from Anna says calmly, "I believe Gallagher has stumbled across a real hornets' nest. Whoever is responsible for their disappearance is doing it under orders from on high."

"How high?"

"Maybe as far as the President."

"Is there any way we can find out?"

Helen thinks for a moment. "The Snake."

***

Later that day at Mary Ann's Gift Shop...

The delightful spring air is bringing out the tourists in droves. Flowers are in bloom creating an invigorating floral scent throughout the valley.

Restaurants and Inns are bustling with patrons and hikers are roaming the many trails sprinkled across the countryside. All is looking very typical until two Federal agents enter Mary Ann's Gift Shop.

"Excuse me but I would like to speak with the proprietor," asks one of the agents who is a distinguished looking man wearing a white Fedora.

Mary Ann replies very innocently, "That would be me. My name is Mary Ann Blair. What can I do for you gentlemen?"

The man hands her a sealed envelope. "Your property has been confiscated by the Federal Government. You are to leave the premises immediately."

Mary Ann can't avoid the look of shock and surprise as she opens the envelope and reads the contents. She looks at the two men after reading the legal document and asks puzzled, "I don't understand. How can you do this? What have I done?"

The other agent steps forward and says, "The document says it all very clearly. Because of National Security our reasons for doing this must remain confidential."

Mary Ann throws the document at the man and says in anger, "I'm not going anywhere until I have legal representation. This is my business and until I know of the reasons for this outrageous action I'm staying put and you will have to leave right away or I will have to call the police."

Both men look at each other with a grin and then look at Mary Ann. The man wearing the white Fedora says, "We were hoping you would understand and cooperate." He then waves to a waiting car outside and says without hesitation, "We are shutting this place down immediately."

At that moment two more agents enter the shop and one of them placed cuffs on her and says, "You are under arrest for suspicion of treason."

Mary Ann struggles then realizes there's no use and says, "Aren't you even going to read me my rights?"

***

Later that evening...

Anna and Helen are cleaning up dishes when the phone rings. Helen quickly runs to the phone hoping it's Gallagher. "Hello...Gallagher?"

"I'm sorry Helen but it's not Gallagher, it's Paul Anderson."

"Oh... Paul we are so glad to hear from you!"

"I'm sure you are. We know where Gallagher and Jonathan are being held but getting them out of there is going to be tricky."

"Paul...can you tell us what this is all about?" Helen asks showing her frustration.

"I understand how you feel. If I could tell you more I would. All I know is Gallagher is on the verge of disrupting a top secret plan designed by our government which if revealed, could have terrible consequences on the entire world."

Helen is stunned at his revelation and says, "I'm not sure you have been told the whole picture.

Gallagher would never interfere with the governments plan. What he's trying to do is stop the Russians from acquiring the antidote."

Anderson remains quiet for a moment. "Helen...I have a member of the president's staff on the other secure line and I want you to tell us what Gallagher found out."

"I'm not comfortable with that idea. Gallagher has kept certain details of what he has come to know because of an uncertainty with everyone he has been dealing with including yourself. His detainment is a perfect example. He trusted you and wanted the meeting to take place and now we have not seen him for more than ten days. So you want me to tell you more? Why don't you tell me what you know and we will go from there."

"I can't go into it right now but trust me. I am... and have always been, on Gallagher's side."

"Well then you will have to wait for Gallagher to be released before I tell you anymore."

"Helen, I know I can't fool you. Gallagher is obviously a product of your training and I'm not going to insult you. Things are happening fast and out of control. One of the reasons why I called you is because earlier today Mary Ann Blair was taken into custody for her own protection. Her shop was seized and has been searched."

"What are they looking for?"

"Helen...I think you know."

"Do you?"

"To be honest, no. That's why I'm appealing to your sense of duty to this country. I know your father's legacy and I know the man Gallagher is and what he was able to do to stop the Fifth Column. We need your help or I'm afraid more people will be hurt including Gallagher and Jonathan."

"You have to promise me you will do whatever you can to get Gallagher and Jonathan out of wherever they're being held."

"That's already in the works. It's the other reason why I called. A very large spy ring, which is right under the nose of the White House, is undermining our government. Gallagher unwittingly has crossed the line and his life is in jeopardy. We are in the process of extracting him."

Helen paused for a moment. "You say unwittingly. Gallagher knew exactly what he was doing. I might as well tell you what he found out."

Anderson is silent for a moment. "Go ahead. What did he find out?"

"There are Russians working right here in the valley."

"Please tell me more."

"The man they found dead in Livermore had a tattoo on his lower back in the form of the Soviet hammer and sickle. Also, the harbor policeman working at Camp Ellis in Maine also had the same tattoo. He was found dead at the bottom of a cliff in Maine with a chunk of skin removed at the base of his lower back where the tattoo had been. It was obviously removed as a cover-up. Also a man by the name of Gerald who was working at the morgue was found dead at the bottom of Arethusa

Falls and there was evidence of a tattoo on his lower back just like the policeman."

"Gallagher revealed all that to me and that's why a meeting was held with top officials from the government but something went very wrong. I was kept out of the hearing. Let me ask you this; why did it take so long for Gallagher to tell me all this? I think I know but I would like to hear it from you while I have others listening in."

Helen cleared her throat. "Remember...for awhile we didn't know whom we could trust." Helen pauses for a moment to catch her breath then continues, "I read the letter you sent to Gallagher. It stated there were two names missing from the list that was found in Echo Lake. Gallagher believes that at least two of the three who were found dead with the hammer and sickle tattoo may have been working with the Cause. The Russian scientist was simply a spy and not actually connected with the other two."

Anderson pauses for a moment before speaking. "If I'm getting this right, Gallagher believes two of the ones found may be connected to the missing names."

"I'm not sure what he's thinking but I present these facts to you."

"Alright...I will tell you what we know. A retired CIA agent contracted by our government assassinated the man called Gerald. The agent who carried out the assignment was on what is called a RED list."

"Red list?"

"Retired and extremely dangerous. We found out Gerald was an American who was dishonorably discharged from the Army during the Korean War for allegedly selling top-secret field operations to the North Koreans. He had a top-notch lawyer who got him off on a technicality. Somehow the evidence was compromised during the trial. It looks like he's held a grudge ever since. Two years ago he was arrested for murder and was placed on death row in Arizona."

"Wait a minute Paul. I wasn't born yesterday. If he was on death row how did he ever end up working at the morgue?"

"It's complicated."

"Okay, how about the harbor policeman?"

"A man by the name of Ishmael took care of him. I believe you know him."

"He's CIA?"

"Yes. He's also classified as RED. The policeman known as Andy was part of a major drug ring in Boston but had the knack of never getting his hands dirty until three years ago when a drug bust went wrong and two police officers were shot and killed. He was also given the death penalty."

Helen paused for a moment, "I know it's complicated."

"Yeah it is. As far as the Russian spy is concerned we only know of him as Boris and you know what happened to him."

"Paul...what in the name of everything that is sane and wholesome in this world is going on here?"

"All I can tell you is this; there is a group within our government that is working apart from the Kennedy administration and they are working with the Russians. That is why Livermore and Goodrich Falls were used for a pseudo research project for an antidote. It was to flush them out. It's too early to tell who they all are. We had to use Dredmeyer and Jones on the project for credibility so the formula would look legitimate to other scientists, particularly the Russians. The formula was missing a vital ingredient on purpose. Dr. Dredmeyer had deliberately concealed the formula with the missing ingredient in two books. I believe you know what I'm talking about."

"Yes I do. So are you talking about this country preparing for a nuclear war?"

"It's a possibility. We know current relations with the White House and the Kremlin are not going very well. Tensions have been rising ever since our government placed Jupiter missiles in Turkey in 1959. Then the attempt to overtake Castro in Cuba in 1961 was added to the list. It was a great embarrassment to our country. Khrushchev and Castro have become political bedfellows not because of any respect for each other but for military logistical purposes. Constant surveillance has been going on in spite of what happened to Gary Powers. Where this will all lead is anyone's guess."

"So where does that leave everyone?"

"We understand Dredmeyer has been taken to a secret facility with the hope he will reveal the missing ingredient but he has been unable to function because of the accident so we need to know where the real formula is so it can be kept out of the hands of the Russians. Unfortunately our agents had to shut down Mary Ann's Gift Shop for her own protection. We couldn't say anymore to her at the time."

"The formula is not there."

"We know. Do you know where it is?"

"Wait a minute. If you know the formula was not there, why shut down her shop; it make no sense."

"It makes perfect sense. First it eliminates the possibility of the formula being in her shop, which protects Mary Ann from any overt action on the part of the interested parties. Secondly it forces the interested party to show their hand by seeking alternative places to hunt down the formula. So I ask you again; do you know where it is?"

"I can't say that I do. Gallagher is very discreet about what he does, which sometimes drives me crazy. So you better get Gallagher and Jonathan out of wherever they are."

***

PART FOUR

Extraction

34

One week later - Saturday – May 26, 1962

Through secret channels Paul Anderson was able to locate Gallagher and Jonathan. They were being held at Fort Myers Military Base in Arlington Virginia. Extraction was almost impossible accept for a CIA field operative working inside who was very familiar with the entire layout of the base and was able to find out where exactly they were being held. Paul Anderson's reputation in the Bureau and his close connection with the first family was enough for 'Shadow' to come out of retirement and work the extraction without detection.

On the outside Frank 'The Snake' Margetti was poised to cause the disruption needed to facilitate the confusion inside the base. In the meantime Gallagher and Jonathan were being held together in the same secure prison facility and were told that escape was futile. They had been beaten several times and had been given drugs but neither one caved in. During the time spent in confinement Gallagher had a lot of time to think out what has been going on.

"Jonathan, as I think about our situation I've come to the conclusion we are in the wrong business because we tell the truth. It seems to be a liars world."

"Does that include Paul Anderson?"

"I believe Paul has become a victim of the ever eroding system of corrupt politics. He works for

238

people he trusts but they only give him small morsels of intelligence to carry out their agenda. It makes it very hard because without the whole truth of a matter he's shooting in the dark most of the time."

"For what purpose does leaving him in the dark serve?"

"The corrupt ones who are pushing the buttons are able to manipulate events to fulfill their own egotistical plans."

"Are you saying the current administration is corrupt?"

"Power corrupts."

"I follow you. This country places missiles in Turkey as a deterrent so Russia behaves herself. Russia in turn sides with Cuba to create a threat to the United States."

Gallagher nods and says, "And the beat goes on."

"Where's all this heading?"

"I'm afraid to even contemplate the answer to that question. I only know this, if an antidote is needed for radiation poisoning and its being used as bait for a foreign power, something big is in the works. We have to find the book collector and his partner the giant."

"The giant?"

"I didn't tell you but the book collector has been seen around the museum on a few occasions and the last time I saw him he was with a rather large man who could wear a size fourteen boot and strangle a man as easily as John Russell. This further shows how someone else besides Little Hands can fit the description of Ben's murderer."

"What you are saying is the book collector could have had something to do with Ben Willard's death."

'It seems to fit and I may be going out on a limb by saying it but it's what I'm thinking."

***

Nightfall....

The glider flew stealthily across the night sky low enough to be invisible to radar. Frank Margetti equipped with a Mitchell Wing hang glider leaped at the precise moment from the plane and sailed quietly into the blackness of night and landed softly in the middle of the base undetected.

He quickly disposes of the glider and runs to the rendezvous point where he connects with the Shadow. The sky is moonless and mostly overcast, which is to their advantage. While Frank rests against the side of a small building in the far west section of the base where Gallagher and Jonathan are being held, the Shadow approaches from behind and says in a whisper, "Don't move," as he presses a knife in Margetti's back.

"I can't see a shadow in the dark?"

"Best way to catch a snake."

After they both pass their identity test they move together stealthily around the back of the building where it faces the back fence.

"When should it strike?" asks the Shadow.

Frank looks at his Hawk wristwatch and says, "I estimate it will arrive in about forty-five seconds."

Right on time the specially modified glider plane equipped with explosives crashes into the mess hall sparking a huge fire when it pierces the gas line leading to the kitchen. A huge fireball emerges lighting up the sky followed by a thick plume of black smoke.

Frank and the Shadow move quickly inside and find Gallagher and Jonathan locked in a dark cell where only a small light is lit. Gallagher and Jonathan had already jumped out of their bunks and were waiting by the door. Frank quickly pries the metal door free and all four of them escape around the back where two specially trained agents had already bypassed the electrical fence with jumper cables. They cut an opening big enough to allow them to pass through without triggering the alarm. A waiting agent in a military truck is parked in the nearby woods and immediately drives up when they are in sight and picks the four up and they drive off into the night while the chaos at the mess hall keeps everyone occupied.

Gallagher recognizes Frank immediately when he gets into the truck but can't make out who the other man is because of his cloaked disguise.

"Frank...both Jonathan and I want to thank you for getting us out of there. We thought we were in line for execution the way they were treating us."

Then Gallagher looks at the Shadow and says, "I'm sorry but I don't know who you are but thank you so much for helping us."

The Shadow removes his wool cap and wipes the black soot off his face. Gallagher's eyes open wide and says in complete surprise, "Paul Anderson?"

"Yes it's me. You seem to bring out the youth in me these days but I have to tell you; I've had enough and I'm ready to go back to my desk job."

***

The trip back to Quantico from Fort Myers was only a straight 33 mile drive south on Rte. 95. Anderson had notified Quantico of their planned route back. Several agents were stationed at five-mile intervals to monitor any attempt of a chase emanating from the base. They arrived without incident in a record time of twenty-five minutes.

***

Sunday morning – May 27, 1962

After a day of rest and recuperation Gallagher and Jonathan were summoned to a large room to be debriefed. Four FBI agents along with two high-ranking senators from the Foreign Relations Committee are sitting across from both of them and start firing several questions their way.

"What reasons did you have Mr. Brady to attempt to enter the military base at Owl Mountain?" asks Senator Booth from Illinois.

"I'm not sure I can answer that question without legal representation."

"I don't understand. You are in the presence of several law enforcement agents and two United States senators. How much legal support do you need?"

Gallagher forces a smile and says respectfully, "It appears you have the support, not us."

"I beg your pardon."

Gallagher, already showing signs of losing his patience says, "We have been through this before and not with the best results. I will not cooperate with you until Paul Anderson is by our side."

Senator Booth looks at a guard standing on duty by the door and says, "We need Anderson. Get him in here right away."

Within five minutes Paul Anderson enters the room and sits next to Gallagher and Jonathan.

"I'm sorry Senator Booth. Mr. Brady and Mr. Henry have been through a similar hearing recently with very negative results. Please pardon Mr. Brady's apprehension."

"Now do you feel like you're now being represented Mr. Brady?"

Gallagher nods and says, "Yes Senator. It has come to the attention of myself, our police department in Jackson and Jonathan Henry who is seated beside me of some secret and dangerous experimentation being carried on, possibly by our government in our own backyard. As a result our fish and wildlife have been dying. The result of that happening has caused Mr. Henry and myself to investigate the reasons for the fatalities. In the process we've uncovered an elaborate sting operation to catch and arrest Russian spies."

Senator Williams from Arizona speaks up looking directly at Jonathan, "According to our information you are a journalist and also an investigating reporter for the Jackson Observer; is that correct?"

"Senator Williams, I'm a freelance reporter and I'm not officially connected to the newspaper. They print my articles if the need warrants it and recently there has been a lot to report on but I have held back any information to the paper for security reasons."

"I don't understand?"

Gallagher interrupts and says, "It's very simple. We don't know who we can trust."

"Mr. Brady...why do you feel that way?"

Gallagher is getting real impatient with the questions and showing his irritation replies, "I know what you know regarding what had gone on in Mount Washington Valley back in 1960 with the resurgence of the Nazi's in the form of a Fifth Column organization called the Cause. The FBI was very much involved in the capture of the remaining Fifth Column members that were on the list, which was recovered from Echo Lake last year. I also know what you know about the missing two names that were somehow permanently scratched off the list found in Chicago. Agent Anderson had warned me with a letter he sent me informing me of their existence."

Senator Booth looks at Anderson, "Is this true Agent Anderson?"

"Yes Senator. I felt it was necessary for Mr. Brady to know of the possibility of some remaining members of the Cause to surface in his area."

"Did you reveal the purpose of the Aricona Project?"

"Senator I couldn't because I didn't know of the existence of the project at the time."

"Mr. Brady, please continue to tell us what you know."

"I have learned that two of the men who have recently been eliminated by our government were not originally on the Chicago list at all. So they were not working with the Cause and they were not Russian spies."

"What are you trying to say Mr. Brady?" asks Senator Booth.

"It's too much like Hollywood. Tattoo's in the shape of a Soviet symbol on their lower backs above the buttocks. We are not fools Senator Booth. The only legitimate victim with a tattoo was the Russian named Boris. The other two never had tattoos but it was made to look that way. Patches of their skin were removed right above the buttocks to look like they had one. It was a bogus cover-up."

Anderson starts squirming in his seat at what Gallagher was revealing. Jonathan immediately looks at Gallagher and whispers, "You don't think they were Russians?"

Gallagher ignores Jonathan for the moment and replies, "I don't know who is behind it but there's something in the works and this government doesn't want it to leak out. I can understand national security but I can't understand polluting our rivers in the process and I don't condone using criminals as sacrificial lambs."

.

"Mr. Brady, we can assure you there is nothing being kept from the American people by this current administration. We appreciate your zealous concerns over the contamination of your rivers. We have assembled a team to cleanup any chemical pollution and restore your delicate ecosystem. We know tourism is the lifeblood of your valley. But this accusation about using criminals as sacrificial lambs, please elaborate."

Paul Anderson interrupts and says, "Could I speak with Mr. Brady in private?"

"By all means. We can take a break and continue in fifteen minutes."

Paul Anderson escorts Gallagher and Jonathan to a private room and speaks before sitting down, "You should have quit while you were ahead. I believed at one point they were going to dismiss this case. They are obviously oblivious to what is going on in their backrooms. Let's leave it at that for now. After things cool down we can talk about any next move that needs to be taken."

Jonathan looks perturbed at Gallagher for revealing his thoughts about not believing they were Russians. "Who are these guys if they're not Russians?"

"I believe Paul should answer that question."

Paul shook his head and said, "I'm not in agreement with this whole thing but as Gallagher said the Harbor policeman named Andy and Gerald the morgue attendant were criminals on death row and given a free get out of jail card if they carried out their assignments. This is where one half of our government doesn't know what the other half is doing. Contracts were put out on both of them and our friends at Langley carried out the task.

246

Sacrificial lambs are definitely the right description for it."

Gallagher adds, "Like I said before, it's Hollywood. I think they were working with another individual whose name is missing from the list. They have been puppets in a very deadly game."

"Any idea who?" Anderson asks perplexed.

"The book collector."

"What do you think we should do now? Remember my hands are now tied because of this hearing. I will be taken off the case immediately by the Director."

"We need to talk to Dredmeyer or Jones. They would know who to finger in all this."

Anderson acknowledges Gallagher's solution and says, "Dredmeyer and Jones have unfortunately disappeared from our radar."

"Are you telling me everything?"

"What I know, you know. Trust me. It's for your own good you don't know. Right now I need to talk with the senators to ease their minds on what you said about sacrificial lambs."

***

After more than a half hour everyone gathers back into the room and Senator Booth speaks first. "In further considering of what you have candidly revealed to us we find your actions are not an overt threat to our National Security but we advise you to keep what you have found out confidential. That's an order coming from the Attorney

General's office. We will not pursue this with you any longer. We believe your intentions were honorable and we seek your assistance in the future as this continues to unfold. Without sounding philosophical what our world may be facing in the very near future is a crime against humanity itself. It was short sighted on many believing the bombs dropped on Hiroshima and Nagasaki was the end of madness. It has just begun I'm afraid. You are free to go."

***

35

Friday morning two days later...June 1, 1962

Gallagher and Jonathan landed at the Concord Airport and after some last minute shopping on Jonathan's part they quickly boarded the train and headed back to Jackson.

Gallagher looks at his watch and says, "We have about an hour and a half to talk about our next move. I did a lot of thinking last night and I came up with a couple of ideas. First of all we know that Livermore and Goodrich Falls were places where experiments were conducted to produce an antidote or vaccine to cure radiation poisoning. Secondly we know the project is called the Aricona Project. Thirdly we know both sites were a subterfuge to lure Russian spies and members of the Fifth Column; the ones whose names were missing on the Chicago list. Fourthly we know one half of our government doesn't know what the other half is doing. We also know that Dr. Philip Jones may be working with...for the sake clarity, the dark side. The kidnapping of Tobey and the condition he left his wife in is proof of that fact. Dredmeyer has been the victim from the start and he is priority number one."

Jonathan interrupts and asks, "Where does O'Reilly fit into all this?"

"I believe he was working with Randolph Morgan who is one of the missing names on the Chicago list, which was originally scratched off. It fits with the fact that one of the first things O'Reilly did, as Chief was to suspend any routine surveillance of Goodrich Falls allowing for the research to take place so they could get the formula. When it was clear the whole operation was a bust he disappeared."

"What about the book collector?"

"He's the next one on the list to find."

"What about the giant who wears a size fourteen boot? Was he working for Morgan too?"

"It would be a very big coincidence if he didn't and you know what I think of coincidences."

***

The train pulls into the Jackson Train Station at 3:00 in the afternoon. Anna, and Valerie are waiting in the lobby. As soon as Anna and Valerie catch sight of their returning heroes they rush over and fall into each other's arms. After much hugging and kissing Gallagher exclaims, "What a welcome. We should go off and get ourselves into trouble more often."

"Don't get any ideas you two," Valerie replies as she holds Jonathan tight to her side. "Anna and I have been talking and we think it would be a wonderful thing for another wedding to take place without delay."

Jonathan perks up and says, "Who's wedding?"

Valerie squeezes Jonathan tighter and says, "Ours silly!"

"I thought I was the one to propose?"

Valerie laughs and says, "I've been waiting for you to pop the question for what seems like an eternity. I figured I needed to speak now before I get too old to care."

"Then we have to do this right."

Jonathan gets down on his knees and before he says another word he surprises everyone by taking out a small blue box from his coat pocket and says, "Valerie...will you except this ring and be my wife?"

Valerie immediately breaks down in tears of joy and happily accepts.

***

The four of them start driving toward Eagle House where Helen, Bill Waters and Chief Peterson are waiting. As they drive up the long driveway they notice Mary Ann's car in the driveway.

Anna speaks up first and says, "They released Mary Ann!"

Gallagher and Jonathan, not being aware of her arrest, look at each other puzzled. "What do you mean released?" asks Jonathan. "Released from what?"

"It's a story you should hear from Mary Ann herself," exclaims Valerie. "We can only guess what she went through. We were not allowed to know where she was taken when she was arrested for suspicion of treason."

After everyone was greeted and hands were shook and hugs were offered Gallagher quickly goes over to Mary Ann and asks her to explain what happened.

"It all happened so fast but I was arrested because they said I possessed highly classified documents of a scientific nature. All I could think of was what you found in the cover of one those books."

Gallagher nodded and said, "That's exactly what they were trying to find."

"They asked me where the books were and I said I had no idea. It was the truth because at that moment I did not know where you had placed the books because I hadn't yet set foot in the museum and even if I knew I wouldn't tell them."

Gallagher places his hand on her shoulder and says, "You did good. There's someone who thinks he knows where the books are and he has been poking around the museum site asking questions."

"Who?"

"Our infamous book collector."

"What's so valuable about those books for someone to be so persistent?"

"If you only knew?"

Mary Ann sighs and says, "Well I don't want to know. They finally released me right after your hearing at Quantico. Helen got the call from Paul Anderson saying I had been released."

After some refreshments Gallagher, Jonathan and Chief Peterson gathered in Gallagher's library and began planning on what to do next.

***

36

About a month later...Monday - July 2, 1962

It took about a month for everyone to return to his or her normal everyday routines. Gallagher was finally getting back to overseeing the construction of his new museum. Mary Ann and Valerie were busy making plans for the upcoming wedding in six days. John Peterson accepted to stay on temporarily while they searched for a new Chief. Helen and Bill Waters started seeing each other more regularly for tea and were seen on occasion taking in a movie at the Majestic Theatre. Penny Jones finally left Eagle House and went back to her home on Hurricane Mountain Road. She was very grateful to Helen for allowing her to stay for as long as she did. There had been no word from Philip or Tobey but she felt maybe Tobey would find his way home somehow.

It was 10:30 in the morning and Gallagher was busy at the bookshop looking over the books Professor Meridian had donated to the museum when Tobey Jones stumbles through the front door with two of his buddies, Charlie and Ernie.

Gallagher looking amazed to see his little friend standing before him says, "Tobey...where in the world have been all this time? Your mother has been worried sick and the whole valley has been searching for you for weeks."

Tobey is trying to catch his breath when Ernie speaks up and says, "I was in front of our shortwave radio early this morning when I heard Tobey's voice. I immediately answered him and found out where he was being held. You're not going to believe this but he was being held captive by his own father in an old AMC shack about six hundred yards deep into the woods off of Black Mountain Road."

Tobey continues, "I was able to get on the radio for the first time since I was taken. My father went outside to get some water by the stream when I took the chance and called for help. Ernie and Charlie started a brush fire near the shack and my father ran out to cover it over with dirt when I took the opportunity to jump out the back window and run off."

"We need to call your mother right away," Gallagher declares.

"Before you do that I need to tell you something my father revealed to me when he had too much to drink one night. His real name is not Philip Jones."

* * *

The following Saturday...

Gallagher and Jonathan were not going to allow the latest developments to interfere with Jonathan and Valerie's special day. They gathered at the Village Tavern along with Anna, Helen and Mary Ann, who was Valerie's maid of honor. All of them witnessed a wonderful ceremony with the added feature of four members of the Boston Symphony playing Vivaldi's Four Seasons as they walked down the aisle.

Gus and Lars Swenson went all out for Jonathan and Valerie converting their outdoor flower garden in the back into a beautiful spot for a wedding and providing all the food as a gift to the newlyweds.

After the reception the happy couple said their goodbyes to everyone and headed for Lake George in New York for their honeymoon.

***

After many days of searching, the police finally found Philip Jones in a large ditch barely alive. He had wandered off after having had too much to drink and jumped off a small ledge with the hopes off ending his life. A detailed letter was found in the old shack stating his sorrow for what he had done to his family. He wrote that Penny had no idea of his secret activities for the United States government. His work on the Aricona Project was a privilege especially being able to work with Wallace Dredmeyer. He indicated there were others who were principally involved but was afraid to reveal their names for the sake of his wife and son.

Tobey and Gallagher took the portable shortwave radio from the old shack and brought it to Tobey's home. Gallagher gave Tobey the job of trying to locate Dredmeyer in case he had access to a radio. It was a long shot but anything was possible. Doctor Mathews informed Penny that Philip had sustained a serious concussion and with the combination of drugs that were found in his bloodstream it was going to take some time before he would be able to talk.

***

37

Twelve days later...July 19, 1962

Jonathan and Valerie had returned from their honeymoon and decided to sleep in late when they heard a knock on the front door.

"Good morning Jonathan. I've been trying to reach you but for some odd reason your phone has been off the hook," Gallagher says with a hearty laugh.

"Gallagher...please come in. I was going to call you last night when we got back but we were both exhausted from the trip home and retired early."

"You don't have to explain to me my good friend. I just thought you should read this morning's paper as soon as possible. Reality sadly has to come back to your life."

They both enter the kitchen and Valerie comes down and starts brewing some coffee. "Morning Gallagher. What brings you by so early this morning?"

Jonathan starts laughing and says, "Did you notice the time?"

"Wow! I don't think I've slept this late in my life. It's almost noontime."

Jonathan begins reading out load from the front page of the Observer:

The Jackson Observer

Castro announces that Cuba is taking measures
that would make any direct U.S. attack on Cuba
the equivalent of a world war. He claims that
the U.S.S.R. has invested greatly in helping
to defend his country.

Jonathan stops reading and says, "So it begins."

"That means we have to end it before it's too late."
Gallagher declares. "I've had Tobey monitoring his
radio listening for any word from Dredmeyer.
About 5:30 this morning Tobey heard this:

"Whoever is there... I hope you are able to hear this
transmission. This is Dr. Wallace Dredmeyer. Please
stay silent because I do not have much time to be
interrupted. Please get this message to Gallagher
Brady as soon as possible. He will be able to figure
it out. The message is this: "I am parked in a
Cadillac in a bar surrounded by maniacs."

The transmission ended without further comment
from Dredmeyer.

"That's it? Can you figure it out?"

"There was a lot of static according to Tobey. He
said it was hard to make it out but he was sure he
got the whole message. I told him to keep listening
for other messages. Dredmeyer may only have a
short time to send what he can; there may be
more."

***

Gallagher left Jonathan's and headed back to Eagle
House. Anna joined him in his study and asks, "Was
Jonathan able to figure it out?"

256

Gallagher pauses to think before speaking. "I don't believe this is from Dredmeyer. I think it's a trick to throw us off. I know what the message is saying. It almost sounds like a child's prank."

"Please fill me in please."

"Cadillac must refer to Cadillac Mountain. Bar stands for Bar Harbor and maniacs, really spelled Maineiacs, refers to people who are native to Maine."

"Why do you think it's not from Dredmeyer?"

"Too simple. Dredmeyer is a genius and he would've thought up a more cryptic message."

"Maybe that's the point. Maybe he did it that way so as not to draw too much attention to it. You think it's childish, maybe others would think so too and ignore it."

"You might have something there. Whatever the case someone wants us to go to Cadillac Mountain."

* * *

38

Friday - July 20, 1962

Gallagher and Tom Perry leave early for Bar Harbor to find out if the message they received recently was actually from Dredmeyer.

Thunderstorms are predicted throughout the day as Gallagher and Tom drive towards Cadillac Mountain. Gallagher is very apprehensive about the trip because of the strange cryptic message but the whole thing intrigues Tom.

The trip takes a little over four hours. They approach Cadillac Mountain from the southern route of 179. Narrow roads lead to the base of the mountain, which sits in the middle of Arcadia National Park. Gallagher had called ahead to the Parks Service to let them know of their intentions and received the full cooperation from the rangers.

"What are we looking for?" Tom asks.

"The call came from a shortwave radio so we need to look for the main office."

Tom spots a ranger station set back off the main road with an antenna protruding from the roof. Pointing to the station he says, "What about that building over there? It looks like someone's there."

Gallagher enters the building and sees a woman sitting at the front desk, "Excuse me Miss. I'm Gallagher Brady from Jackson New Hampshire. I called ahead to let you know I was coming to investigate a possible abduction. That person may be somewhere on your property."

"Oh yes. I have a note here Mr. Brady. How can we be of help? We checked out all our buildings and didn't find anyone there who may have made the call. Some of our stations throughout the park are closed today because of the heavy rain. We don't expect too many tourists today and the fire threat is low."

"We noticed a building about two miles back set deep into the woods. It has an antenna which indicates it has a radio."

"The woman smiles and says, "All twelve stations throughout the park have shortwave radios; take your pick. Here's a list of the locations. The ones marked in red are the only ones currently occupied."

"Thank you. You've been very helpful."

Gallagher rejoins Tom and they head back to the station they had first past and approach the entrance.

"What are the chances of finding him here?" Tom asks.

"About one in twelve is my guess. Let's find out."

After spending several hours inspecting seven of the twelve unoccupied stations Gallagher is about ready to give up but then he remembers how he didn't give up on Jonathan when he found him barely alive in Ravenswood Cemetery trapped in a tomb. He needed to press on to the finish. Dredmeyer had to be found.

They drive up to the furthest station from the main lodge and notice three vehicles in the lot. A tall man was standing by the door and says, "You must be Mr. Brady."

"That's right. Who are you? You're not dressed in a ranger's uniform."

"You're right because I'm not a ranger but I'm the one who sent the message."

Gallagher quickly asks, "Where's Dr. Dredmeyer?"

"He's on an island named Tonga in the Pacific recuperating from his injuries."

"Why the seclusion?"

"In Livermore he was used as bait to lure the hunter."

"Who's the hunter?"

"You know him only as the 'book collector'. Please sit down and let me explain. Have your friend join us."

After Tom Perry joins them he begins. "Dr. Dredmeyer is alive and well. We have been taking him to one place after another so he can continue his work. We don't stay long because there are several interested parties who want what's in his head."

"Wait a minute. Are you saying you are responsible for removing him from the hospital?"

"We are! We are working for the government and our identity has to remain classified. I can tell you a little of what is going on but it must remain confidential or many lives will be in danger."

"I understand...please continue."

"Wallace was working on a top secret project called Aricona. It stands for 'Antidote Research In Case Of Nuclear Attack'. He was working with Russian scientists who were unsympathetic to the Khrushchev administration and had knowledge of Russia's intention of helping Cuba after the Bay of Pigs incident. They were willing to share their knowledge with our scientists to develop an effective antidote for radiation poisoning in case of a nuclear exchange. If this was to get out in the open we would not have the upper hand on the Soviets."

"We were informed that the Aricona Project was a trap?"

"Exactly."

"How come the rest of our government is not on the same page? They claim to have never heard of Dredmeyer or Jones."

"It's complicated. The director of the FBI and the President do not see eye to eye. Much intelligence is being ignored putting this country in grave danger. The Attorney General has commissioned a special task force to make sure this trap works. There's no love lost between the Attorney General and the Director. That's all I can tell you."

Gallagher scratches his head and says, "So you're telling me the Livermore and Goodrich Dam sites were not government sanctioned but were a secret project set up by the Attorney General?"

"Correct. The antidote was made two years ago shortly after we placed missiles in Turkey. It was a secret operation and those involved were kept isolated from any outside contact and remained anonymous. Dredmeyer was the chief scientist on the project."

"If that's so why was Dredmeyer working at Livermore and Goodrich Falls. What was he doing there if the antidote was already made?"

"It served two purposes. It wasn't long after the original batch was made that we found it was becoming unstable as it sat in storage. Dredmeyer with the help of Soviet scientists discovered the missing ingredient to achieve stability. In the process it served as a trap to lure those interested parties who Agent Anderson had warned you about in his letter."

"Did our finding out about the two sites spoil the trap?"

"In some respects yes but it also achieved a very positive result as well."

"How so?"

"It flushed out the book collector whoever he is and thanks to you we know that Randolph Morgan is the other one on the list."

Gallagher acknowledges and says,, "So we need to find out who this book collector really is."

"Agent Anderson, who is a good friend to the Attorney General, will brief the two of you on what you can do from now on to help end this political nightmare."

"Can I ask just one more simple question?" Gallagher asks showing a slight grin.

"Go ahead."

"Why the odd message?"

"It got you here, didn't it?"

***

39

Saturday morning- July 21, 1962

Gallagher and Jonathan arrive at the Village Tavern to enjoy an overdue breakfast from the Swenson's. Gallagher pulls out of his pocket a small piece of paper and hands it to Jonathan. "Read the latest from Anderson."

"CIA Director John McCone sends a memo to Kennedy expressing his belief that Soviet medium-range ballistic missiles will be deployed in Cuba."

"Wow. It looks like something big is really going to happen."

"Something big is definitely in the works but I'm getting very frustrated with all the secrecy."

I know. You get lured out to Bar Harbor and meet with a very official looking man who remains nameless and we are given an amazing story about Dredmeyer's secret location."

Jonathan remains silent after saying those words, which catches Gallagher's attention. "You're all of a sudden very quiet. What are you thinking?"

"If Dredmeyer found out about the trap, does that mean the formula he placed in the Baskerville book was a phony?"

"Not at all. It's the real deal. It's why he delivered it so inconspicuously."

"Dredmeyer knew what he was doing."

"That's right but it almost cost him his life at Livermore."

Gallagher got up and starts to pace back and forth while sipping on his coffee. Gus comes over and says, "Gallagher can I get you some more coffee; you look restless."

"Gus, I am restless but not in a physical way. Something is not right in my mind."

Jonathan overhears him and asks, "What are you thinking?"

"I can't put my finger on why I'm so uneasy about what we have just learned. I'm happy that Dredmeyer is safe and well but there's something missing. Something we have not discovered yet."

***

Later that night...

Gallagher is tossing and turning in bed because he can't get the person he is thinking about out of his mind. After many restless moments he get up and goes to the phone.

"Who are calling at this hour?" Anna asks as Gallagher's movements had wakened her.

"I'm sorry if I woke you but I think I know who the book collector is."

"Who?"

"First of all let me ask you this question. Has anyone ever met Randolph Morgan to your knowledge?"

Anna thinks for a moment. "I know Jane Willard has talked a lot about her father but come to think of it, I personally have never met the man."

"Neither have I."

"Who are you calling?"

"Chief Peterson."

"His wife will never forgive you for calling him at this hour. Why not call Tom Perry. He should be able to help you and he doesn't have a wife that will scream at you for calling so late."

"Peterson has been on the force for decades and may have met Randolph Morgan on more than one occasion. Morgan does own several properties throughout the valley, which may have afforded them the opportunity to meet."

"My I ask who's calling at this late hour?" a voice asks on the other end.

"I'm sorry Mrs. Peterson but I need to talk with the Chief; it's urgent."

"Of course it is Gallagher. These calls always are urgent. Just a minute."

"Gallagher, this better be good. Remember, I retired once from all this grief and I can't wait for my replacement and continue where I left off."

"Sorry Chief but your replacement won't be able to help me on this one."

"What do you want to know?"

"We now know that one of the missing names on the list is Randolph Morgan. We also know about the book collector who has remained nameless may also be on the same list. My question is; have you ever met Randolph Morgan personally?"

The brief silence on the other end is broken by Peterson's sigh, "You woke me up for this?"

"I know Chief but I have been racking my brain on this and your simple answer will answer a lot for me."

"Never have! Now please let me go back to sleep."

'Click'

***

40

The next morning – July 22, 1962

Gallagher and Jonathan make their way to Jane Willard's home. As soon as they drive into her driveway there is a sense of uneasiness going through Gallagher's mind.

"Jonathan, do you notice anything?"

"No. What should I notice?"

"A barking dog."

Jonathan shrugs his shoulders and says, "I don't hear any barking. Maybe she's walking the dog."

"I would like to think so myself but I have a feeling Jane Willard is on the run and has taken the dog with her."

"Please tell me what you're thinking. You haven't said one word about why we needed to see Jane Willard."

266

"Let's go inside and take a look before I end up eating words I have omitted to say."

"I know, you are remaining quiet and thought the fool than to speak and remove all doubts."

"You are catching on my friend."

Gallagher tries the door but it's locked so he does the next best thing and smashes the window then reaches in and unlocks the door. They made there way throughout the house and nothing seemed disturbed.

"I don't see anything suspicious do you?" Jonathan asks.

"Just one thing."

Gallagher bends down and picks up something and holds it in his hand."

"What did you find?"

"A morsel of dried dog food."

Jonathan starts laughing and says, "I'm sure if you're that hungry we can find something a little more appetizing to eat."

"Gallagher couldn't help but return a laugh then says, "The dogs food bowl and water dish are usually right in this spot. You can tell by the remnants of dog fur around this area where the dog spends a lot of its time eating and drinking. This means Jane Willard is not walking the dog but has left without telling anyone. We need to go through her personal belongings and look for a picture of her father. She's bound to have a picture of him lying around somewhere."

"Why is that so important?"

"Because all we have ever heard regarding Randolph Morgan is he being her father but no one has ever met the man; not even Peterson."

They both begin pulling boxes of photos from her closets and drawers out of dressers and begin sifting through the many family pictures but not one shows who could be her father.

"We need to find her wedding pictures. Her father has to be in some of those photos."

Finally Gallagher pulls a large photo album from the closet and finds what he was looking for right away.

Jonathan takes the album and stares for several seconds at the photo then finally says, "The missing finger!"

"I knew it. Randolph Morgan is the book collector. This means so far we only have one of the missing names on the list. Morgan and the book collector are one and the same. This means there is still one out there somewhere who must be found or this nightmare will never end."

***

41

One week later – July 29, 1962

Gallagher and Anna ware halfway up White Horse Ledge enjoying an early Sunday morning climb when a voice from above catches Gallagher's attention.

"Gallagher can you hear me?"

Gallagher can't see the top and yells out, "Who are you?"

"It's Paul Anderson. I need to talk with you right away."

"Right here and now? I'm in somewhat of a precarious situation to carry on a conversation."

"I realize that but it's urgent. We need the formula."

"Why do you think I still have it?"

"It was in your possession last."

"No it wasn't. Professor Meridian was the last one to possess it. I'm sure he still has it; why the concern?"

"To our knowledge so far from what you were able to ascertain the formula was intended to be picked up by the book collector but was distracted at Mary Ann's gift shop. So his first attempt failed. I must say Mary Ann is quite the savvy one; she's no push over. The second time was when he was poking around your museum asking a lot of questions but Harry didn't give him anything to work with."

"So what are you getting at?"

"We believe Dredmeyer only had one copy of the formula. If your right in saying Professor Meridian is still in possession of it, he's in grave danger."

"Is that all the wonderful news you have to tell me?"

"No. We received word that there's now evidence of Soviet missile installations in Cuba. The Senate is urging Kennedy to take action."

***

PART FIVE

The Sleeping Indian

42

One month later - Monday morning - September 3, 1962

Gallagher and Anna are relaxing in their library listening to Van Cliburn performing Rachmaninov's third piano concerto when Gallagher is struck again by a nagging thought he can't get out of his mind. He quickly rises from his chair and goes to the telephone.

"What are you up to?" Anna asks showing her suspicion of whom Gallagher was calling.

"I have to call Paul right away."

"I thought we were done with this nightmare. Everything has been quiet for about a month now. It's out of your hands."

"I know but there is a third sleeping Indian Paul should know about."

"You're kidding?"

"I wish I was."

Gallagher dials. "You have reached the office of Paul Anderson. If you know the code please dial it now."

Gallagher punched in his code and waits.

"Yes Gallagher. Have you found out anything?"

"Yes but its not good news. We found out Meridian destroyed the formula believing it was best to be out of the hands of any government because it allowed a careless disregard for life. His thinking is we can press the button and they can fire back but we have an antidote; too deadly of a game in his opinion. Paul, I can't help but agree with his thinking."

"I know, we have been through this discussion already and I agree with you as well but what are you getting at here?"

"Well for what it's worth I finally got back to reading a western novel I have been trying to finish since all this trouble began. The book is titled Shane. The story takes place in Jackson Hole, Wyoming."

"Okay. Why are you telling me this?"

"Usually when I read books I like to look up certain details that are described in the book. So what I did was, I looked up the geography of Jackson Hole and guess what I found?"

"I can't imagine."

"There's a third sleeping Indian."

"What...?

"Our government has known for quite some time the intentions of our Russian friends. As far back as the Warsaw Pacts of 1954. A few months ago Jonathan read me a synopsis of a speech he was preparing to read to the senior class at Jackson High School. In it he mentioned the Warsaw Pacts, which was the beginning of the breakdown of trust between Russia and the United States."

"Okay I'm following you. What else?"

"I don't believe there's nothing other than a military base at Owl Mountain. I believe the legitimate sleeping Indian is at Jackson Hole, Wyoming, which is the one Dr. Jones was referring too on his map even though he had no clue as to what it really meant. This means the elaborate operation in our neck of the woods of developing an antidote was not only a subterfuge and a trap for the Russians but it served as a screen for the real location where the antidote had been manufactured and stored. The same strategy applied to Owl Mountain. All the traffic with the planes and the trucks and all the other distractions were all designed to throw everyone off track. Our country is about ready to defend itself against a major attack and it's looking more like the Russians are the ones to press the button from Cuba's backyard."

"Okay let's say you're right. Why do we have to be concerned about Jackson Hole?"

"Because I believe it's one of the targets. If missiles are ever launched from Cuba they will be able to reach Jackson Hole and destroy the antidote. I believe they found out about the sleeping Indian from Philip Jones. When he escaped from his captors he obviously was caught again after taking Tobey and Penny to Dredmeyer's house. I believe he was drugged and was forced to reveal his knowledge of the sleeping Indian even though he had no clue as to its meaning like I said before, but someone did, the book collector, the infamous Randolph Morgan. That's what put Anna and I on the radar when we were flying to Colorado and eventually hijacked."

"Okay, so what you are saying is Harmon may be in with Morgan?"

"It's a very good possibility."

Anderson thought for a moment. "If Owl Mountain was not the sleeping Indian being referred to on Jones map why were they so intent on preventing you or anyone else from finding out that fact."

"It's only logical. It made us think it was the sleeping Indian where the antidote was being stored. There would be no need for us to look any further."

Anderson remains quiet for several seconds.

"Paul, are you still with me?"

"Yeah I'm here. Let me get this straight. Jones' notation of the sleeping Indian on his map was really referring to Jackson Hole, Wyoming not Owl Mountain in Colorado?"

"That's right."

"I don't believe all this. It sounds impossible."

"When you eliminate the impossible, whatever remains, no matter how improbable, must be the truth."

"What? Oh, never mind, just answer me this question. What does all this mean now?"

"If the antidote is being stored at Jackson Hole; it has to be moved without delay. With the latest news coming out of Washington the Russians mean business."

"I need to relay this to the Attorney General right away. I will be in touch the usual way."

Later that night...

Penny Jones called Gallagher and told him she had just received word that Philip was recovering."

***

43

Behind closed doors...September 11, 1962

In a speech to the UN, Soviet Foreign Minister Andrei Gromyko warns that an American attack on Cuba could mean war with the Soviet Union.

***

Friday...October 5, 1962

Gallagher is summoned to the White House to attend a special hearing from the Attorney General's office to explain his knowledge of what he knows about Russian spies and the Aricona Project.

Gallagher is escorted into a large room, which was all too familiar to him because of the last two hearings he attended. He was escorted to his seat and beside him on his left was Paul Anderson and on his right to his shock was James O'Reilly. Gallagher looked twice to see if it was really O'Reilly but said nothing. O'Reilly looked back and Gallagher and revealed a slight smile.

The panel was made up of members Congress, National Security, CIA and key agents of the FBI. The Director of the FBI was interestingly not present.

Senator Collins who is also a member of the Foreign Relation Committee asked the first question.

"My first question is to Agent James O'Reilly. For the sake of those in this room I would like you to be clear and to the point in answering. Is that understood?"

"Yes Senator Collins."

"Please explain the reason why you were sent to Jackson, New Hampshire to take over the position of Police Chief."

"I received a directive from my superiors of the need for me to have hands on knowledge of the Aricona Project in Jackson. By keeping my cover as the new Chief I was able to maneuver my time without question, at least I thought. Also I was able to change some routines performed by the force in order for certain operations to take place without creating suspicion."

"Can you be more specific?"

"One major change was the routine surveillance of the Goodrich Falls site. I suspended all police presence in that area by explaining the financial hardship and wasted use of manpower as the reason. No one questioned my decision, again so I thought."

"When did you recognize it was time to remove yourself from the operation?"

"It was actually two events that made me realize my usefulness in the project was over. First it was the work of Mr. Gallagher Brady and Jonathan Henry in finding the Livermore site because of the contamination of the fish in the Swift River and the residual deaths of wildlife in the area. Secondly it was the continued contamination of fish in the Saco River, which enabled them to piece things together and find the Goodrich Falls site. It was at that point I decided to disappear."

"My next question is what was the catalyst in creating the contamination?"

"It was from an experiment gone bad. We believe a Russian spy posing as a scientist purposely sabotaged the project by cutting the drainage pipes leading to the recovery tanks at both locations after finding out the project was just a front and not the real site of the Aricona Project. We also have concluded that he purposely caused one of the dogs to have a violent attack on Dr. Dredmeyer by injecting it with the fake serum but he got the worst of it in the end. It wasn't until Mr. Brady was able to discover a partially eaten piece of flesh from the lower back of the dead spy to absolutely know he was Russian. I believe you have a photograph of the remains of the tattoo."

"What is our understanding of how this Russian was able to infiltrate the site?"

"I believe Mr. Brady is best qualified to answer that question."

"Fair enough. I direct that question to you Mr. Brady."

"Senator and members of this panel I believe Randolph Morgan was instrumental in enlisting the Russian into the project."

"Are you accusing Morgan of treason?"

"Yes. We have come to know his name is listed on a roster of Fifth Column members found in Chicago. For some reason it was partially scratched off but we were able to put the missing pieces together."

"I'm very well aware of the list found in Chicago and it's duplicate, which was found by you in Echo Lake. My question to you is this; are not the names on those lists accompanied by their pseudonym?"

"Yes that's true. I believe the missing alias is just simply, 'book collector'."

Senator Thompson from Arkansas raises his hand and asks, "I would like to direct a question to Mr. Brady. What do you believe has become of Dr. Wallace Dredmeyer?"

"Senator, it's not a matter of belief. I know Dr. Dredmeyer is alive and well as we speak."

Paul Anderson looks at Gallagher surprised at his statement but remains silent to hear his explanation.

The Senator, showing his surprise asks, "Why do you say he is alive and well when the last report of his whereabouts was on the Island of Tonga in the Pacific. How do you have this knowledge?"

"Propaganda!"

"Excuse me. What are you saying?"

"Because I now know it was not Dredmeyer on the island of Tonga."

"Why do you say that?"

"In thinking about it I believe our government would not purposely allow Dredmeyer to stay on Tonga knowing the Russians frequent that part of the world. I think Dredmeyer was taken from Livermore and has been recuperating right here in Washington. It only makes sense because you already have the antidote he developed two years ago and his usefulness in the phony Aricona Project was over. He was extracted from the hospital in North Conway and brought here for further recovery."

"Mr. Brady I have to admit your perception of this whole case could make anyone of us think you're a spy."

"I don't know if I should thank you for thinking it but there's one thing you need know and you don't have to be a spy to figure it out. There's still one name on that list still unaccounted for and he's on the lam."

***

The hearing concluded after two more hours of questioning and the panel was most enlightened by Gallagher's synopsis of the situation. Work was in progress to remove the antidote from Jackson Hole and distributed near key locations, which are likely targets of a nuclear strike where the antidote could be administered. It was the intention of the government to disperse the antidote in time but the recent escalation of tensions between Russia and the United States and the current information from Gallagher prompted an earlier distribution.

***

Gallagher and Paul Anderson walk out of the hearing together and Paul pulls Gallagher aside and asks, "Where did you get the idea that Dredmeyer is here in Washington?"

"That was easy. When I called the professor about the formula I left something out. He told me he had heard from Dredmeyer and that's how he knew he could destroy the antidote."

"Why did you leave that out?"

"Never mind me leaving something out. What's the story with the resurrected O'Reilly?"

"I'm sorry about keeping it from you but it was orders from Langley. O'Reilly is a retired CIA operative and his disappearance was needed because of the accident. What I have just found out through closed door hearings was O'Reilly was to meet with the man you suspect to be Ben Willard's killer. When he got there all he found was the note you discovered."

"What about the jeep?"

"O'Reilly purposely caused a small explosion to get everyone off his trail. He was picked up by another agent before you got there."

"What about his military record?"

"It's a phony for security purposes."

"So you had nothing to do with his appointment as Chief to replace Peterson."

"I was told by my friend at Langley to go along with the arrangement. Because I had no prior knowledge of the purpose of the Aricona Project I didn't suspect a thing."

Gallagher's mind begin to work and it finally hits him. "O'Reilly's rendezvous with the man who wears a size fourteen boot makes sense. He was also after Ben Willard's killer. Can it be arranged for me to talk with O'Reilly?"

"Out of the question. Because of security reasons O'Reilly is not allowed to discuss the case especially because it has to do with activity on US soil. He's already left on another pressing assignment."

***

October 9, 1962... behind closed doors

Kennedy orders a U-2 reconnaissance flight over western Cuba, delayed by bad weather.

***

October 14, 1962... behind closed doors.

A U-2 flying over western Cuba discovers missile sites.

***

Early morning ...October 15, 1962

Gallagher convinced he has freed himself from the recent chaos in the valley because the Aricona Project is shut down and all respected parties have gone back to their normal assignments, drives to the bookshop optimistic of having a normal day.

Gallagher walks through the door and sees Kathy minding the store. "Good morning Kathy. What's the good word for today?"

"It's Columbus Day weekend and the leaf peepers have been flocking in spending their money and enjoying our little paradise in the mountains. Thanks to you and Jonathan the contamination of the rivers has been cleared up and the shopping center at Hart's Location has been dissolved. That's the latest gossip around the village."

"Speaking of gossip, I'm going to run over to the Tavern for breakfast and see what they have been hearing."

"Is Anna coming in today?"

"No she making arrangements for our second honeymoon."

"Second? You didn't even have the first."

"Precisely. We need to finish what never got started in Colorado."

"Anywhere in particular?"

"Not sure yet. But I know one thing; it won't be Colorado."

***

The Village Tavern was busy as usual with the local patrons starting out their day with a hearty breakfast and a good cup of coffee along with a little village gossip. Gus Swenson catches sight of Gallagher and comes over to his table right away. "God middag' my friend. Good to see you back in your regular routine. I will bring you over the usual."

"Thank Gus. Have you seen Jonathan this morning? Now that he's married I don't see him much anymore. I think we need another mystery."

"Are you serious?"

"Not in the least."

Overhearing the conversation Professor Meridian wanders over and sits across from Gallagher. "Gallagher, can I talk with you a second."

"Good morning Professor. I'm surprised to see you in here. You're not a regular in the morning. Did Louise forget to make you breakfast?"

"I wish that was the case. I asked her to leave home for a while and spend some time with her sister Pam in Sugar Hill."

"Is Pam not well?"

"No...she's fine. I don't want her around because I've been getting a lot of phone calls but no one says anything on the other end. It has Louise nervous and I thought she should get away for awhile till this person gives up."

"How long has this been going on?"

"For about two weeks."

"Did you call Peterson about it?"

"No, not yet. I called you at your home earlier and Anna said you probably were here having breakfast. I think this has something to with the formula."

"You destroyed it I thought."

283

Meridian was silent.

"Professor...are you with me? You did destroy it, didn't you?"

"Oh yes. I'm sorry. What I said to you earlier about destroying the formula was not true. Dredmeyer told me to say that if questioned. You see; it's the only copy of the formula in existence."

"You think your being checked out by this individual to see if your home?"

"Yes I do. You know me. I don't go anywhere these days for any length of time except a little fishing with John. Louise works out of the house with her sewing classes so she's here most of the time. Every time the phone rings I have been out checking the mail at the post office or picking up something at Rawlings Super Market. Louise ends up answering the phone almost every time. Once I answered and it was the same; silence on the other end. It's becoming rather unnerving."

"I'm trying to think positive here. Is it possible Louise has a secret admirer?"

"If you told me that two years ago I might have agreed with that hypothesis but I've become more of a cynic these days."

"What would you like me to do?"

"Normally I would go to the police but if it's someone local they would recognize anyone on our small police force. It has to be someone who's not from around here."

Gallagher's wheels start turning. "You really think it might have to do with the formula?"

"Yes I do."

"I don't know if he would do it but I have a possible candidate. He's good at working in the shadows."

"That would be greatly appreciated."

***

After breakfast Gallagher returns to Eagle House and goes into his study and dials Paul Anderson's number on the special phone line the FBI had set up.

"Gallagher...I'm not sure I want to hear from you" Anderson replies on the other end.

"It's all your fault. I have this hotline that goes directly to your office. I can't use it for anything else so I might as well put it to use from time to time. I really wish your guys would've installed a red phone."

"Very funny. What's up?"

"It's the book collector. He may have surfaced."

"I hope so. Our agents have been following every lead they get but have come up empty each time."

"I think Shadow needs to make another appearance."

***

44

The next day…October 16, 1962

"Paul Anderson's office. How can I direct your call?"

"This is General Bradley at EX-COMM. I need to speak with Agent Anderson a.s.a.p."

"Just one moment."

"General Bradley…I was hoping I would never have to hear your voice."

"I understand and I won't take it personal. We are having an emergency meeting this afternoon 1400 sharp in the Situation Room. Your presence is required per order of the Attorney General."

* * *

Later that same day…

"Gallagher…can you talk?"

"Yes Paul. Have you made arrangements?"

"If you can believe it, something more urgent has come up so I will not be able to help you on this one. It's out of my hands. "

"I understand. I will take care of it myself. I fear for the Professor's life."

"Why don't he just destroy it?"

"I don't think it's that simple. Unless there was a public burning of the formula no one is going to believe he destroyed it. If he tangles with these guys he will be tortured along with his daughters until they get what they want. I'm sure they have both houses staked out by now."

"I have an idea. Tell Meridian to leave his home right away. Before he leaves tell him to place the formula in envelope marked Aricona and have him leave it in his desk; preferably the top drawer."

"You want me to set a trap?"

"Not exactly. Let whoever it is steal the formula and see where he takes it. It might lead you to the group he's with. They never work alone."

"I'm on it."

***

45

Behind closed doors…October 17, 1962

Throughout the EX-COMM's discussions, the Joint Chiefs of Staff and especially the Air Force strongly argue for an air strike at Cuba after another U-2 flight discovers intermediate range SS-5 nuclear missiles.

***

Professor Meridian does exactly what Gallagher instructs him to do. He leaves his home and travels to his daughter's home in Sugar Hill. From there they were all instructed to leave together including his son-in-law and his twelve-year-old grandson. A police escort followed them to a safe house somewhere in Gorham about twenty miles away.

With instructions from Paul Anderson, Gallagher and Jonathan staked out the Professor's home watching for signs of the book collector. A technician was able to rig a portable phone hookup so Gallagher could answer the phone when the collector calls while hidden in woods behind the house. Jonathan was the point man and as soon as the collector was spotted approaching the house he was to signal Gallagher.

Darkness is beginning to cover the valley. Gallagher and Jonathan wait patiently for the call then at 7:00 p.m. the phone rings. This time no one picks up the phone. It rings several times but Gallagher waits and lets it ring. The ringing finally stops and then another call two minutes later and Gallagher lets the phone ring several times and then the ringing stops. The whole thing happens a third time and then silence.

A half hour goes by and Jonathan spots a short man approaching the side door hidden from the road. Within seconds he's inside and both Gallagher and Jonathan are tempted to seize him with the goods but per Anderson's instruction they are to let him leave without incident.

Ten minutes goes by then the book collector emerges from the house and leaves the area on foot and disappears. Gallagher and Jonathan are about ready to follow him on foot when all of a sudden a massive explosion occurs in the house and fire and smoke engulf the entire house. Firefighters and the police are on the scene within minutes. Gallagher watches as he thinks about all the books and papers and the Professor's research are all going up in flames. Gallagher has to clear his mind of the Professor's loss and refocus on the collector. He had gotten away with his clever scheme to distract anyone who may have been watching. Gallagher quickly uses the portable phone and calls the North Conway Airport. As he expected a small military jet called a Marvel is waiting to take off. The flight plan is to take three passengers to Miami International Airport.

Gallagher all of a sudden is in a quandary on what to do. Anderson wanted the collector to steal the formula with the intentions of finding out who his connections were but he was playing hard to get; he had to let him leave or it would spoil the trap.

Gallagher meets with Jonathan and they drive off and head for Eagle House. Gallagher looks in his rear view mirror and feels sick to his stomach has he sees his friend's home burning to the ground. The rare emotion of anger is stirring within him. He is at loss on where to turn. They arrive at Eagle House and Anna and Helen are waiting in the living room. They had heard on the news about the Professor's home. After explaining what happened Anna speaks up and says, "How about the Snake?"

***

Behind closed doors...October 18, 1962

The Soviet Foreign Minister Andrei Gromyko and President Kennedy meet for two hours. Reading from notes, Gromyko assures Kennedy that Soviet aid to Cuba has been only for "defensive capabilities of Cuba."

***

Gallagher searches through his desk drawer and finds the lists of numbers Anderson had given him if he needed help. He finds the number and calls..."CIA Headquarters at Langley.

"How may I direct your call?"

"Connect me to CIAWH/3 please."

"Division 3... your code please."

"Mountain Eagle 001."

"Who do you wish to contact?

"Shadow's friend."

"Please stay on the line."

After about five minutes Gallagher gets connected. "This is Shadow's friend and am I speaking to Mountain Eagle 001?"

"Affirmative."

"What can I do for you Mr. Brady?"

"I need the help of the Snake."

"Would this have anything to do with the book collector?"

"Yes it does. How could you...?"

"How could we know? You underestimate the CIA. We can find out what's going on in everyone's backyard if we choose too."

"Why have you chosen ours?"

"I have come to understand you're not the naive type."

"I know it was a stupid question but I had to ask for my own reasons."

"Fair enough. To help you out here Shadow gave me the heads up you might call."

"Nothing gets by him I guess."

"Well that's not what he told me. He said you had a better handle on what went down in Jackson than anyone else.

"He's being kind. But getting back to my request, can the Snake help us?"

"You are to meet him at Brown's Airfield outside of southern Miami at 1200 tomorrow. It's a small airfield that was once used for crop dusters. It's no longer open but we have monitored drug dealers using the airfield flying at low altitudes to avoid detection from radar to smuggle their drugs in from Columbia. He will tell you what the plan is when you arrive."

***

The next day at 1200 hours - Brown's Airfield

Gallagher gets out of cab and see's a black sedan parked behind the traffic tower. The cab leaves the area and he slowly walks over to the sedan and Frank Margetti gets out and greets Gallagher with a hearty handshake. "Good to have a chance to work with you again. Here's the plan so far. Our intelligence has revealed the man you call the book collector landed at Miami International and rented a small Cessna 172 and flew out heading south and we believe he plans to hold up here temporarily. What I need from you is a positive ID before we move in for the kill. Take my binoculars and try to stay out of sight when he lands. If we are dealing with the kind of people your familiar with in the last case you were involved in this should prove very interesting."

"You mean the Cause."

"That's right. Shadow's friend filled me in on how you broke up the Fifth Column group, which had a ripple effect across the country. I even heard about it in Alcatraz. You're actually famous amongst the prisoners. I guess no matter what kind of crime they had committed stopping Hitler's brood was okay in their book."

"I would have never guessed."

Frank moves behind the tower and Gallagher follows. The Cessna is in view and touches down about a hundred yards from them. Two men get out plus the pilot and head for the small building next to the tower. Frank taps Gallagher on the shoulder and says, "That's the old storage building where the pesticides are kept. If you go around the back you might get a good view to positively ID the man."

"Why don't we just barge in on them and take our chances?"

"One big reason not to is if he's not our man we may disrupt their plans."

"What are you getting at?"

"We believe whoever is in there, plans on flying to Cuba at nightfall. The package may have been transferred if they catch wind of our trap."

Gallagher moves to the back of the building and sees two men sitting at a table starting to play cards. The pilot then joins them with three bottles of beer. Gallagher is able to get an excellent view of their hands. After about five minutes Gallagher rejoins Margetti. "He's not there."

"How can you be sure?"

"The book collector is missing the middle finger of his right hand. The three of them have all their fingers intact."

Margetti nods and says, "We were afraid of that happening. He must have passed on the formula to one of them."

Gallagher starts thinking. "Is there any way of finding out what flights took off after he left the airport?"

"Yeah...we can find out but what's your thinking?"

"This might be a diversion."

"I've been given updates by the Attorney General's office ever since we shut down the Aricona Project."

"Well I have a feeling their stealing the formula was just a planned deception to hide their real plan."

Margetti scratched his head and says, "What are *you* thinking?"

Gallagher looks at his watch. "Today's the 19th. Where's the President today."

"If memory serves me correct he plans on delivering a campaign speech in Cleveland."

Margetti grabs Gallagher and says, "We have to get to a phone right away. I think I know what you're thinking."

Three blocks away was a small gas station. Margetti quickly gets out of the car and heads for the phone booth. Ten minutes later he returns and says, "Three flights left within a hour after the book collector's plane landed. I was able to find out he booked himself on the next plane to Cleveland. He's in the air right now."

***

Behind closed doors...October 19, 1962

The Presidents flight on Air Force One to Cleveland has been diverted. The President is said to be suffering from an upper respiratory infection and has cancelled the remainder of his campaign trip.

***

Later that night...Brown's Airfield

From a Miami hotel room Gallagher turns on the television and the news comes on the air; "We are reporting from Brown's Airfield outside of Miami where just one hour ago two U.S. Marshals arrest three suspects reported to be involved in a major drug sale. In other news President Kennedy's trip to Cleveland was cancelled earlier today after he complained of having discomfort in his chest. It was later diagnosed as an upper respiratory infection."

Gallagher turns the television off and picks up the phone and calls home.

Anna picks up, "Hello."

"Anna...its Gallagher."

"Where are you?"

"I'm in a sleazy hotel in Miami."

"What are you doing there? I thought you were on some covert operation with the Snake?"

"It's a long story. I'll fill in when I get home. I only had fifteen dollars on me and the banks were closed. I had to settle for this dump called May's Starlight Hotel. I will get to the bank tomorrow morning and fly out of Miami at noon. Can you have Jonathan pick me up at Logan at around 2:30?"

"I will pick you up myself. I have a lot to talk to you about."

"Great I'll see then. I love you!"

"I love you too."

***

46

Gallagher and Anna are huddled close to each other on the couch anticipating a special news broadcast from the Oval Office.

Helen walks into the room with Bill Waters who has recently become a frequent visitor and joins them.

"From the Oval Office...

Good evening my fellow citizens:

This Government, as promised, has maintained the closest surveillance of the Soviet military buildup on the island of Cuba. Within the past week, unmistakable evidence has established the fact that a series of offensive missile sites is now in preparation on that imprisoned island. The purpose of these bases can be none other than to provide a nuclear strike capability against the Western Hemisphere."

Gallagher gets up from the couch and refuses to hear anymore and goes into his study and makes a phone call to Paul Anderson.

"Gallagher, I'm surprised you are calling at this time. The President is on the air right now speaking to the American people. He's going toe to toe with Khrushchev."

"I know but I don't want to know. We've done all we can and what's going to happen is going to happen. All the pieces are in place except one."

"The man with the missing finger."

"You mean the book collector."

"That's right. He was never apprehended in Cleveland. He's somewhere out there ready to strike; I can feel it."

"I realize he gave everyone the slip in Miami but it's all over. If his intention was to confiscate the antidote, he was too late; the shows over."

"I don't think so."

Anderson pauses and says, "Go to your television set and at least hear the rest of his speech and then we will talk tomorrow."

Gallagher goes back into the living room and sits down next to Anna and listens.

"The path we have chosen for the present is full of hazards, as all paths are—but it is the one most consistent with our character and courage as a nation and our commitments around the world. The cost of freedom is always high-but Americans have always paid it. And one path we shall never choose, and that is the path of surrender or submission.

Our goal is not the victory of might, but the vindication of right-not peace at the expense of freedom, but both peace and freedom, here in this hemisphere, and, we hope, around the world. God willing, that goal will be achieved."

"Thank you and good night."

***

Gallagher remains silent after Anna turns off the television. Anna and Helen retire to the kitchen to prepare some coffee and dessert. Bill stays with Gallagher and breaks the melancholy mood that was filling the room. "Who would have thought finding dead fish in two of our rivers was a warning signal to something even far more sinister like nuclear war."

"No matter how much I've tried to stay insulated from the rest of this Devil ruled world I seem to find myself further drawn into the fight to stop it."

Bill nods his head in agreement and says, "I remember talking with your grandfather so many years ago and I remember his description of what he wanted the Thorn Hill Covenant to achieve. He of course had no idea of the extent this world would be plunged into the depraved state that it's in but he had a close enough picture in his mind, which amazes me. I think if he could see you now he would be proud of you for the ideals you have held close to your heart and how much you desire to look the other way but you always end up coming through and meeting the challenge."

"I sometimes don't know if what I do really matters but I know my life and my loves are here in this valley and I'm determined nothing will get in the way of their happiness."

***

47

Three days later...October 25, 1962

Dr. Wallace Dredmeyer steps off the train at Jackson station and Gallagher and Jonathan are there to meet him and take him home. During the drive to Mirror Lake both Jonathan and Gallagher are filled with questions for the doctor. Jonathan speaks first and asks, "I know there's a lot to tell but can you explain to us what really happened at Livermore. It's really only speculation on our part if we were to tell someone."

"It's rather a long story but I'll do my best. It all started when I received a letter from Washington about the plan to set up a laboratory at Livermore and Goodrich Falls and make it look like a legitimate research operation so it could fool other respected scientists with the intention of exposing suspected spies. It was called the Aricona Project, which I've been told you already know it's meaning and purpose. We had already developed the antidote in California two years before but in order to make it look authentic we went all the way with animal experimentation and antidote production."

Jonathan interrupts and asks, "Was the formula you placed in the Conan Doyle book the real formula?"

"Yes it was because working with the other respected scientists we couldn't take the chance of having a bogus formula."

Gallagher's decides to interrupt and asks, "What actually went wrong?"

"There were five of us scientists involved in developing the formula and we regularly traveled back and forth to both sites along with two government agents who served as our escorts and protectors. Each site was involved in different stages of the formulation of the antidote. Two of our scientists left the project after their work was completed so that left three of us at Livermore. The man we now know as Boris overheard Dr. Jones and I talking about the deception. At that time we had no idea he was a spy. We had known each other for many years and we suspected nothing. Boris didn't indicate to us he had overheard our conversation but he began his work on sabotaging the project."

In showing his undivided attention Jonathan asks, "When did it become obvious?".

"We had an incomplete vial of the formula that hadn't had enough time to stabilize which at that point could cause severe mutation in the cellular structure of the recipient, particularly the brain. Without warning Boris injected the whole vial into the dog, which was four times the amount of the formula, which was to be prescribed and as a result within minutes the dog went wild and attacked Boris. Then the dog attacked me and started biting me in both my legs. The dog's saliva had entered my blood stream almost immediately and I started to get disoriented. That's when I went to the radio and sent out the message for help. I realized after sometime during my recovery the message must have been extremely incoherent. We both ran into the refrigeration unit for safety but the dog followed. I must have gone into shock and that's all I can remember."

"Where was Philip during all that time?"

"He had run out of the building in a panic when it all started to happen."

"If Philip was with you why did you send the message to his radio at home?"

"The frequency was already set on his radio at home because he would talk to his son Tobey from time to time. He never let on as to where he was because of the secrecy of the project. I was hoping Tobey would do the right thing if he heard the message."

Gallagher is totally mesmerized by what he is hearing first hand from Dredmeyer asks, "What were you referring to when you mentioned the sleeping Indian in your message?"

"I knew the antidote was stockpiled at the sleeping Indian in Jackson Hole, Wyoming because I was involved in the original legitimate project. It was a long shot but I figured someone might figure it out. I knew Tobey liked going to the Turning Page to hear your stories and I was hoping he would tell you about the message. I figured if anyone could figure it out it would be you."

Gallagher laughs and says, "Did you realize there are two other locations in the country named the sleeping Indian?"

Dredmeyer returns a laugh. "I was certain you wouldn't think it was Mount Chocorua; that would be ridiculous."

Jonathan rolls his eyes and says, "It sure would."

Gallagher then asks, "What happened on the island of Tonga?"

"I never was on the island of Tonga. It was simply a propaganda ploy and the Russians fell for it. They wasted much time an effort trying to find me."

For the next several minutes Dredmeyer continues answering their questions and then they eventually arrive at his home on Mirror Lake. Waiting for them inside was Professor Meridian and his daughter Louise.

"Look who's here!" exclaims Jonathan as they enter his home.

Dredmeyer quickly goes to Professor Meridian's side and says, "I heard about what happened and I want to offer you and Louise my home until you can rebuild. It's the least I can do and besides; I've been a bachelor all my life and I could use a woman's touch in the kitchen."

"I was deeply touched when I heard about your offer and we both don't know what to say."

"Please, I don't want to hear anything about it. You both will my guest for as long as it takes."

At that moment a truck pulls up and two men begin unloading its contents.

"What do we have here?" Gallagher asks.

"Professor Meridian smiles and says, "When I started getting the prank calls I decided to ship all my books and papers to your museum for safe keeping. Harry Fuller was more than happy to accommodate."

***

October 28, 1962

Khrushchev announces over Radio Moscow that he has agreed to remove the misses from Cuba.

***

48

Early evening... Sunday - Nov 4, 1962

The limousine pulls into Philip Jones's driveway. Philip steps out and sees his wife and son standing on the porch. At that very moment Gallagher and Anna are coming up the walkway and witness the happy reunion.

It was the conclusion of a long and very troubled time for the Jones family. After they all made their way inside Philip starts to break down. "I don't know how to begin to say how sorry I am for all that I did and the hurt I caused. I wasn't myself and I need to know that you understand and it wasn't me who acted in such a terrible way."

Penny holds Philip's hand and says, "All along I knew it wasn't you but at that time Tobey and I were at a loss as to what was happening to you."

Wallace Dredmeyer is sitting in the far corner of the room and says, "Penny and Tobey, Philip was drugged with the same serum, which killed several other people but for some reason one of the medications Philip takes regularly counteracted the serum and prevented his death."

Dr. Matthews walks into the room as Dredmeyer is describing what had happened to Philip and adds, "That's right and instead of it killing him it caused an extremely toxic effect in his system."

Tobey had been very quiet and had not said anything to his father since he had walked into the house but finally asks, "Dad, why did you tell my me Philip Jones was not your real name."

"Philip smiles and says, "I don't remember saying that to you but I assure you I've always been Philip Jones and I've always been your father and I always will."

Tobey runs over to his father and begin hugging him tightly. Penny joins them in the hug and the rest of the evening is filled with much joy.

***

After some refreshments Gallagher and Anna leave with everyone else to let the Jones family heal from their ordeal. Helen is waiting in the living room enjoying a robust fire when they arrive at Eagle House.

"The warmth of the fire feels so good," Anna declares as she sits beside Helen on the couch. Then she realizes what's going on after noticing a glass of wine on the table in front of her. "Oh, I see I'm taking someone's seat."

Helen looks at her with a big smile and says, " Bill decided to keep me company on this cold November night."

Anna gets up as Bill enters the room from the kitchen with a plate of cheese and a loaf of fresh

Italian bread and says, "You're just in time to celebrate."

Anna looks at Gallagher and says, "What's there to celebrate?"

Gallagher smiles at Anna and says, "I meant to tell you but it slipped my mind."

Anna smiled and said, "What slipped your mind?"

Helen speaks up and says, "Bill and I are engaged."

Anna immediately goes back to the couch and gives Helen a big hug. "I'm so happy for you both."

Helen holds Anna close to her. "Everyone has been getting married around here. There must be something to it. I've been a spinster all my life and Bill has been windowed for many years and time is slipping by so we felt if we feel the way we do about each now, it can only get better."

Gallagher and Anna join the two of them for wine and cheese and they all enjoy the fire and pleasant conversation the rest of the evening.

***

PART SIX

Revelation

49

Monday – Nov 12, 1962

Gallagher arrives early at the Turning Page and notices Daisy Saffron waiting for the doors to open.

"Daisy, you're out early this morning."

"I wish it was for my usual reasons for coming in and seeing you but I have some disturbing news and I need your help and advice."

Gallagher can see the anguish on her face and says, "Let's go inside and I'll make us some coffee."

Gallagher escorts Daisy to a small reading area where he offers his customers the opportunity to sit and chat over fresh coffee and muffins. Fresh donuts and muffins are delivered to the bookshops backdoor from Molly's Bakery every morning.

After Gallagher brings a fresh cup of coffee to Daisy she hands him an envelope. "I found this slipped under my door when I got up this morning. I can't believe what it says."

Gallagher opens the envelope and starts reading. Daisy interrupts him and says, "Could you read it out loud? I'm getting old and I might have misread something."

"Dear Daisy,

"I hope this letter finds you well. I'm sorry I haven't been in lately. My life has taken a terrible turn starting with Ben's death. I would normally not share such news with someone else but this needs to be shared with you because of what I have learned regarding your son Mario."

Gallagher looks at Daisy and notices tears forming around her eyes.

"Gallagher, please continue," she urges.

"My father has been involved in some risky ventures in his day but what I've recently found out about the true nature of his most recent activity has totally shocked me to the core, to the point where I have left my home and staying with a friend who will remain nameless for my own protection.

Your son Mario has been working with my father secretly for a number of years. Their activity has always been kept inconspicuous to the point where Ben and I had no clue of how deeply entrenched their activity was in acts of disloyalty to this country.

It all came to light when my father and Ben continued to have disagreements over purchasing the land at Hart's Location. Ben was put in a very awkward position to please me and also remain in my father's good graces. I was going through some of Ben's clothes to get them ready to give to charity when I found a disturbing note in one of his coat pockets. The note was from my father threatening Ben if he didn't carry out the purchase of the property. It said his life would be worth nothing if he didn't cooperate with his request."*

Gallagher stops for a moment and looks up from his reading and says, "What does this have to do with your son?"

Daisy hands Gallagher a piece of paper and says, "Read this first."

"Mother I'M SORRY!"

Gallagher's demeanor suddenly changes. "Where did this come from?"

Daisy clears her throat and says, "Mario finally came back home two weeks ago. He was not my Mario; he had changed. He would not talk to me about anything as to where he had been since he left the military. He said simply it was not important. He stayed for three days and then he left without a word. I found this note tacked to my front door."

"What do you think it means?"

"Continue reading Jane's letter and you will find out."

"My father never stays with me when he secretly comes by to see me accept recently. He would always say to me, "Someone in his line of work has many enemies." I never could figure out what he meant by that statement, but now it's clear to me.

While he was taking a nap I went out to his car and curiosity got to me and decided to look through his personal things he keeps in the trunk. What I found made me sick to my stomach. I found the muddy hiking boots with the red paint that Ben's murderer had worn. I began thinking and realized they didn't belong to my father because he wears a size nine shoe. I looked further and found a check receipt from the North Conway Bank in the amount of $10,000.00 dollars paid to Mario Caruso. I have kept this to myself in fear of what my father could do if he found out what I knew. Please give this information to Gallagher as soon as you can. Don't have him look for me because he will be wasting much of his valuable time."

Gallagher rubbed his chin and says, "I wouldn't think it was a waste of time. I fear for her life and she needs protection."

"I know and I agree but read the last paragraph."

"I searched further and found a detailed schedule of campaign stops by the President. I don't know what it means but I thought Gallagher should know

because he has friends in high places. I'm sorry your son has gotten tangled up with my father. If there is any truth to be found, Gallagher will find it."

Sincerely,

Jane

Gallagher put the letter down and sits beside Daisy and says, "You know what this means for Mario."

Daisy nods and says, "I knew in my heart Mario was heading for trouble. He never got along with his father Angelo and they always argued about politics and the government's foreign policies. I was surprised he joined the military but now I see his reasoning. He got the training he needed to work for a man like Randolph Morgan."

"Daisy, what appears on the surface may not be the reality of the matter."

Daisy looks at Gallagher perplexed. "You mean there may be more to it than what it appears to be. Just like in those mystery novels I read all the time."

"That's right. Let me find out what I can and please don't tell anyone about all this. I'm getting tired of people rushing to judgment. Jonathan and I will pursue this and I'm confident we will find the truth. The first thing that must be done is finding Jane Willard"

***

50

The next morning...

Jonathan arrives at Eagle House exactly at 9:00 in the morning. Gallagher tells him all that he heard from Daisy.

"It sounds like a setup to me," Jonathan declares.

"My thoughts exactly and here are my reasons. First of all why would Mario implicate himself by leaving his boots and a note at Liberty Cabin and a similar note at Daisy's? It makes no sense unless he's being framed."

"I tend to agree but how do you explain the check receipt?"

"I believe he wrote out a check with Mario's name on it but was it ever cashed? Did Mario ever see the check?"

Jonathan looks at his watch and says, "The banks are open. I will run to the local branch of the.... you didn't tell me the bank."

"North Conway Bank."

"What are going to do?"

"I'm going to see the Chief and fill him in on what we found out."

"Are you going to get in touch with Paul Anderson?"

"I'm keeping the FBI, the CIA, the military and all other branches of this government in the dark on this one for the simple reason I still don't know who the good guys really are. The government agencies are split on their loyalty. As I've said before, power corrupts and the ones who get corrupted are the people carrying out that power."

***

Early afternoon of the same day...

Gallagher found out from Jonathan the information he needed and suspected. Mario never cashed the check. So with that out of the way Gallagher walks into the police station and sees Chief Peterson absorbed in his latest copy of Fishermen's Monthly. As soon as Peterson sees Gallagher's face he raises his hand and says, "Don't tell me. I don't want to know. Tom Perry right now is taking his final exam to become Chief. According to my watch he should be back in two hours with his results."

Gallagher was about to say something witty when Jonathan unexpectedly walks in to join them and says, "Gallagher, your feeling about Mario was right. Little Hands called me after hearing from Mario and said Mario told him he is on the run."

Peterson looks up from his magazine and says, "On the run from whom?"

"You're not going to believe it but from a man much larger than Little Hands. Mario told him he's working for Randolph Morgan."

Gallagher's wheels start turning and says, "The man with the size fourteen boot."

Peterson perks up. "I see what you're saying. We find Randolph Morgan and we find Ben's killer. So you are definitely ruling out Little Hands and Mario Caruso."

Gallagher nods and says, "Exactly! The book collector a.k.a. Randolph Morgan needs to be stopped because I believe from what Jane Willard said in her letter to Daisy he has plans beyond our lovely valley. He's very interested in the Presidents campaign schedule."

"Do you have any other evidence to support your claim?" Peterson asks revealing some skepticism.

"I do because on the day I was with Frank Margetti at Brown's Airfield outside of Miami waiting to nab the book collector we found out he had changed planes and was heading for Cleveland where the President was stopping on his campaign tour. It's not a coincidence, it was planned but it was foiled because of the Presidents illness. We need to find out where the President is going next and beat

Morgan there before he carries out whatever he's planning."

Peterson starts to shake his head in disagreement, "I don't like this one bit. Call Paul Anderson and tell him the whole story. It's too much for us to get involved in."

Jonathan was listening very patiently to their conversation and finally speaks up and says, "Gallagher, why don't you tell the Chief the whole story?"

Gallagher looks at Jonathan then at the Chief and says, "Okay, this is what I've gathered so far. It all goes back to the incident with Ben Willard and Little Hands."

Jonathan looks at Peterson. "You want some coffee? This could take awhile."

"Sounds good."

Gallagher begins: "I will leave out the non-essential details. Ben Willard purchases a parcel of land at Hart's Location because of an ultimatum given to him by his father-in-law Randolph Morgan. If he didn't buy the land Morgan would withhold the funds Ben needed to build his dream ski resort. Ben is now caught between a rock and a hard place. He doesn't like the idea but he goes along with it. Then Little Hands comes onto the scene and complicates matters. Randolph Morgan gets wind of it somehow and recruits an unknown giant of a man who wears a size fourteen boot. Then by being linked with an argument with Ben, Little Hands is conveniently accused of Ben's murder. This works in Morgan's favor and frees up his giant friend to perform other duties."

Peterson interrupts and asks, "What other duties?"

"This is where it gets complicated. Agent Stephen Harmon who was identified as a mole by Paul Anderson but claimed to be working for the Bureau to trap a mole named Paul Anderson. This is where the government was split down the middle. Harmon was working for the Director of the Bureau and Paul Anderson was working for the current administration primarily the Attorney General. The reason why the covert operation by the Attorney General was because of specific intelligence he received leading him to suspect Russian and or Fifth Column infiltration of our governments military operations particularly the Cuban and Russian relationship. Now this is where the Aricona Project comes into play. The Attorney General sets up a subterfuge to create the idea of an antidote for radiation poisoning being formulated when in reality it was already manufactured two years earlier in California. The reason for the ruse was to draw in suspected Russian and Fifth Column interested parties. Here is where O'Reilly comes into the picture. He was placed in our valley to oversee the Livermore and Goodrich Fall sites so the antidote could be manufactured without any glitches. The big glitch was the accident. This is when O'Reilly's usefulness ends at Livermore and

Goodrich Falls so he disappears but his new assignment was to get the book collector a.k.a. Randolph Morgan who is one of the missing names on the Chicago list."

Peterson interrupts again and asks, "Why the purchase of Hart's Location to build a shopping center?"

"Randolph Morgan's motive was to allow himself the opportunity to get close to the Livermore site and possibly steal the formula, which he almost did when he found out Dredmeyer had hidden the formula inside one of the Baskerville books."

Peterson nods and says, "I'm following you, please continue. To be honest with you I thought I was going to be bored silly with all this but I'm hooked."

Jonathan now speaks up and says, "I need some more coffee."

After a short break Gallagher continues, "Here comes another twist. With Little Hands behind bars Randolph Morgan needs another scapegoat. He attempts to recruit Mario Caruso, who nicely fits the description of a strong and very large man who could be Ben's killer. Poor Mario is suffering from some kind of depression associated with his past military experience and has become despondent to his own mother and is now on the run from Morgan's hired thug, the unknown giant."

Peterson asks, "What do you think Morgan is up to now and why?"

"It's my belief he has a strong dislike for this country and will do whatever he can to spoil its prosperity. First he attempted to steal the formula, which would have made this country vulnerable to nuclear attack from Cuba. Now with the evidence of his interests in the Presidents campaign schedule I believe he and his giant friend have plans to harm the President; to be more precise, assassinate him."

"Well now I've heard enough," Peterson exclaims. "We have to get Paul Anderson involved right away."

Gallagher bows his head and shakes it back and forth and says sadly, "I received a call this morning from one of my contacts at Langley who was a good friend of Anderson's. Paul's dead."

"What!" Peterson exclaims in shock. "How? What from…?"

"He was struck down by a car on Pennsylvania Avenue."

***

51

Saturday – December 1, 1962

Jonathan walks into Gallagher's study and places a copy of the article he had written for the Jackson Observer for his endorsement. Gallagher picks up the article and begins reading it out loud:

"On November 23, 1962 Gallagher Brady's big day had arrived to witness the grand opening of the Jonas Blackthorn Antiquarian Museum. Gallagher is the owner of the Turning Page Bookshop located in the center of Jackson and is the grandson of Jonas Blackthorn who was one of the founding fathers in the valley. A light snow began to fall as the doors to the museum were opened at 9:00 a.m. All day long the locals in the valley came and viewed the many works of literature, which Gallagher had collected along with most of the books his grandfather had collected during his lifetime. The museum was dedicated to his grandfather, Jonas Blackthorn, who was instrumental in putting the desire in Gallagher to read at a very young age. Professor Meridian was instrumental in donating most of his collection of scientific works and gave a speech to the audience that had gathered in the Science Wing. As he spoke he sounded more like a philosopher than a scientist. He stated and I quote; "In this troubled world of ours the need to focus on the simpler things in life, which has been captured so completely in this magnificent museum. When I say simpler I mean wholesome and innocent. The great works of poetry and prose, which enrich the

mind and heart, have been preserved for our future young readers and writers that will walk through the many aisles of books that were once dusty and forgotten on the many bookshelves throughout our land. Gallagher Brady has sacrificed his time and resources, as did his grandfather before him to preserve the fine literature you see here today for our enjoyment. We know that Gallagher in recent times has been drawn into the troubles of this world, which I mentioned before in order to stop the chaos that at times robs the joy these very works of literature can create. We hope in time man will learn what is most important in his short life on this planet by his taking the time to spread some joy and peace by sharing a verse or two with one another."

After the professor spoke those words Gallagher was asked to say a few words himself and he began by saying, "The professor stole my thunder. It's a hard act to follow but I will try to express my feelings about what has been accomplished by the opening of this museum. From the first page of the first book I ever read, The Swiss Family Robinson by Johann David Wyss, I have loved the printed page. It seems most fitting I was introduced to such a work of literature because it had to do with survival. The books that line these shelves have survived time and the elements, which can erode the treasured thoughts of the authors that penned the many words these books contain. Time can allow those words to be forgotten and the elements can destroy their message. As the professor so aptly put, my time and energy lately has been drawn into the corruption that has so permeated our world. My grandfather taught me a very valuable lesson in what he tried to do with his Thorn Hill Covenant and that is to protect our heritage. In line with my grandfather's ideals I will be initiating a weekly classroom discussion right here in this museum of current and past great literary works. Once a month a guest author will be invited to read and discuss their work and invite the audience to ask any questions they my have."

A hand was raised in the audience and Gallagher stopped his speech and said, "Yes, do have a question?"

"I was wondering if you and Mr. Henry are finished in your investigation on what had happened to our rivers recently?"

Gallagher formed a smile and said, "I believe our rivers have been restored to their original pristine condition and efforts are in place to never have such a tragedy happen again by creating an environmental agency to oversee our lakes and rivers."

Gallagher looked at his watch and said, "I would like to take more questions but I don't want steal the show. Chief Peterson would like to say a few words. Chief, the floor is yours."

"Thank you. I don't have much to say other than I thought this was a good time to announce my second retirement and hopefully my last and to *announce the promotion of Tom Perry as our new Chief."*

After much applause the audience continued to mingle for the rest of the day enjoying the many exhibits that were on display.

Gallagher puts the draft down and says, "Jonathan, you have a way of capturing exactly the way the day turned out. I think it should go to print."

As soon as Gallagher finishes those words the buzzer at the entrance gate sounds. Anna walks into Gallagher's study and says, "You're not going to believe this but it's Paul Anderson."

Gallagher's demeanor changes in an instant from shock to utter joy to hear his good friend has come back from the dead. Jonathan is speechless as Anna escorts Paul into Gallagher's study.

Paul raises his arm and says, "I know what you're thinking but before you say anything I want you to know I took a lesson from Gallagher on the wisdom behind staging ones death. It allows a lot of freedom to roam about and gather valuable intelligence."

Putting sentiment aside Gallagher asks, "What have you learned?"

"I was able to track down Jane Willard. She was questioned and she was told her cooperation was greatly needed in finding her father."

"Is she willing to cooperate?" Jonathan asks.

"She has more than cooperated. She has told us everything regarding her fathers activity with the Fifth Column organization the Cause."

Gallagher's eyes widen. "Anything to do with my parents death?"

"Indirectly he was responsible for it because he was the mastermind behind the organizations northeast cell and their corrupt agenda."

Gallagher remains silent and was trying to hold back his justified anger. After some awkward silence on everyone's part Gallagher looks at Paul and asks, "Where's Randolph Morgan?"

"We have him in our sites right now in New York City."

"What do you plan on doing about it?"

"Wait."

"Wait for what?"

"To draw out the man that strangled Ben Willard. This was the only reason why Jane told us how to find her father."

***

52

New York City – February 10, 1963

Six weeks had past since Paul Anderson's surprise return from the grave. He had remembered how Gallagher faked his own death during the Thorn Hill Case in order to be able to move about freely behind the scenes and felt it was the only way to find Jane Willard and possibly her father. It worked and Jane was found in Boston living with a cousin. Upon seeing Paul Anderson on her doorstep it caused her much anxiety and yet at the same time much relief. She couldn't go on any longer with the knowledge about her father and his responsibility behind her husband's death and many others through the years. Her father kept in touch with her not ever thinking she would ever turn him in. But he was misled because the love for her mate was far stronger than a daughter's love for her father.

***

Operatives working in New York were keeping close watch over Randolph Morgan's every move. Jane had received a call from her father on February 9th and in conversation he revealed in passing his plans to attend the play 'Beyond the Fringe', which was playing on Broadway in New York City at the John Golden Theatre the following night. Bells went off when Jane told Anderson of her fathers recent plans to attend the play because the President and First Lady were to attend the play on the same night.

***

53

John Golden Theatre – New York City

Paul Anderson is stationed one street away from the John Golden Theatre when a very large man dressed in an usher's uniform is seen standing by the back entrance of the theatre. Paul's mind begins to imagine all kinds of things including the assassination of President Lincoln at Ford's Theatre.

Gallagher described the man's appearance in detail to Anderson and there was no doubt they had their man. Was it going to be a gun or an injection of radiation or was it going to be up close and personal by strangling?

When people begin arriving at the main entrance of the theatre the man scoots in through the back door after some stagehands exit the building to take a break before the performance begins.

Paul then makes a call. "Little Hands, he's gone inside. Do what you need to do without creating a scene; we can't cause a panic."

Little Hands is a little apprehensive when Gallagher first told him of Paul's need to have an equally strong man apprehend the giant. But after considering how it was Randolph Morgan who was responsible for his imprisonment he gladly accepted.

The lights dim signaling everyone to take their seats. Little Hands moves into position. The President and First Lady have balcony seats and Little Hands is hiding behind the curtain, which separates the balcony seats from the foyer.

***

Eagle House...

Gallagher looks at his watch as Anna, Helen, Bill and Jonathan wait for the call from Anderson. "The performance should've started by now."

Helen, needs to pass the time and starts reminiscing about hearing her father Jonas Blackthorn on one occasion talking to a man in his study and the words she remembers began to cause a chill go up her spine. It all fit now in her mind. It was an argument that echoed throughout the house it seemed. The man accused her father of protecting someone. The man threatened to make him pay someday for his actions; that someone was the Abenaki people and that man must have been Randolph Morgan. He had designs on the land at Hart's Location way back then for his own economic gain.

***

John Golden Theatre...

The giant makes his move towards the curtain. Little Hands wastes no time and wrestles the man to the floor. He holds him in a body lock called a Full Nelson until security shows up and he is taken into custody. The performance continues without interruption.

Outside in a black sedan is the book collector a.k.a. Randolph Morgan. Paul Anderson and two of his agents approach the car and with guns drawn open the passenger side door. Morgan is taken without incident.

***

EPILOGUE

Two months later... Swift River at Hart's Location

John Little Hands Russell is doing what he loves to do best; fish. All the events in the previous year are still fresh in his mind. He has had a lot to be thankful for and a lot to be happy about. Gallagher was able to reactivate the protection of Hart's Location for the Abenaki people by drawing up new documents securing his grandfathers original intentions and desires and submitting them to the State House, which were quickly accepted.

After the exposing and convicting of Randolph Morgan of treason and murder he was sentenced to two consecutive life sentences in prison without parole. In court it was revealed his large companion referred to, as the giant, was the other name on the Chicago list. His refusal to reveal his actual identity added to his many convictions, which by his own admission included the murder of Larry Nelson, the freelance reporter and Ben Willard.

Mario Caruso returned home to his mother Daisy after his long exile and began working for her at the Trading Post. The reason for his self-exile was never explained to his mother. She accepted it and never questioned him about it again.

Larry Harmon was cleared of any wrong doing because he was only following orders from the

Director of the FBI who was not in sync with the current administration due to personal conflicts.

***

Jonathan stops typing the details of the 'Tale of Two Rivers' and decides to take a rest. His account of all that had transpired in recent days and months will just have to wait for another day.

Valerie enters the room and says, "I stopped hearing the typewriter. Are you coming up for air?"

"Let's take a walk. The sun is out; the air is fresh and crisp. Flowers are starting to poke their heads through the thawed out ground and I'm hungry."

***

Camp Ellis – Maine...

Gallagher and Anna make a trip back to Camp Ellis in Saco, Maine to spend some time together and to visit an old friend by the river. Ishmael is tending to his boat ready to sail out when he catches sight of Gallagher coming towards him.

"Well I'll be. I never thought I would see you again."

Gallagher smiles and says, "Good to see you Ishmael. I've had this nagging question going through my mind and I need to hear the truth from you."

"What may that be?"

"Are you RED?"

Ishmael laughs. "You mean retired and extremely dangerous?"

"Yeah."

"Do I look extremely dangerous?"

"Not at all."

"Then why don't I take you out with me at first light tomorrow for some fishing like we talked about?"

Gallagher shows him a big smile. "I will be here before sun up."

***

Later that night...

Gallagher and Anna are sitting by a fire in their rented beach house and Gallagher looks at Anna and says, "I'm a little nervous about going out tomorrow on the open sea with a man who could be considered extremely dangerous."

Anna just shakes her head and says, "With all that has happened to you in your life you have become a real cynic."

"Oh no. A cynic is one when he smells flowers he looks around for a coffin."

"Where did you get that little tidbit?"

"H.L. Mencken."

"Who's he?"

"Come by someday and visit the new museum. You will be amazed of what can learn from a book!"

THE END

Acknowledgements

I want to thank my wife Suzanne for believing in me and encouraging me to continue writing. Also I want to thank her for being a second set eyes in the editing process. I also want to thank the many readers of my first book 'The Thorn Hill Covenant' who have encouraged me to write my second novel.

Specifically on this second novel I want to thank Michelle and Giovanni Gulli for helping me find the many of the locations depicted in this story.

David W. Firmes

About the author.

David Firmes was born and raised in Worcester, Massachusetts and resides with his wife Suzanne. He is currently working on his third novel, The Great Unsolved Mystery of 1826.

***

Other books written by David W. Firmes.

The Thorn Hill Covenant©

Made in the USA
Lexington, KY
01 November 2014